To Peter

PYRAMID

PAULA LOVE CLARK

Always ask questions
Always fight to stay free.
Always have faith ♡.
Happy reading.
Love
Paula ♡

PYRAMID

'I fear the day that technology will surpass our human interaction. The world will have a generation of idiots.'
 ~ Albert Einstein.

INTRODUCTION

Once the tubes had been pulled, the child was classed as 'born' and ready for labelling. Swaddled in the official drab grey colours of the Baby Nation, depending on gender, they were carried by nursing robots to the Labelling Room. Light grey with a hint of metallic blue for the boys and light pink/grey hue for the girls. The metallic, white robots, with non-animated face coverings, perfunctory in their movements, had no substitute parenting role. They were merely carrying out their orders and performing their tasks.

The newly created babies were placed in metal basket cradles, lined with synthetic soft fur and a white cotton material. The baskets were then slotted onto one of four metal conveyor belts, with the nursing robot determining which line the child would join. This was simply a systematic decision, without conscious thought or reasoning as to which line the child would join. At the end of each of the conveyor belts, was a large white sign with black writing. Each child would be labelled with either a P, D, C or F, depending on which line they joined. The system from start to completion, was simple, clean and efficient.

PROCESSING

DOMESTIC

CONSTRUCTION

FACTORY

Despite the creation of babies, this was no maternity ward. No small human cried, and no caring hands existed to gently touch in wonder, its soft new flesh. No celebrating, exhausted parents to fuss over their long-awaited child. These children would never know love, or kindness, or compassion, or the warm touch of another human being. Those emotions and desires were long ago removed from the controlled human creation process. Desire, ambition, passion, creativity and achievement were also long ago extinguished, and designated obsolete character requirements for the New Human.

The babies made no sound, since there was no one to answer their call. No mother to soothe them, no father to be held close to, heart beating against heart. Whether it was a programmed feature, or a naturally occurring evolution trait, the babies instinctively knew not to make a sound.

At 11.11am one Thursday, on a typical grey day with no sun (since exposure to the sun had been prohibited for almost a decade), another child was born into one of the factories of the Baby Nation. A boy. Despite ridding the New Human of all its internal reproduction organs, the Controllers decided to retain their basic genders. The genitals were impacted, since there was never to be human to human contact but could not yet be entirely removed. New Humans were still works in progress, but the Controllers were pleased with what they had thus achieved. Genders were not strictly male or female, as no distinction was actively encouraged for the New Humans. The colouring of clothes had more to do with sexual preference for the levels of Controllers, than for the human's benefit,

The boy was taken by a nursing robot and designated a line for labelling. PROCESSING. However, when it was the child's turn to have a 'P' laser burned onto his skin, the child did something not heard in that room for a very long time, he screamed. He felt the pain from the laser and hollered loud and shrill. Time stopped. Silence followed.

The robot who was responsible for placing the child, paused the laser machine and walked towards the human. It regarded the screaming infant and stood staring quizzically at the writhing human child. Protocol called for the child to be placed into the Reject Bin. Yet the robot did not move. It simply stood there transfixed by the sobbing child. Something was triggered inside it, a glimmer of a memory. It momentarily stood transfixed and confused. The memory did not compute with what it knew and with its daily instructions.

Thus, instead of following the directive protocol, the robot reached out and offered a finger to the boy. The child, instinctively grabbed the digit and held on tight. Then he stopped crying and looked up into the face of the robot. For a moment, the two regarded each other. Something like recognition, kindness, or understanding, passed between them. It lasted but a moment and yet would impact the two forever.

The robot withdrew its digit and the baby, now soothed, had already dismissed the pain. Instead of rejecting the child, the robot restarted the machine and allowed the child to pass. That simple act saved the boy's life, but also meant that he would grow up craving and striving for that touch for the rest of his life. Alternatively, the robot would try to ignore the fact that despite its programming, a human memory within its make up, had been triggered. And, despite how much the system would discourage it, that one shared moment, would change both of their lives forever.

1

A NORMAL DAY

The alarm hit 6.15am as usual for a weekday. Thursday, almost the weekend. Not that it mattered, when one day seemed to lapse into another, without ceremony or adventure. Jake hit the snooze button. Routines. His awakening state left him somewhere between Forget and Remember. He groaned as his consciousness rolled him into the lap of Remember. He lay on his back and stared at the ceiling. Dread filled his soul from his feet up to his chest, greedily, silently, chomping away the brief peace gifted by deep sleep. As the minutes ticked away on the timer of his phone, he lay in the half light of early Spring, which seemed determined to creep through the sliver of the not quite closed curtains, exposing the awakening of the dawning sky.

A sigh was expelled from the depths of his being, as he contemplated another day of survival. *What's the point?* He whispered to his soul. *What's the point?* As usual, no response echoed back.

The alarm trilled again beside his right ear. Reactions

swift, he leaned over and stabbed the 'Stop' with his left index finger. Silence and nothingness for just a brief moment. Then the floodgates from the dam, that held back the Remembering broke and pain washed over him as it had done for the past few months. Sleep, awake, remember, on repeat day after day after day.

That smile. Huge, wide, incongruous, insouciant and indubitably infectious. The giggle that leapt forth at random times, filling his heart with all that was good and all that mattered. He recalled the way her dark hair curled down over her right eye as she sat colouring in her book, or playing with her dolls. It stayed there until it bugged her enough to swipe it away with the soft, perfect back of her young hand, or momentarily lift up in flight with a puff of air from her mouth. Eyes huge and blue, earnest, trusting and full of love, colouring into his own. And then he felt it, that tearing pain as his heart tore into a million pieces; the Remembering.

He pulled a pillow over his face and wondered how long he could hold it there before the memories escaped into the dark nothingness. How many times had he asked himself this very question the past few days? Was it too much to ask life to stop reminding him of why he wanted life to just stop?

He couldn't do it, just as he couldn't do it the many other ways he had contemplated ending his life and getting off the planet. Would he remember on the other side? Would she be there waiting for him? 'Argh!' he shouted out as he threw the pillow onto the floor and bolted upright. He couldn't go there. Not today.

He forced himself out of bed and went to the bathroom. For the longest time he stood under the shower. Nothing took it away. Neither the heat, nor the cold; not music, nor the television; not work, nor friends. Not even his other children, now grown up and living lives of their own. Nothing. Only the darkness of sleep and switch off of conscious thought, that he craved.

The commute to the office was same as it was every other day. Drive to the station, train, walk, people, buses, cars, tube entrance, more people, step on, be jostled, step off, join the caterpillar heave of commuters heading towards the same destination – up and out of the tube station. Out into the fresh air. Traffic, buildings, people, noise. The same routine every day. And what for? To sit in front of a computer, shuffle documents, share information, do the research, meet the people, have the small talk, work to deadlines and then the meetings, a never ending queue of meetings.

'THE WORST THING ABOUT GRIEF,' he once told the counsellor, 'is that nothing matters except the loss. How can anyone reach in and connect when you are continually swirling around in this whirlwind of a vast ocean of meaningfulness? How can someone who doesn't know what that's like, understand? I can't tell them. I can't show them. And God knows I don't want them to experience this, but sometimes, just sometimes, I wish, for just a moment, that they could feel it. To feel what and how I feel.'

"JAKE!" he was pulled from his thoughts by the emergence of Henry his manager in front of his monitor. "Is the presentation ready?" Jake nodded. "Great, we need you in the boardroom in five."

. . .

It had been only nine months since he had lost Eloise and life for everyone else, carried on as normal. But for him, the days melted into one another, creating a crunching slow caterpillar trail slime of barely-there existence, with no hope or desire of transforming into something else. He craved the cocoon, but not the re-emergence.

"Yup, it's good to go." he replied opening the top drawer of his desk with a key and grabbing a file with the title, 'IMMERGE', typed out in large black letters. He sighed as he thought of all the work he held in his hands and how he had been encouraged to plough himself into the project to cope with his overwhelming loss. He had been working on the concept for years, yet it was only after the accident that he managed to create the breakthrough he was looking for. In just over five minutes, he was about to present that breakthrough to a boardroom of people, informing how he had successfully discovered a safe way of combining Artificial Intelligence with the human brain. It was his hope that the work he pioneered, would ultimately prevent the metastasis of cancer cells and prevent or inhibit the growth of other life threatening diseases. Jake also knew from his proven research data, that there was evidence to suggest that this technological advancement could also prevent the development of mental illnesses and severe addictions by manipulating cognitive behaviours and re-routing dangerous thought patterns.

This work was highly coveted and the race to be the first company at the finishing line was intensely competitive. Time was only slightly advantageous to his company and this project, because of the funding from their investors. He hadn't been told who they were and truthfully, had no desire to find out. But they seemed to have an unlimited amount of funding. And the bonus he was promised, was enough to financially secure his girls and family for the rest of their lives.

"Well done Jake. Top job. I'd say that was in the bag, wouldn't you?" Edward the CEO declared, as they walked alongside each other post presentation. He was a portly man in his early seventies, with a penchant for Cuban cigars, fine whisky and young secretaries, which his three marriages and two costly divorces, paid testimony to. His latest personal secretary whom he had recently married, was half his age and according to everyone who gossiped at the company, quite the gold digger.

He placed his left hand flat against Jake's back and leaned into him, like fellow conspirators discussing post battle. "I have inside knowledge that the government are considering us as their top contender," he declared with a knowing wink. "Big bonus for you!" Then he grinned like a fat Cheshire cat, patted him and walked away.

Jake stood there for a moment and watched him with disdain. He secretly despised the man. He listened to the company whispers as much as anyone and he knew that Edward was as far away from a saint in a suit, as he could be.

He noticed as he watched Edward, that the older man's gait was slightly out of balance to his left. 'War injury' he often joked. But everyone knew the truth. His second wife ran him over with a golf buggy, crushing his left ankle. He didn't pursue any vengeance against her and paid full alimony. Jake wondered what type of man must he be, to have a wife deliberately try to run him over with a golf buggy?

These thoughts trailed back to his own ex wife and then to Eloise's mother. He shook the unwelcome thoughts away and instead focused on a line from his presentation.

'IMAGINE IF YOU CAN, ladies and gentlemen, an immersive chip implanted into the fluid of the brain, with the ability to link AI command to human consciousness. With the IMMERGE chip, we can control bodily functions and human thoughts. And once we are in, we have the capacity to control brain function by use of electromagnetic pulse frequency. Thus, we can send direct messages to the brain and effectively control what we want the brain to tell the body. Imagine a future, where we can look forward to the elimination of disease, mental illness and addictions; where the eradication of disease and cell imperfections will provide a greater, more centralised and aligned direction for the human race.'

AS HE STOOD WATCHING the CEO, this man, who professed to have everything money could buy, except moral conscience and a good heart; a man who most people despised, including, it seemed, his own wives, he wondered what made a person truly human? He couldn't help but travel with these thoughts, since he had just presented his work to a board of narcissistic, ego centric people with an agenda for self attainment and increasing their bank balances. This new mergence of technology with the human brain, would be a tool like no other. Whoever gained control of the human mind, could control the progression of the human race. It was a huge advancement for human civilisation. And he was there at the very heart of it; not just in the race, but firing the starting gun.

But, he hesitated as a new voice rose up from a place deep inside of him, *But...could it also have the power to obliterate the very essence of what makes us human?*

"Hey Jake! "A call from behind extracted him from following that particular thought process. He turned around and saw Henry holding open the door to the boardroom he had just exited. "Team briefing."

He sighed inwardly, as he reluctantly retraced his steps back towards the boardroom. However, he couldn't shake of the feint, questioning voice asking, *Is this progression? Is this right?*

It was early evening, by the time the team meetings had subsided, phone calls made and emails replied to. He finally got the opportunity to check in on his personal messages. He had left all groups, bar the ones his name had to remain visible, namely family, golf and work related. He sent some standard bland replies to work and an upcoming golf meet he chose to opt out of, then headed off towards the tube station. It was almost seven on a Thursday evening and the thought of being home alone again, gutted his stomach and sent his heart into a dangerous free fall. He was so close to leaving the planet, that he was barely hanging on by his fingernails. Just had to wait for the bonus to be applied and get some final details sorted, then he was good to go. He hoped for the second time that day, that she would be there waiting for him on the other side. Only his most inebriated and darkest self would have no boundaries holding back the possibilities of pursuing that wish.

His phone pinged. Automatically he pulled it out of his jacket pocket and glanced down. It was Amy. She wanted to talk. He felt his heart pull apart as though it were an elastic band. She was the only person who could help with his pain and yet his pain was too great to be with her. He went to place the phone with the unanswered message back into his pocket, but it pinged again. 'Please. Please Jake. We have to talk. I need you. I miss you.' Then another message. 'She was my daughter too!'

His eyes clouded with the storms of all the broken yesterdays. The urge to allow the emotion to spill out, threatened to buckle his legs in the street. So he headed to a bar on a side street. He spotted a free standing space to the far left of the crowded bar; a perfect hiding space for anonymity.

He ordered a beer and placed his face into his hands. If he held his eyes tight enough, the storm would wash itself away. He took deep breaths as the therapist had taught him. He only went a couple of times, but he utilised what he had learned for moments just like this. There were many moments like this recently. Lost in the concentration of breathing in and forcing back the threatening flood of emotion, he didn't notice that time had stood still.

"MIND IF I JOIN YOU?"

. . .

He glanced up and followed the direction of the voice, which led him to connect with the gentle, warm face of a very old man. There was something vaguely familiar about him. It was a deeply lined, yet beautifully inviting face. Jake found his own eyes meandering over the many cracks and crevices of his features until they led up to the clearest, sparkling crystal blue eyes. His hair was full and white and his smile easy and quick. He wore a brown suit with white shirt but no tie ('terrible inventions,' he would declare later). Lean and purposeful, yet relaxed and with the air of someone who had all day to spend in that space and no desire to be anywhere else. He drank what looked like beer from a tall half glass.

"Ah that's better." he said smiling and wiping his mouth with the back of his right hand. "I missed that taste. So refreshing don't you think?" he said nodding towards the younger man's beer glass.

Jake took a gulp from his own glass. Burped inside his mouth, apologised and returned to stare back at the man. "I hate beer. I prefer lager." he said without thought.

"So why did you order a beer?"

Great question. Jake had no answer, so shrugged instead. The old man laughed. Really laughed. So loud and hard that it filled the room. Jake was shocked and looked around him in embarrassment. Then he stopped and stared.

Nobody moved. Nobody spoke. Everyone was frozen doing whatever they were doing. He shook his head and rubbed his eyes. Nothing changed. With utter confusion, he walked around the bar looking into peoples' faces. They were all frozen, unseeing; trapped in a moment of their life. Hands were stuck in mid air during conversation, a woman reaching into her bag, a man with a finger poised above his phone. The bartender about to empty a measure of spirit into a glass. All frozen mid motion, mid sentence, mid thought. And silence filled the room.

He looked over to the old man at the bar. He wasn't stuck, he stood there watching Jake as he ran around in a panic.

"What the f...?" Jake said running his hands through his hair trying to make sense of what he was experiencing. "Am I hallucinating?" he asked the man, searching his face for answers. "Have I died and am experiencing a weird flashback thing?"

The old man simply smiled and drained the liquid from the rest of his glass. When the glass was completely empty, he placed it gently and with great concentration, on the bar. Then he turned to Jake, placed his crinkly hand onto his left arm and guided him towards the door.

"Let's take a walk." he said.

When they exited the door, the scenery changed. No longer was it the bustling streets of London City spewing out its exhausted work force, or depositing them from work building to social building. No huge red buses or black taxis, no beeping delivery scooters or bikes. No tourists standing at street corners following phone maps, no news stand sellers shouting out to grab the free paper. In fact, that world had disappeared. They were walking along a sandy beach in the middle of a warm spring day, with only the sound of the playful ocean crashing against the shoreline and the sing song of seagulls calling out above their heads.

Despite the nonsensical situation he found himself in, for the first time since losing his little girl, he felt something akin to peace transcending his whole being.

"Ah, the smell of the ocean. Is there a better smell out there?" the old man announced.

"Bread. Fresh bread. My grandma used to bake bread every other day for us growing up. She had one of those range cookers that warmed the kitchen and seemed to have endless room to feed my huge family." That's strange, he considered to himself. *When was the last time I thought of grandma?*

"Oh yes, Edna's bread was legendary. She could feed a family of eight on one loaf of bread. And that jam she made..." the old man said kissing his fingers and smacking his lips. Jake stopped dead in his tracks. He studied the man again, but this time searching his face for clues.

. . .

"Who are you? What's going on here? What do you want from me?"

"Relax. Breathe in the air. It's beautiful isn't it? The ocean, the sand, the sky...life?" the old man said as he stood looking out to the sea and breathing in deeply.

"What is this?" Jake shouted.

"Close your eyes."

"What?"

"Close your eyes." he repeated, in a stern, command tone. Jake, for no other reason than feeling totally discombobulated, closed his eyes as directed.

"Now open them." the man's voice was gentler this time. Jake opened his eyes, but took a while to adjust to the view. From standing on the sand of a sprawling beach, they were sitting on the edge of a high cliff overlooking a huge city surrounded by countryside and roads from all directions, that fed like veins, into the vast grey jungle below them.

. . .

"What? How did we get here?" he cried out in utter confusion. "Will you please tell me what the hell is happening to me? Did I die?"

"Hah!" replied the old man. "No not yet."

Jake shot him a sharp look. His mind went into overdrive. *Does he know my plans? But if so, how? And what the fuck is happening to me right now?* The old man seemingly replied to his thoughts.

"Do you know who I am?"

Jake thought for a moment, studying the man's face, seeking clues in the etches of his skin and searching for layers in his eyes. But his skin did not yield secrets and the eyes remained clear and icy blue, giving nothing away. "Are you God?" he asked incredulous.

The old man burst out into laughter. "Oh my! No, I am not God." Then looking to the sky, he added, "Did you hear that? He thinks I am you!" Jake looked up and around him. No words rose up and forth. He knew not what to do or say, or how to extract himself from the ridiculous situation he was in.

. . .

"Do you remember Uncle Teddy?" the old man said, breathing deeply and drinking in the view below. They were hundreds of feet above ground, yet despite Jake always struggling with vertigo, he felt neither fear nor exhilaration. The moment was what it was. Apart from confusion, something akin to peace and acceptance sturdied him inside.

"Who went to war? Grandma's older brother?" The old man nodded. "I never met him. He died in France a year before the war ended I believe, why do you ask?"

"I will never forget the day I left. Mother had made me some scones and a flask of tea. She was convinced that the army wouldn't feed us well, so she saved some of their weekly rations and sneaked them into a pouch with the scones. I will never forget the taste of the homemade strawberry jam and the softness of the cake as I dipped it into my tea. Mary your mother, got the baking knack from our mother. She taught both my sisters how to bake. She tried with me, but I was never one to be told. I would rather be off spearing fish with a homemade rod, or collecting wood and coal for the stove! Money was always tight, so we made do. We were happy with the little we had, because the best thing my parents gave us, was love and a warm home to live in. All our needs, no matter how basic, were always met."

Jake's mouth gaped as he turned to stare at the old man. "You're Uncle Teddy?" The old man nodded. "But how? He died in battle. At the age of twenty-three! It's impossible.

Besides," Jake said mentally attempting maths, "you'd be like a hundred or something now right?"

"A HUNDRED AND four to be precise!" corrected the old man.

"I'M JUST SO CONFUSED. This is a real mind fuck right now. I don't get it. I don't get any of this." Jake lifted his hands up and spread them out before him. "Why am I here? On this mountain. With seemingly, a ghost of the dead uncle I've never met, who is old yet should actually be half my age! I just...I don't...what the...?" He buried his head in his hands and rubbed at his eyes with the palms of his hands. "What is this? Please...just tell me?" he implored.

THE OLD MAN sighed and looked up. He was told it wouldn't be easy. But he had volunteered and knew what was at stake. "Son, you have to destroy your work."

"WHAT? My work? What the fuck does that mean?"

"IF YOU DON'T MIND young man, I would appreciate you not cursing. It hurts my ears."

"IF I WANT to say FUCK, I will say FUCK! You get it, you crazy old man?" He stood up and gestured. "You bring me up here without asking, tell me you're my goddamn dead great uncle I never met and then ask me to destroy my work and therefore my career and then you ask me not to curse because it hurts your goddamn fricking ears? And you expect me to say what? Oh yes Uncle Teddy, what a great idea. What a wonderful idea you have there. You know what, fuck you! Fuck this hallucination I'm having; this....this...fucking mad brain trip I'm on! That's why I said yes to the bloody project in the first place! So we can do away with mental health issues and addictions and disease and all that fucking crap, so we can have nice happy lives and not destroy the lives of other people! You hear me. NO FUCKING WAY!"

The old man sighed as he watched his great nephew walk away from him. He knew it wasn't going to be easy. He knew it had the potential to be a fruitless task when he asked to be assigned. But he wasn't one for giving up. He decided to have one last try. He caught up with Jake. "Let's go back to the beach." Before Jake had a chance to speak, they were returned to their original spot.

"Do you know where we are?" the old man asked him. Jake sighed with exasperation and looked around him. He felt exhausted emotionally and physically. He wanted to sleep. Not just for a few hours, but forever.

"No. I have no clue."

"Normandy. We are standing in the exact location where thousands of men lost their lives during one of the most vicious moments in war history. More than four hundred and twenty five thousand men lost their lives here. Both German and allied soldiers. Over twenty two thousand British men. I lost friends and family members on this beach. It was a day forever etched in my memory, no matter how many lives I live."

JAKE LOOKED into the face of his relative and saw darkness swirling into the blue, like melting liquorice. His heart softened as he thought of the young soldier and his friends facing scenes that he would probably never have to encounter in his lifetime. "Can I ask you something before I ask about the work thing?"

"SURE." the old man said, as the memories faded away into silent whispers.

"YOU MENTIONED you lived other lives. I...I don't get any of this, but I want to try to understand. At least I think I do anyway. What do you mean? How can you look so old, yet you died so young? Do you age in death?"

"GREAT QUESTION JAKE. Now you are thinking! Actually," the old man stated, "it's all rather complicated and I don't have definitive answers to that question I'm afraid." he glanced at Jake who looked disappointed. "However, what I can tell you, is that we get to choose how we appear if we come back to visit one of the living."

. . .

"Really? Like, could you have been a woman?"

"Erm, I don't know about that. Truthfully, this is my first time and I guess I wanted to come back close to the age I would have been if I didn't pass early. I think I'm meant to look about eighty years of age right now?" He looked to the younger man for affirmation. Jake shrugged and nodded.

"Yeah around that I guess." he thought again for a moment, his mind scrabbling to make sense of it all. "So why did you come? Why were you sent?"

"Ah, now I *can* answer that one! The Council sent for me."

"*The Council*? What kind of council?"

"Mmm. I've got a question for you. Did you know I was a war hero?" the old man asked with a sparkle in his eyes.

"No. Were you?"

"I sure was." the old man announced with delighted glee, "I saved a whole battalion of US soldiers from a convoy of German troops waiting in ambush for them."

. . .

"Wow! How come we never heard?"

"Ah. Well, I died in the process. Me and my mate Billy Smith were sent on a reconnaissance mission to check the position of the enemy. I saw the yanks coming, but knew there wasn't enough time to warn them before they were spotted by Jerry. We had minutes to decide what to do. We could have made our way back to camp and let the war do it's thing, but if there's one thing the war taught us, is that you do right by others, no matter what."

"So what did you do?"

"We made ourselves known to the Germans."

"How?"

"We sang 'Don't Fence Me In' by Bing Crosby and the Andrews Sisters. Ah, I was a real fan of that song. And my voice weren't too bad neither!"

"What happened?" Jake was caught up in the story, hanging on his great uncle's words.

"Oh well, Billy and me we poured our hearts and souls into that song. And Jerry poured their bullets into us. It did the trick though. The sound of their guns alerted the yanks and our own camp. Many lives were saved that day. You know,' the old man said with a smile, 'we never know how valuable our life is to others until it's too late.'

"Wow!" Jake declared with a smile. "You guys really were heroes." He looked into the calm, warm face of the old man and added, "I'm really proud of what you did for those men Uncle Teddy." The old man smiled back. How long had he waited to hear those words, and he took a moment to savour them before he was asked to answer the same question he was asked earlier. "So come on tell me, what's this all about?"

THE OLD MAN SIGHED, focused his thoughts, breathed in deeply then, in a balanced and even tone declared, "It's your work."

"MY WORK? You said that earlier. Why? What about my work? Is it the company I work for or my actual job role?" Jake was trying to keep the hysteria from rising again, but it flittered in his chest and he felt the panic escaping at the end of his sentences.

"YEAH. BOTH."

"LOOK UNCLE TEDDY. Boy that feels weird saying that, but look here. I have no idea where you are going with this, so please explain. And I promise I will try to keep a lid on my language." Jake said offering a half smile.

The old man instructed him to sit on a large nearby rock at the edge of the sand. He picked up a stick and started to speak.

"This is where humanity is now okay?" he said drawing a circle with the stick on the left in front of their feet. Jake nodded. "And just say this 'X' is the chip thing you and your company are proposing to be fitted into the human brain." he added drawing an X to the right of the circle.

"The chip is called IMMERSE and it won't go into every human brain, just the ones identified with mental illnesses or disease." The old man did not respond, but instead looked solemnly into Jake's eyes holding his gaze until Jake felt forced to look at the markings in the sand.

"These smaller circles here, are human beings. And this IMMERSE chip you helped create will be connected to one main computer right? Kind of like an AI brain? Am I getting that right?" the old man asked, as he drew smaller circles on the right of the X and a large box above the X. He then marked lines leading from the square box to the X and from the X out to all the smaller circles.

"Yes, I guess in layman's terms, that pretty much sums it up." Jake said nodding. "And?"

. . .

"And...who now has control?"

Jake furrowed his brow. "Control of what?"

"The human being with the chip inside their head."

Jake thought for a moment. It was obvious from the drawing in front of him, but he knew that it was far more complicated than the old man had described. "It doesn't work that way."

"Doesn't it? Tell me Jake, once this chip is in, can it be taken out?"

"Well no. I guess it could, but it would be dangerous. It's designed to interact with the brain by electromagnetic pulse activity in the brain fluid, or EMP. Once inside, it's meant to remain as a permanent feature."

"And who controls this EMP? The individual?"

"No, of course not. It's an external control. The person with the chip has no access to any control. That's kinda the point really." he explained and looked up at the old man. "So what's the issue? The chip is our chance to eradicate humanity from disease and mental illnesses; addictions, crimes and evil intent. With this chip, we could become more perfect than we were before. Can you imagine what the future of the human race would look like?"

"Yes I can. We all can." the old man said nodding to the sky with a serious expression. "That's the problem Jake. Whoever has control of this chip has control over the human race." He watched as Jake processed the words he had just heard, shaking his head and poking the ground with the stick the old man had dropped before his feet.

"No. You don't understand, it doesn't work that way. It's meant for good. It's a good thing. It is!" Jake couldn't stop the hysteria creeping into his voice. "It's a good thing for humanity."

"We know you have the best intentions. You have such a sharp and clever brain and a great soul. Your heart is kind Jake, but you have allowed your mind to be led by those who aren't as kindly as you and whose actions aren't to help humanity to progress for the better. Their intent is more nefarious and psychotic than you can ever imagine."

Jake thought of the immoral limping CEO, of his own manager neglecting his marriage and his children because of his work. He thought of the amount of time he himself, had spent pouring over his monitor, the time in research or in the lab with the technicians and engineers. Of all the failed experiments, until finally the day they had a breakthrough. It felt so good to succeed after all the failures.

Could he simply walk away from it because he was having some sort of lucid psychotic hallucination?

"I don't understand what you are asking of me." he said in a calmer tone.

"We want you to take a long look at what you are doing. And to ask yourself where it could go. If the X is the chip and the box above that is the main computer that controls the chip, who controls the computer?"

Jake furrowed his brow. He never asked the question. He assumed it was the government. "The project is for the government. Whoever wins the contract gets the go ahead and the funding from them and the project is hot."

"And where does the government get the funds from? Who does the government work for?" The old man knew he was pushing it, but time was running out. Gently gently wasn't working.

"What do you mean? The government funds it!"

The old man sighed and looked up. This was far more exhausting than he had hoped. Maybe he really was getting old. His old soul was feeling ready to hang up its boots. "It doesn't work that way. There's always someone else pulling the strings. You don't think politics is that simple do you?

One thing I do know about men in power, is that there's always someone further up the money chain!"

Jake lay back against the rock. "I can't do this man. I'm too exhausted. I put everything I had into this project to make it work and now it looks like we've finally got the get go. What are you asking of me?"

"You have to destroy it. Everything. The files, the back up files, the paperwork, the chip, everything pertaining to this project has to be destroyed. No evidence of it can survive. It's imperative for the survival of the human race as we know it, that this project does not go ahead."

"What? Are you off your fu...flipping head? Do you know what you are asking me to do?" Jake jumped up and stood with his arms outreached, shocked at what had just been asked of him. "If we take me out of this, my work, my career, the bonus, everything about me, there are others who will suffer too. All the team including my direct manager, will probably lose their jobs. And let's not talk about the amount of money spent on this over the past five years. God...they'll probably kill me if I do what you are asking!"

"Is that really an issue? I thought you wanted out anyway?" As soon as he spoke the words, the old man regretted it. *Sorry Council I think I just blew it.* He held his breath as he awaited the younger man's response.

· · ·

"Damn you. You have no idea how I am feeling! I lost my daughter. I lost my little girl. You have no right. No right do you hear? Take me back." he shouted. "We are done talking. I no longer want to play make believe. Take me back NOW!"

The old man sighed long and deep. "Okay, okay." he said nodding to himself in resignation. "She told me it wouldn't work. But it was worth a try."

"Who is *she*?" Jake asked shooting him a quizzical look.

"Oh, you'll find out soon enough." he said clearing away the diagram he had drawn in the sand with his left foot. "Do me a favour though boy?" Jake looked up aggrieved, hurt and confused. He levelled his gaze to the old man's. "Say hi to your mother."

When Jake opened his eyes, he was in his bedroom. He could not recall how or why. He looked around him and it was exactly how he had left it that morning. Bed unmade, discarded and dirty clothes strewn around, cups on the dresser and clean garments hanging out of unclosed drawers. He sighed. *Phew! It was just a dream.* He looked down at himself and noticed he was still in his work clothes. He must have got drunk at the bar and somehow got himself home and collapsed on the bed. *Weird dream* he whispered to himself as he sat up against his pillows and ran his hands through his hair. *Strange, I don't feel drunk and I can't taste alcohol on my breath* he thought aloud.

He sought his phone. He found it on the inside of his pocket, exactly where he saw it last at the bar. He checked the time. Twenty-three eleven; eleven-eleven. Huh! He thought to himself. That time was always celebrated by his mother and sisters. A magical time they said; a time for angels. He yawned and stretched and checked for messages. A message from his boss congratulating him and the team for the presentation that morning. It looked like they were the main contenders to win the contract. They would find out tomorrow. He had mixed emotions now. Residue feelings from the dream he decided. No doubt he'd feel better by the morning.

He decided against replying to the work group chat. Some things are better left unsaid he decided, particularly when there wasn't anything conclusive to say. Next he moved onto the family group chat. His name came up often. There was a private message from Suzannah his younger sister. 'Check your messages numbskull!' The message she was referring to was about their mother's seventy-fifth birthday the following weekend. His job was to get the cake.

He replied to her direct message and then to that particular group chat that excluded his mother, since it was a secret surprise party they had planned. He simply had to turn up with a cake. Of course he hadn't organised it, but he would do that tomorrow at work. A job for Cynthia his secretary. She remembered all his family's birthdays the past few months. If she hadn't, nobody would have got so much as a card. With all messages replied to, he thought of his mother. The words from his dream chimed like a soft ringing bell in his head. *Say hi to your mother*. He sat for a moment and recalled the dream. It was so odd; so realistic and didn't feel like he had been dreaming. Yet here he was, in his room, on his bed. And Uncle Teddy died at twenty-three not in his eighties.

He rubbed his face with the palms of his hands and decided to lay off the booze. He'd been working so much and not sleeping, that he must have created some kind of mental imbalance within him he decided. During his research and testing on the chip, he wondered if certain emotions could be extracted from the brain, or numbed? Emotions like grief and loss. And if it could, would he want to not miss her? To not think about her anymore? He shook his head. As much as it tormented his mind, missing her was all he had left of his sweet Eloise.

He sighed and picked up his phone again. It was five minutes to midnight and he was up at six, so he should hit the sack soon. But first he was impelled to do something. He found his mother's name on WhatsApp and pressed record.

'HEY MUM, how are you? I know it's late and you'll get this in the morning, but I didn't want to leave you a text message (pause). You know I love you right? I...I know I don't tell you enough. And I'm really sorry Mum. You deserve so much more (long pause). Since...since Eloise left, I've been in no man's land; totally lost. I miss her mum. I miss her so much (sobs). I...I wish I could bring her back or change what happened, but I can't. I just have to go on living with this terrible loss inside me. It's like this angry black hole that threatens to eat me and I'm tired of fighting it. I don't know how much longer I can keep fighting mum. I wanted to tell you this because I thought you should know. I love you so much and I'm so sorry.'

. . .

He stopped recording and started to re-listen to the recording before he deleted it. He had recorded so many of these late at night when he knew his mother would be asleep, but he had always deleted them before she listened to them. He stopped and pressed pause on his voice. His ears alerted him to a noise coming from the kitchen. He listened intently. Someone was in the house. He placed his phone into his pocket and looked around for something that would serve as a weapon. He chose a hanger from the wardrobe and a work shoe which he held at the softer toe end, so the heel could serve as a blunt instrument.

He slowly crept out into the hallway. "I've got a weapon. I don't want to hurt you." he shouted. He could hear the fear crackling his voice. He inched his way towards the kitchen, where light poured into the hallway. He glanced beyond the kitchen to check on the front door. It was locked.

Jake's brow furrowed as his mind scrabbled around for answers and explanations. Then he stopped mid step, as he heard the fridge door open and then close again. And what was that sound? He inched closer. Humming. Whoever was in his kitchen and helping themselves to his food, was humming! With one huge step and the shoe held in his right hand above his head, the hanger pointing out in front with his left, he threw himself into the room.

"Well hello. You must be Jake? Here, I made you frittata. I hope you don't mind, but I used what I could from your fridge. There wasn't much, but it does look appetising, don't you think?"

. . .

Jake stood aghast. The hanger fell to the ground and his right arm slowly lowered to hang limp at his side. Apart from the fact that the kitchen was looking more immaculately clean than it had been since moving in and the table laid out for dinner for one, standing just in front of him, stood a tall, glowing light blue angel figure. A beautiful female form with long icy blue hair and the darkest, deepest blue eyes, unlike any eyes he had ever seen before. She looked like an angel, but she had no wings.

"Wha...who...?" was all he could muster before he was being ushered into the chair.

"Eat! We have a very long night ahead."

2

THE MESSENGER

It was by far the best frittata he had ever eaten. Soft, with red pepper, mushrooms, ham and just the right amount of seasoning. Despite his curiosity as to the presence of his strange visitor, the desire to eat was too overwhelming. Where did she find the bread? It was delicious.

"It was in your freezer. Your mother dropped it over the last time she visited. She separated the loaf into packs of two and placed them in your freezer. Of course, you wouldn't have noticed, since you don't notice anything these days."

He looked up and intently regarded his visitor. "Who. Or what are you? And why are you here?" She did not answer. Instead she tidied around him, clearing plates and somehow also made him a cup of tea, though he never saw or heard the kettle being boiled.

"As I mentioned," she said with a knowing smile, "you haven't noticed much in a while."

"Okay. I give in. I'm having psychotic hallucinations right? Is that what this and the whole Uncle Teddy dream thing is about? I'm finally going mad?" he asked leaning back into his chair. Despite his fear of entering psychosis, he felt strangely calm and satiated by the frittata. It was just so perfect for the moment. And the tea was just how he liked it. Not too much milk and just a half a spoonful of sugar. The perfect cup of tea.

"No. You are perfectly lucid. Teddy was real. As am I." she answered as she sat in the chair opposite him. She did not eat or drink he noticed. But she did glow. "I'm glad you enjoyed the meal. And the tea." she added with a warm smile and a wink.

"Am I dead?" he asked in shock.

"Hah! No. You have not yet passed. It will be a while yet before your time comes to pass, despite you thinking that is what you want. Though you have the gift of freewill, so it will always be your choice.' The visitor looked at him with a curious and searching expression. *How does she know so much about me? And what the fuck is happening?* He thought. "I can read your thoughts Jake. In fact, I know everything about you."

"What the f...?" he refrained from cursing. The admonishment from Uncle Teddy still lingered in his conscience. "Please. Please...," he asked softly, "please could you explain what is happening?"

"Teddy already explained did he not?"

"He said something about wanting me to destroy my work." Jake said shaking his head.

"Yes. That's right." affirmed the visitor with a curious smile.

"But you know I can't right? It's impossible. And besides, why would I?"

"Indeed, why would you? That's why I am here. To show you why." the visitor replied. She stood up and held out her long hand, with fingers that seemed to stretch forever. "It's time to go on a journey Jake."

"A journey? What do you mean? It's late. I...I have to get up for work in a few hours. I can't go anywhere. What is this anyway? I am going crazy right? It's hallucinations or psychosis or something similar right? I've been working too many hours and my mind has flipped. Yes, that's what this is. You're not real; I'm just crazy."

"No Jake. This is real." she stated in a serious expression. "It is time for you to wake up and see Jake, just how real this is."

"What am I supposed to see?" he said as he grabbed a hold of the outstretched hand.

Suddenly, he was flying through a vortex of colour. A whirlwind of different hues of purples, then blues, then pinks and so on until the colours faded together and lightened to pure white. The light was so bright, that he felt forced to close his eyes. He felt the swirling, travelling motion and the gentle feathery touch of a hand. There was no weight to him, no sense of imbalance; simply a comforting feeling of floating through clouds. Just as he was starting to enjoy the sensation, he could feel that they were slowing down.

When he felt their feet land on solid ground, he opened his eyes. It took a few moments before he realised where they were. They were inside the living room of his older sister Helen's house. He glanced around him. It was tidy, yet edging on scruffy. The sofa had seen better days, with mismatched cushions scattered along it in a haphazard fashion. Scuffs on walls that were in dire need of repainting. Scratches and cup stains on the wooden furniture. It breathed neglect. He glanced up at the blue visitor. "Can I talk?" he asked. She nodded.

"They cannot hear us. We are invisible to them. Here, but not here so to speak."

Jake turned to look at her. Curious now, he asked, "Who are you? And why are we here?"

The visitor explained that she was a messenger from the Council of Angels. He could call her Avorra. In her world, that meant 'way of truth '. The Council of Beings had chosen Teddy as a preliminary messenger before her. They hoped not to involve the Council of Angels, but since time was crucial and humanity was running short of it; they had no choice. Jake's stubborn refusal to listen to Teddy, coupled with Jake's desire to end his own life, meant that the only option was to show him the consequences of what may befall the human race if Jake did not destroy his work.

"So am I in the future?" he asked indicating his sister's home.

"No Jake, this is the present."

"The present? I am sure Helen's house was less, less, er...tired last time I visited?"

"When was the last time you *did* visit her Jake?" the messenger asked. Her large midnight blue eyes bore into his own, as though seeking deeper dimensions within. He felt seen, transparent, exposed. He tried to pull away from her stare, but there was nowhere for him to escape to.

"I...I don't recall."

"Three days before the accident. That's when. Do you remember why you visited?" Avorra did not break eye contact. Jake stood frozen. He had placed all memories pertaining to the time and situations around that period into a deep, dark secret closet inside him. Truthfully, he did not want to remember. "When Jake? When?"

"Please don't. Please don't do this to me." he begged, feeling his knees buckle. He was so tired of fighting the emotion and the memories; so tired of running. He looked down and allowed the tears to fall, some landing on his shoes. It was impossible to prevent their arrival, so he gave in to their escape.

Avorra placed her hand on his arm and in a flash, he was there on that day, in this very room with his sister and her children. There was laughter and tea and cake. So much cake! Then into the room walked Amy, beautiful, glowing and radiant. Watching the memory, his heart leapt with joy. She was so beautiful, so perfect. On seeing her again, he was reminded of all the reasons he fell in love with her. A stab of regret like a dagger, shot through his heart. Then it was crushed by grief again, as little Eloise exploded into the room in a flurry of giggly excitement, surrounded by balloons of different colours. 'This one Daddy, I like this one!' she exclaimed holding a light pink heart shaped balloon and kicking her feet around the unchosen balloons scattered around her. Despite his grief, the memory of the moment brought a smile to his face and heart.

"We were here choosing cake for our wedding." he said still facing the ground. Then he looked up, eyes filled to the brim. "Helen was our designated wedding planner."

"She still has everything in a box under her bed. She still has hope for you."

Jake shook his head. "Is that why we are here? To persuade me to make it up to Amy? To go back to the place we were? Because if so, I can't. I...I...*can't*." he said the last word as a whisper.

"This is the present Jake, or very close to. We'll be visiting the past sometime soon." Avorra said with a knowing smile.

"Hang on! Is this some kind of Christmas Carol thing? You know, the past, present and future revealed? Wait...am I the Scrooge guy?" Jake stood aghast. "Is that what this is? I'm the bad guy?!"

The messenger said nothing. Instead, she looked to the clock that hung on the wall to the right of his head. Then she beckoned him to follow her up the stairs. Jake, both bewildered and affronted by the unspoken assumption, watched the strange, icy blue figure walk past him and head towards the staircase. He wanted to say more, but instead, led by intuition, followed her. Just before he started walking up the staircase, he zipped back into the living room and checked the time on the clock. It must have been significant for Avorra to look there. It was four thirty in the morning. *That's odd*, he thought. *What is so significant about this time?*

The house was quiet except for the hum of the refrigerator and the tick of a clock. Then he heard an alarm go off. It wasn't loud; barely audible and then it stopped. Avorra stopped him outside Helen's room which she shared with her husband Peter. She met his questioning gaze and held it. He wanted to ask why they were there, but he didn't have time. Helen emerged carrying clothes and a bag. He didn't have time to move and she was set to walk straight into him. He held his breath expecting her to shriek or scream, but she simply carried on walking. He shot a questioning glance at Avorra who stood to his left, but she simply smiled that gentle, knowing smile she wore frequently.

Approximately ten minutes later, Helen emerged from the bathroom fully dressed. She wore loose black trousers and a branded grey polo shirt. Her hair was tied back and her face clear of make up. He drank in her features. She seemed to have aged since he last saw her. She was slimmer too, not that she was ever overweight. And she looked tired. Not just tired, but ragged and missing something she always possessed in abundance – radiance.

He followed her down the stairs and into the kitchen; a silent ghost in her presence. She opened the fridge and grabbed a water bottle. Then she made herself a flask of coffee. Jake heard her tummy rumble and watched as she instinctively touched where the sound came from before reaching out for a banana. But after seeing that only three remained, she placed it back and sighed. Then she grabbed her coat and keys from the hallway, opened the door and left the house. It was still dark outside. Jake checked the time. 4.45am. All this happened in just fifteen minutes. He turned to look at Avorra and saw that she was watching him intently.

"Where is she going at this time?" he asked.

"Why don't we find out?" Avorra said, placing her hand gently onto his arm. The next moment, they were stood in the middle of a brightly lit office. Confused but no longer discombobulated, he walked up to the huge floor to ceiling windows and looked out. They were many floors up in the building. He had a sense of familiarity for the place, as though he had been here before. He was just about to ask the messenger a question, when Helen entered the room carrying a Henry type hoover. She wore rubber gloves and a blue apron, with pockets bulging with various cloths and sprays. She was singing to herself. Then he noticed the ear pods. His gift to her for the Christmas just past. He smiled as he saw that he'd managed to get her something useful. It was Cynthia's idea to get all the women in his life an expensive set of ear pods and a designer handbag. *That woman deserves a raise,* he said to himself and made a mental note to reward her in some way. She was yet another person in his life whom he had been neglecting.

He watched as his sister, lost in her world of music and whatever else filled her head, made her way mechanically from desk to desk. Dusting, wiping, lifting, swiping. Then she plugged in the hoover and swerved her way around the carpets. When she had completed that task, she unplugged the machine, glanced around her and switched off all bar one light then exited the room as deftly as she had entered.

Jake turned to Avorra. "Helen has a full time office job. Why is she here? Did she lose her job?"

"No. She still has that job." she replied.

"I don't understand Avorra. Why does my sister have a cleaning job if she still works at her office job?" At that moment, his heart ached for the beautiful soul that was his best friend growing up. *What had happened during the past few months that I missed?*

"It's been nine months Jake. You haven't been engaged with anyone around you in all that time. I suppose you could say that despite being alive, you have not been experiencing the present, not in your life or in anyone else's."

He forgot she could read his mind. He studied Avorra then. He noticed how delicate the features of her face were compared to most women. And her eyes. They were huge and dark and full and deeply mysterious. He looked closer. No lashes or brows. Her lips were small yet perfectly formed, with a pink blush as though she had just kissed a rose. Her long icy blue hair, stroked with white highlights, was just a lighter shade than the winter blue, cold hue of her skin. Whilst her fingernails hung like azure teardrops at the end of long, slender fingers that trailed along the outline of a dress that seemed to have no ending. He wasn't sure if she actually stood on feet, or floated like a whisper just above the ground. She moved silently, yet her presence filled the space around them.

"What's going on with Helen?" he finally asked.

"Isn't it obvious? She is trapped. Peter lost his job and is drowning in guilt, anger and regret. He drinks to mask the feelings of failure that cripple him, but once sober, the avalanche of emotion crushes him, so he drinks again to escape the feeling. And this debilitating cycle continues day after day. Helen is then forced to work two jobs to keep the wheels turning, since her daytime job alone is insufficient for their family expenditure. However, the demands on her are vast and she knows she can only keep this up for so long. If it continues, she will get sick and then her family will really struggle. Hence why she feels trapped. And of course, she misses you." Avorra said gently. Jake winced. Guilt flooded him and he looked down at his feet. He was starting to realise how absent to everyone he had been the past few months. Still, that would not account for why his sister got up at 4.30am to clean offices.

"Poor Helen." Jake replied with sadness. "Does she work here everyday?"

"Weekdays only. The weekends she babysits as often as she can. It pays well. She keeps a portion of that money for herself."

"Why?"

"Because Peter takes any extra money for his habit. Helen does what she can. Besides, her daughter, *your* niece's eighteenth birthday is coming up soon. And she wants to treat her to something special. She is saving the money for that. Did you notice that she did not eat that banana despite being hungry?"

Jake nodded. He was too scared to ask why, since he had already guessed the answer.

"That's right. She won't eat if there isn't enough. She's losing weight and getting tired Jake. She needs a hero don't you think? Or at least her best friend..." Avorra reached for his arm again. "Let's go and see Suzannah now shall we?"

"My younger sister? Oh no, what's going on with her? Is she okay?" Avorra looked into his eyes. He saw curiosity and wonder, but also something else: sadness. Then she touched his arm. He was about to find out.

Unlike their older sister, Suzannah was single and childless. Having spent the first nine years of her life watching her father regularly get drunk and beat her mother at weekends, she swore she would never marry. Even after her mother divorced him when she was barely a teenager and despite the death of her father not too long afterwards, her decision was resolute. She came close to reneging on that promise when she was twenty-seven and sporting a beautiful solitaire ring on her left finger. However, the discovery of his affair with one of her close friends, reminded her of all the reasons she made the decision in the first place. Men were weak and could not be trusted and thus, she was better off alone.

This had been working well until she turned forty-one five months ago. And the tide of regret kept washing her up against the rocks of her life. It wasn't until the grief of the passing of Eloise had subsided, that she realised how much love she had poured onto her niece as a substitute for being childless. And with her brother also missing in action, she felt the combined weight of grief overwhelming. Alcohol had become her late night friend and it was beginning to affect her life. When Avorra led Jake to a wine bar close to where Suzannah worked, alarm bells triggered.

"Who wants another one? My round!" his sister announced rather too loudly. Jake watched as she grabbed hold of the man's arm beside her and in a demonstrative way tugged him towards the bar.

"Stop. I don't want another drink. And we had better go." the man said, trying to gently prise the woman's fingers off his arm. But she would not relent. "Come on Suze," he cajoled in a deliberately calm tone, "I think you've had enough don't you?' he pleaded.

Jake watched the scene unfold in horror. He could not believe this was his sweet, determined, ambitious and fun loving sister. He could feel the tension in the group and hear the exasperation in the man's voice.

"Oh don't be a spoil sport Andy. Come on. Have another drink. One more and we go okay? Just one more little drinkie. Okay?" Jake could see that one more would be one more too many. He found himself approaching to hold her, but he was invisible. He was there, but wasn't. He looked to Avorra in desperation. Avorra nodded for him to continue watching.

"No Suzannah. You've had enough!" the man declared, a little too loud and pulling his arm away from her grip. The circle of people at their table stopped mid sentence. They too watched as the drama unfolded before them. Jake felt helpless. He could feel what was coming and yet he couldn't stop her. He knew from their childhood, that it was impossible to reason with a drunkard.

"Suzannah? Oh it's Suzannah now is it?" she shouted loudly. "Funny," she started peering into his face and almost falling over in the process, "it isn't Suzannah when you want some loving is it? No...you men! You're always the same."

Jake lowered his head in shame. For her behaviour, for himself for letting her down and for their childhood. No matter how long their father had been deceased, his ghost still haunted them. He sighed and looked to Avorra for help. "I don't want to be here." he said slowly.

But his words were not acknowledged. Instead he was forced to watch as the man pulled her close and whispered into her ear. This quietened her and she looked sad and then lowered her eyes. The man then turned to their acquaintances and apologised. He grabbed his wallet and keys and the coat on the back of an empty chair. One of the women in the group reached for a handbag that sat beside her and placed a phone that lay on their table, inside the bag. Then she handed the bag to the man. She smiled condolences and they all said their farewells. The man then gently held Suzannah's arm and guided her to the front door. Jake watched his sister look back with regret at the table she had been walked away from, mouth the word sorry to no one in particular, then exit with the man through the door.

"Why aren't we following her?" he asked Avorra. He was saddened and heartbroken to see his beautiful younger sister become so lost. "My family is broken." he finally said in realisation.

"Everyone is a little broken Jake. But not everyone has to remain that way. It's always a choice." the messenger added. He heard the wistful tone in her voice and wondered just how much they knew and saw in her space above, watching the humans below. He had so many questions. With a tender touch on his arm, she took him to another place; a surprisingly familiar place.

"My mother's garden. Why have you brought me here?" Avorra placed her finger to her lips and looked to the right beyond where he stood facing her. He slowly turned around, his heart pummelling inside his chest. He prayed it would not be another scene with his youngest daughter. Instead, he came face to face with a memory. He turned back to Avorra. "I thought you said you weren't doing the past yet?"

"There's no set rules in this Jake. I need you to listen." she replied in a solemn tone, adding, "It's important for you to hear this."

Sitting on a picnic blanket on a warm day, sat two young children, crossed legs and facing each other. The boy was deep in concentration, making a daisy chain. The girl, around four years younger, sat mesmerised as she watched a stem being wrapped around the neck of a small, white and yellow daisy.

"There!" the boy exclaimed in triumph. "Finished."

"Oooh Jake." gasped the girl in wonder and joy. "Is it really for me?"

"Yes. I made it for you Suzi Blusey." said the young boy, who, no more than ten, placed the white and green garland around his little sister's neck. He was careful to not get it caught in her hair and gently cautious to not break the delicate necklace. "There you go." the boy declared feeling proud of himself. He had broken the first one and hoped this would last longer than the one he had made on their family walk a couple of weeks earlier.

"I love it Jay. I truly do." said the girl as she tenderly fingered the flowers that sat on top of her pastel pink tee shirt. "You're so clever. When I grow up I want to be as clever as you."

"You're already clever silly billy. You're cleverer than all of us put together." the boy replied, tutting his teeth and rolling his eyes.

"I wish we could stay like this forever." the girl said. She was both wistful and sad; her face furrowed and her mouth fell into a sorrowful pout.

"Hey you, don't be sad. Everything will be okay. I promise."

"Do you Jay, do you promise?"

"I sure do Suzi Bluesy." he said, which made her giggle. The boy smiled in triumph at chasing away the sadness in his sister. That morning was a Sunday after the Saturday night before. Sunday was always a difficult day for the children at home.

"Pinkie promise?" the girl said with her face alight and holding out her tiny little finger.

"Pinkie promise." replied the boy as he snuck his own little digit into the half circle shape of her finger.

"Promise that no matter what and no matter how old we get to be, that you will always be there for me?" she said in a voice so serious that the little boy was taken aback. "Promise Jay, promise!"

"I promise. I promise that I will always be there for you. No matter what."

Avorra then touched Jake's arm and transported him from the past to the present in his sister's life. They were in her bedroom. It was obviously the morning after the bar incident and it was clear that she had only just awoken. Without make up and wearing her bedclothes, she reminded him of the young little girl he often found sad or crying in her room and how he always felt compelled to chase those blues away and make her smile again. The desire to do that for his hurting sister at this particular moment, was overwhelming. Yet he could not. Instead, he was forced to watch her sob as she read a letter that had been left beside her on the bed.

Suse,

I'm so sorry. I just can't do this anymore. You're getting worse and no matter how much I try, you won't let me in.

I love you and want to spend the rest of my life with you. I know you don't want children, so we'll get a dog, or a cat or a goldfish. I don't care, as long as it makes you happy.

But the sad truth is, since your niece died, nothing is making you happy. Including me.

I can't live this way. I can't stand by and watch you destroy yourself with drink because you are hurting. We all hurt Suse. Every single one of us. And the truth is, that the only one who can ever really save us, is ourselves.

If you decide to get some help, give me a call. I'll help you through it.

But if you choose to stay on this self destructive path, I'm out. Sorry Suse, but I've tried, I've really tried.

Love Andy x

Jake watched his dear sister's face crumple on finishing the letter. Then witness the crashing sobs that followed. He felt his own tears rise and his heart demand that he fix her as he always had. He couldn't face Avorra so he kept his face locked onto his broken sister weeping on the bed. Anger swelled up inside his chest like a bull ready to fight. At that moment, he was angry at so many people and for so many reasons, but mainly at himself.

Out of the corner of his left eye, he could sense the blue messenger reach towards his arm. He was both relieved and saddened to be leaving this scene. But just before the touch came, he heard these words from his sister that tore his heart apart.

"Where are you Jake? I need you more now than ever. Please, if you can hear me, please help save me."

They arrived back in his kitchen. Avorra had made him another cup of tea. *How does she do that?* He asked silently as he gratefully cradled the hot drink in his hands. He had no words, only difficult thoughts. So much to take in and digest. He tried to remember his sisters' lives before Eloise died. *Were they as broken then? If so, why did I not notice?* He sought for answers in the filing cabinet of memories he held about each of them.

Helen and Peter. She loved her job office managing the small group of salesmen in the busy stationery business where she worked. It was a short commute and they were accommodating and flexible on the rare occasion her children required her home. It paid well and often there were small bonuses for treats like holidays, car upgrades or work on their house. She had friends and played badminton for recreation and had a good relationship with each of her three children.

Peter was a carpenter and always busy. He had always worked for himself until around two years ago when he was offered to join a carpentry firm. It was a risk, since the pay was less, but it was regular income and consistent work, so they decided he should do it. He hadn't realised Peter had lost his job. Their children were fourteen and seventeen, younger than their cousins who were both at University.

Jake's oldest girl Mia was completing her MA in Business at Edinburgh and the youngest, Lily was in her second year of art studies at Cardiff University. They both had part time jobs and full time lives. Jake checked in with his girls every few days and felt assured they didn't need him. Besides, they had a very close relationship with their mother and her new husband.

Helen's children and his own, were close. All of the family were close. Eloise was born into a close knit family group, where laughter, conversation and many family gatherings were the norm. Her death exploded the family unit into many shattered pieces. And watching what was happening to his sisters, it was obvious that some of the pieces were left unattended and discarded.

"Talk to me. Please." Jake said finally. Avorra took the chair opposite him. He noticed that she never ate or drank.

"They are broken Jake. Just like you. Eloise's death broke all of you." she explained. Her voice was warm and filled with velvety tenderness. Jake sighed.

"How can we fix this? How can we make it better?" he asked in defeat.

"Well, that's up to you."

'Me? How can I fix their problems? It's obvious that Pete and Helen are struggling financially. And Suzannah has become a drunk like her father. How can *I* make things better?" He thought for a moment. "My bonus!" he exclaimed in wonder. "My bonus will help Helen and take away all their financial worries. Pete could go self employed again if he wanted and Helen wouldn't have to run two jobs. They could pay for couples counselling and get themselves back on track. Pete's a good guy. I've always liked him. He's just fallen on hard times. I'm sure he can get back on track."

"And your little sister?" Avorra asked as she watched him animate himself with ideas on how to fix everyone. "She has money. No kids. Highly paid job as a lawyer, about to be made partner if she doesn't self destruct. She doesn't need the money you are offering."

Jake pondered on this. He knew she was right. Suzannah was focused and determined and had ensured that financially, her ducks were all lined up so she would never have to rely on anyone for anything. Giving her money would be an insult to her. No, she needed help. Counselling maybe.

"The answer you are seeking Jake, is you. She needs you. And you know it." Avorra touched his hand and the memory of the promise he had made to her all those years ago in his mother's garden, came flooding back to him.

"But. I...I..." he stammered, desperately looking around him as he avoided saying what needed to be said, "I have nothing to give." he said finally. "To her, to Helen, to my kids, to Amy, to anyone. Not even to me." he said quietly as he covered his face in his hands.

"You have everything inside you that you need for a

wonderful life Jake. And you are right, Suzannah doesn't need your money. She needs your love. Just like she needs the love of Andy."

He looked up. Of course! She was pushing Andy away as she pushed all men away before him. Yet looking back at the broken woman on the bed, he could see that she was tired of pushing. Tired of running away from love. "I should speak to him. To this Andy guy and get him to stay?"

Avorra smiled. "It's the right direction. But first, she needs you. Pinkie promise." she said with a smirk and holding out her right little finger in a waggling motion. Jake felt the wound where her words stabbed. He knew she told the truth, but it was so difficult to be the brother he needed to be for either of his sisters. He felt so chained to his grief that he didn't know how to free himself in order to help free them; to love on them, connect with them. He sighed inwardly and thoughts again took him to desiring the black nothingness.

Avorra did not withdraw her hand and instead, kept her gaze focused on his face. He glanced up and then back at the outstretched finger. He found himself intrigued by her hand. It resembled that of a woman, elegant and decorated with colour at the tips, but it was also uniquely different. As well as blue. He had yet to meet a blue woman. *What are you?* He pondered. She smiled.

"I have been waiting for you to ask me that." she said as he remembered that she was reading his thoughts.

"I've actually been wanting to ask you since you came, but the timing never seemed right until now. So, what or who exactly are you? And why have you come to see me?" Jake drained his mug and sat back into his chair.

"Firstly, you know why I am here." she replied.

"Ah yes. To try to persuade me to destroy my entire life's work. Uncle Teddy already tried that, remember?"

"Indeed." she replied raising her right brow and holding his gaze. "There is still time. Not much, but sufficient time to help you make the right decision."

"The right decision for *whom* exactly?"

"For the human race." Her words hung in the air like a noxious gas, cascading through the pores of his thoughts and throwing him into a deep pit of indecision. It all seemed so ridiculous. He shook his head and rubbed his palms across his face. Sudden exhaustion swept over him. It felt like he had been awake for hours.

"Can we put that to one side for the moment please? It's just too overwhelming for me to get my head around right now. After all, I have just witnessed both my sisters falling apart." he said with a deep sigh. *How did that happen? Man, life is so bloody hard* he thought to himself. Then he looked up into his visitor's face and realised she could read his mind. *Damn* he thought to himself. Then *damn* again when he realised she heard that too. "So then, now we have established that everyone's life is pretty much as fucked up as mine, who, or what, exactly are you?"

"I'm afraid I am limited in the information I can divulge and truthfully, the human mind is not ready for that level of understanding."

"Why?" Jake asked with genuine interest. After all, wasn't his work entirely focused on the improvement of the human mind?

"We are not talking about brain function here. Not like with your work Jake. This is much more complex. This is about human consciousness and depth of soul awareness. It would take millions of years of humanity's evolution to arrive at the place of understanding required to even begin to comprehend what humans are capable of."

"Try me." said Jake leaning forward. His interest was piqued. Avorra laughed.

"Trust me, it would literally blow your mind." she added with a knowing smile. The two regarded each other. Avorra, deciding on how much she was able to divulge without freaking him out, and Jake wondering how much he could push to extract those explanations from her.

"Hah! I can read your thoughts Jake." she said with a wink. "I'll try to explain as best I can without making it sound too complex.

Jake sighed. "Sure, okay. Fire away."

Avorra explained how the Universe had many layers and incomprehensible depths. There were multi Universes, known as the 'Multiverse', yet only one ultimate God-like creator, which, to simplify it for Jake, they would simply call the 'Creator'. There existed in this Multiverse, a Council of Beings. This Council was made up of superior beings from across the different Universes and there existed various councils affiliated to this main Council of Beings. Avorra belonged to the Council of Angels.

"So let me get this straight," Jake interrupted, "there is one main God type character overseeing all these different planets that make up all these different universes. And under this God, or Creator guy, there are levels of controlling Councils?"

"No. There is no control. No *one* being controls another. This only happens on the planets themselves." Jake pondered this for a moment. "And since I can read your thought process, the answer to your question is many. There are far more planets in the Multiverse than you can imagine. Yet," she added with a furrowed brow, "only a few planets like yours has such complex and destructive control patterns, where despite being sovereign, the beings choose to allow themselves to be controlled. It's perplexing since most other races choose to live in harmonious freedom."

"Tell me about Earth? I mean, tell me what you guys up there," he asked pointing a finger upwards, "think about us mere mortals down here." She regarded him for a few moments before answering. She could feel the mocking in his tone. He was choosing to not believe.

"On the whole, we are disappointed in the human race." she replied. Her words sat in the space between them. He really tried to imagine Earth floating around in a vast Multiverse of untold planets. Each with its own existence, with beings like humans, living their lives oblivious to other species doing the same. It blew his mind. This wasn't real. *I must be hallucinating* he thought. Or in psychosis. *Grief and overwork have pushed me over the edge* he thought to himself. *Yep! I've gone crazy.*

Avorra watched this man before her, exploring his thoughts and conclusions. She sensed the communication beckoning her before she heard it.

The homo sapien is a curious race, she transmitted back to the Council via telepathy. *Even when confronted with truths that answer the deepest questions in their self limited minds, they refuse to consider them, choosing instead to believe untruths. Their inability to confront and explore a deeper understanding of themselves, creates limitations on their progression and evolution. It is curious to witness.*

I advise continuing with the process of revelation of the present, the past and the future. Yet...perhaps continue to combine the timelines for greater impact? I don't think he is yet ready to accept his part in the potential future collapse of humanity. His mind is chained to trauma still. We shall visit that specific time from the past, but first, he has still to see the impact his withdrawal from his own life has caused on others around him. He has yet to know his worth in the world. Only when he sees how he positively impacts the lives of those around him, can he consider the opposite. That his inability to see the bigger picture, will also be responsible for initiating the destruction of the human being as a race. Time is short in relation to humanity's timeline, but I still believe it is achievable. If I do fail in this task, then you will know what to do.

"When was the last time you visited your mother Jake?" He did not have time to respond before she touched his arm.

They arrived in her kitchen. Immediately, delicious memories of baking bread, making cookies and laughter filled his thoughts and caused him to smile. His mother's kitchen, in the only home he had ever known her in; his family home and his happy place. He glanced at the large wooden table. It was bare now except for a vase of decaying pink tulips and a few letters stacked on top of a book. She was an avaricious reader and there was always a book of sorts on that corner of the table. Memories flooded him, of noisy family meals, of large roasts, homemade pies, lasagne, hotpots, sausages and mash with homemade thick gravy and homemade Yorkshire puddings, followed by ice cream, at least two tubs of differing flavours, with various bottles of sweet sauces and flakes or pots of hundreds and thousands sprinkles. Thoughts of her famous Victoria Sponge that won more prizes in village competitions than either he or his sisters had managed to acquire in their entire time at school, caused his tummy to rumble.

He sighed and smiled. These were such wholesome and soul lifting memories to savour. Laughter, tears, joy, heartbreak – it all happened in this kitchen, with the warmth of the Aga adding to the warmth of their family life. It wasn't always like this though. This was after *he* had left, though in fairness to his mother, she ensured the dark times did not obscure the moments of light that filled their childhood.

These memories disappeared in a flash with the sudden entrance of his mother. She wore a look of concern on her face. He held his breath and tried to hide, before remembering that he was invisible to her.

"Jake?" she said looking around her, standing still for a moment. *She can see me?* He looked at Avorra in a panic. He wasn't mentally prepared to speak to his mother at that moment.

"She can't see us, nor hear us. But she can obviously sense your presence. Curious," Avorra said watching Jake and his mother's reactions, "a mother's love perhaps?"

He watched as his mother sighed and pick up the black, heavy bottomed kettle, fill it with water from the tap and place it on the stove. She chose a tea pot from the cupboard and a matching cup and saucer and placed it on the unit next to the stove. Then she picked up a blue flowered tin that sat on the same unit, extracted the lid and took out a scoop of black tealeaves, before placing them into the teapot. He smiled as he realised he had bought her that particular tea set for Christmas. White with yellow tulips. Her favourite flowers. Her house overflowed with tulips in one form or another.

The kettle sang for its tea and she filled the pot. She replaced the lid and carried the pot and the cup and saucer over to the table, where she pulled out a chair and sat. She then took out her phone, put on her glasses and sighed deeply.

Jake panicked. He looked through the window to the outside. It was still dark. Then he searched for the clock on the wall. 12.35am. They had gone forward and back in time to visit his sisters and seemed to have returned to the time just after Avorra had arrived in his kitchen. In desperation, he walked over and looked at the message on her phone. It was his voice note and it had two blue ticks. She had already opened it! His heart sank when he realised she had already listened. *No!* He cried out in his head. *She wasn't meant to get it. I meant to delete it, but then Avorra arrived... Damn!* He shot a look to Avorra, who carried on watching the woman with a curious, intensity. It caused him to turn back to his mother and study her face. Tears welled in her eyes as she quietly whispered, "Oh Jake. My dear dear Jake."

Tears welled in the corners of his own, as he crouched beside her. He wanted to comfort and cajole her, soothe away the sadness and let her know he was there and somehow, everything was going to be okay. He watched as she reached into her dressing gown pocket for a hanky and wipe at her eyes, then blow her nose. She sniffed away the sobs and then picked her phone up. "Now, how do I leave a phone message on here?" she asked herself as she studied the app, turning the phone around as though the back had the answers.

"Press the microphone mum!" he told her hoping she could hear despite him only being a silent visitor. He watched her fail numerous attempts at figuring it out before she shouted, "Siri, how do I do a recording on WhatsApp?" Jake chuckled. She was always asking Siri for help. But then again, so did his girls. He didn't though. He held an unquantified, yet intuitive distrust of intrusive AI tech. Which given his work, made no sense at all.

Siri talked her through the process of recording a message on the app, then Jake watched as she attempted a recording three times, before finally succeeding. What she said both filled and tugged at his heart.

'My darling boy. Where do I begin? (deep sigh). I love you. It's as simple as that. Sitting here in my kitchen, drinking tea from the teapot and cup and saucer you bought me for Christmas, which I really love by the way, I can feel you. It's as if you are here next to me.

There's so much I want to say. So much we haven't said to each other. I know you hurt. Losing your little girl like that was such a terrible thing to happen to you. But it wasn't just you who lost her that day. We all did. I miss her so much. She breathed life back into me, back into this house. She was such a beautiful whirlwind of happiness and joy. Oh that little giggle of hers, somehow seemed to fill the voids in all of us.

She was just coming into her own. Not far off turning five; such a magical age for a child. She loved her school and her friends. I so loved teaching her to bake and we had just started doing Fimo on Fridays after school. You used to love making and baking at her age too. She loved her time with Granny and I adored our Friday sleepovers together. Now my life seems so empty. All of our lives do.

But we can't stop living just because she isn't here any longer. Even for just the short amount of time she had with us, she was a blessing. She left a huge impact on us, both individually and as a family. We owe it to her to carry on living blessed lives and more importantly, just to carry on living.

I know you have thought many times about ending your life. I often read your messages before you delete them. I don't sleep much. I worry about you, Helen, Suzannah, your kids, Amy. Yes Amy. She lost her child and her fiancé in one day. Her life was torn apart that day too, but she continues to work and to live her life despite the huge holes in her heart.

You weren't the only person impacted by her death Jake, we all were. One way or another, we all were. And right now, this family needs you. I know you don't want to hear it my son, but you are the only one who can pull the family back together again. We all need you.

I listened to your message three times. You sound desperate. I am praying you are still alive and not gone and done something stupid.

Remember that I love you. We all love you. She loved you. For the sake of Eloise, stay. And then come back to us. I Love you...I Love you so much. Mama.

Jake watched as his mother sent the message then allowed her tears to wash down her face. It broke his heart.

"We must go Jake. Time is running short." Avorra said reaching for his arm.

He took one last look at his beautiful, sad mother, before asking in a chocked voice. "Where to now?"

They arrived in the middle of a busy college campus canteen. It was a hub of activity and constant chatter. They were surrounded by students bustling around tables; some carried trays of food items, seeking a place to sit and others queuing for the food counter. All the while, the excited buzz of conversation, clinking of cutlery and dishes, as well as the scrape of chairs being pulled in and out against the wooden flooring.

"Why are we here?" he asked perplexed. Avorra nodded to a table in the far right corner of the room. She started walking towards that direction and so he followed. *Should I know this place?* He asked himself.

"Good question." Avorra responded, "Should you?" She stopped in front of a table of students. There were four altogether. Three girls and one boy. At a quick glance, he could tell they were all creative types. Then he gasped as he saw a blue haired girl turn to look his way. Despite her gaze going through him and towards something behind him, he felt completely exposed. And shocked. *Since when did Lily have blue hair?* He shot a questioning glance at Avorra. She nodded for him to continue watching.

"Hey guys." said the boy approaching from behind Jake, before taking up a seat next to one of the girls. Jake immediately disliked this boy. He had an arrogant air about him that he had felt and despised in a certain type of man. Edward possessed it, as did his manager Henry. He found that it usually came from people with money and a sense of entitlement. As he watched this boy command everyone's attention, his lip curled into a snarl. He was working them for his advantage. It was so obvious, but they were all falling for his charm, including his twenty year old daughter.

He studied the way she hung on his every word. The adoration in her gaze and the way her eyes glistened when he spoke. It was obvious that she was infatuated with him. But he did not once look her way. What Jake did notice though, was the way his left hand rested on the top of the thigh of the pretty blond girl whom he had sat next to. It was obvious they were more than just friends. What he did not understand, was why his daughter seemed not to notice.

He and Avorra watched the group's interactions. Jake noticed that every so often, the boy would stroke the inner thigh of the girl beside him, or give it a suggestive squeeze. For some reason, it made Jake's blood curdle each time. The boy was a player. And he vehemently disliked players. Then a bell rang and the noise level of the canteen grew a few more decibels as chairs scraped, crockery clattered and conversations changed.

His attention was drawn to his daughter. The food on her plate remained mostly uneaten. He hadn't noticed that she had been moving it around with her fork, but not actually consuming much. When she stood up, he noticed that she was much slimmer than when he last saw her two months previous. The dungarees she wore all last year, were now hanging more limply. He studied her face. It too was looking gaunt and pale. Alarm bells were triggered. Something was happening to her.

Then he saw the arm of the boy he disliked swing around Lily's waist as he leaned in to kiss her on her lips. It was a proper kiss. *What the f...? I thought he was with the other girl?*

"Love you Lils." he said to her as his fingers slid across her neck, pulling her close to him. Jake rushed to grab hold of him, but Avorra reached his arm before he got there. The next moment, they were in a dimly lit room. Jake squinted in the semi darkness to make out their environment. There was an unmade bed on the right, with what looked like a sleeping body hidden under a duvet, clothes strewn around everywhere and music he didn't recognise humming in the background. He heard a sound to his left and saw a man emerge half naked from a bathroom doorway. It was the boy who kissed lily. Light poured into the room from the bathroom and he recognised an item of clothing on the floor. Lily's dungarees. Jake was ready to swing again, as his eyes darted from the dungarees, to the boy and then, with a sense of dread, to the person lying on the bed.

"Yo Lils." the boy quietly called out. No sound. He walked over to the bed, pulled back the covers and half exposed the girl. Thankfully, she was laying on her front so Jake did not have to witness her upper nakedness. He felt a mixture of emotions blaze in his chest: anger, frustration, fear, shame. He watched with distain as the boy rummaged through Lily's clothes and found a £20 note. *Bastard!* Jake shouted in his head. His hands tightened into fists. Then he saw the ashtray on the side. He recognised the contents immediately: cannabis tokes. This sat beside an open packet of tobacco and Rizla type papers. Then he saw a small, clear plastic bag with what looked like white pills inside. *What are those?* He asked in horror. *What's he been giving her?*

The boy got dressed, took the tobacco, papers and plastic bag containing the pills from the table, along with a half bottle of vodka and left. He didn't wake Lily.

When he had left the room, Jake checked on his daughter. He felt helpless as he watched her sleeping and probably unaware of what was happening to her. He knew she was no doubt high and drunk, which would explain the weight loss. It also explained why she had been messaging more frequently requesting money for 'art project materials' and 'museum trips,' yet putting off coming home. He had been feeding their habits and that boy's pockets for months. Jake felt awash with feelings of anger and guilt.

"She'll be fine for now Jake. She can still be helped, but the boy has plans to introduce her to darker substances. Then..." Avorro said in a soft voice, allowing unspoken words to hang in the air like stale smoke of a hundred cigarettes. She touched his arm and they were in a different place again.

This time, they were walking along a street. It was cold and windy. He looked around him. He recognised the area. They were in Edinburgh. One of his favourite places. He guessed they were visiting Mia next. Other than Amy, she was the only woman in his life that he had not yet made a visit to with Avorra. Secretly, he was hoping they would miss Amy. He wasn't ready. He wasn't sure if he would ever be ready.

"Please tell me she isn't a drunk, a druggie, sleeping with a narcissist pig, down on her luck or starving herself to death. Please God." Jake lifted his eyes upward and placed his hands together in prayer. "Please let Mia be okay?"

"Relax. She's in here." Avorra said entering a restaurant. They approached a table with two people dining. Two women were deep in conversation. He recognised them both immediately. Sarah, his still beautiful ex wife and mother of the older girls, sat intently listening to the young woman in front of her. From the shape and colour of her deep, dark brown hair, he knew that the other woman was their oldest daughter. He smiled at Sarah instinctively. He never blamed her for the affair. And a part of him still loved her if the warmth growing in his heart was anything to go by.

He glanced over at Avorra. *Why are we here?* He silently asked her. She indicated that he should listen to their conversation.

"Mia you are not responsible for anyone but yourself. I keep telling you," Sarah instructed her daughter, "if your father chooses to wallow in that dark place, that is his choice. It is not your responsibility to save him."

"I know, but he's my father. And he's so lost right now. Lily thinks he's suicidal."

Sarah looked shocked. "Really? Why? Has he said anything to her?"

"No, but you know what Lily's like. She picks up on other people. I'm worried about *her* too." Mia said as she moved the pasta around on her plate. Jake watched with growing concern. Apart from the shock of what she was revealing to Sarah, this was her favourite place to eat and that was her favourite dish. He knew Mia. She never ate when she had something troubling her. A throwback to the anxiety after her parents' marriage breakdown seven years previous.

"What's up with Lily? I tried to call her yesterday but she didn't pick up. I feel like she's avoiding me. I've tried to arrange a visit, but she keeps putting me off. What do you know?"

Jake had walked around the table so he could see both of the women's faces. He watched as Mia bit her lip, a nervous trait, then place a forkful of carbonara into her mouth. A well played out ploy to avoid the question.

"Mia...what's up with Lily?" Sarah also knew her daughter's avoidance tactics.

"It's a boy. And..." they watched as she chose her words carefully, "and he isn't good for her."

Jake listened as Mia described the boy perfectly, though he would have added far more expletives than she did. She spoke about her sister's infatuation with him and how she thought he was sleeping with other girls as well as her. *Well that confirms it* thought Jake, remembering the boy's hand caressing the thigh of the blond girl. She told her mother about the weight loss and her worry about her not looking after herself. She wondered if she might be dabbling with drugs and blamed the influence of this boy.

"Oh and another thing," Mia added just before forking another spoonful into her mouth, "she now has blue hair!" The two women raised their eyes as they absorbed the idea. "I know..." Mia added on seeing her mother's shocked expression. "It's not good."

"And that's not Lily! She is the last person to dye her hair blue! Oh my God, she won't even go to the bloody hairdressers. Do you remember all those tears and the cajoling to get her hair cut? What the hell is going on with her?" Sarah exclaimed sitting back in her chair.

Jake watched his ex wife's face. She was devising a plan. She always had a plan. He loved that about her. That was part of the reason he slid into becoming a workaholic: he knew that she could manage the family by herself without him. He didn't know that she would end up managing so well that she no longer needed him in her life. He had so many regrets.

"Okay I have a plan." she announced in seriousness. Mia leaned in. "I have some spare holiday leave at work. I'm going to take her away with me. You okay with that?"

Mia nodded. "Mum, I have my MA finals to work on. I don't have time for holidays. Besides," she added with a wink, "you promised to take me to Florence for my birthday remember?"

"Already sorted!" the older woman added with a knowing smile and a wink.

Good on you Sarah, he thought. *I could always rely on you when it came to the girls.* He then turned his attention to Avorra who was silently regarding the exchange between the two women. He saw something in her face that intrigued him. Was that adoration, recognition? He shook his head to shoo away the notion. It seemed preposterous, but he couldn't entirely shake a feeling that she was more attached to this whole situation than merely getting him to sabotage his work. And for some reason, she remained a silent observer more during this encounter than any of the other family visits.

She caught his eye, smiled with satisfaction and approached him with more tenderness than usual. "Are you ready? Just one more person to see." Before Jake could object, she had touched his arm.

They arrived at a rehabilitation centre. There were medicine balls, various step machines, some cycling equipment, pull hoists and varying machines, mats and tables. The smell was both clean and fresh yet also had the feint must of a workout room. He looked around him and realised that they were situated in an area of a hospital. He threw a questioning glance at Avorra. Then he followed the direction of her eyes.

Behind him three people were walking into the room. A woman and man in blue medical outfits and the other, was Amy. His heart stopped. This was only the fourth time he had seen her since that fateful day. The first was after the accident, the second at the funeral, the third weeks later and now. On seeing her, everything he had been running away from, all the pain, all the memories, in one torrential gush, floored him on the spot. He couldn't breath. His legs wobbled. *I can't do this. I can't be here!* He cried out silently to Avorra. *Please, don't make me do this, please.*

Avorra walked up and placed a hand on his right shoulder and gently squeezed. Then he heard them talk.

"Have you been doing the shoulder exercises I gave you last week?" the male physiotherapist asked. The female physio had walked over to a table where she checked on a piece of equipment. Amy shook her head apologetically.

"Amy, I know it's hard, but the only way your shoulder will improve, is if you strengthen it with the exercises. Now, what about the neck ones? Have they helped?"

"Yes. A little." Amy replied in just a whisper of a voice. The man tilted his head as he assessed his patient.

"Okay, let's concentrate on the shoulder and neck today." he added gently. He advised her to sit on the chair beside the table and showed her exercises he expected her to repeat. As she did them, he wrote on a sheet of paper on his clipboard. "Good. That's good. Try to repeat these twice a day as we discussed last week okay? You will soon see the flexibility return." Amy nodded.

Jake noticed how quiet she was. This wasn't the Amy he

remembered. The bubbly, gregarious, fun loving, light hearted Amy who made the air sing whenever she entered a room. She was the type of person that carried a light energy around with her wherever she went. The person sitting there, in a grey and black tracksuit, pale and subdued, was a mere shadow of the woman he knew.

"You all suffered when Eloise left. But perhaps the one who was most impacted was Amy." Avorra said sidling up beside him. Jake stared at her with incredulity. How could she say that? Wasn't he broken to the point of suicidal? In fact, leaving was pretty much all he could think of before Avorra arrived on the scene. Then he looked back at the whisper of the woman he should already be married to. He studied her face. She looked pale and lifeless and much older than a woman in her late-thirties.

"She's getting help though right?" he asked. He couldn't withdraw his eyes from the woman turning her head from right to left as instructed. Her movements were mechanical. She was there but also not present. He knew that feeling well. *Simply existing* he thought.

"That's right," Avorra agreed, "simply existing but not really present."

"Is she getting any help?" he asked again with growing concern. Memories of why he fell in love with the woman she was, inched into his consciousness.

"She's been offered."

"But..?" he asked confronting Avorra.

"Jake, you know more than anyone that you can only be helped if you choose to be."

"And she has chosen not to be?" he remarked incredulously. Avorra nodded slowly. A look of poignant curiosity shadowed her features.

"Freewill Jake. That's the curious part of being a human.

Choice has both a negative and positive option. As you well know." she added raising her eyebrows.

He stood for a moment watching Amy struggle. Not with the physiotherapy, but with surviving. And then, in a flash, he was transported back to that fateful day. "I can't do this Avorra,' he said clutching the top of his chest. 'I...I can't breathe."

"You have to do this. You have to see the results of pain and neglect and regret. To see it in her, will help you to confront it in yourself."

"But I don't want to!" he cried out, arms outstretched and walking in a circle. "I don't want to." he repeated, his voice snagging on the sobs that had began wracking his chest.

Avorra touched his shoulder again. "It's time Jake. It's time to let go." And just like that, he broke. He fell onto his knees and allowed the past nine months of emotional blockage, to rip forth. The dam had burst and there was no longer the option of papering over the cracks. It cascaded out. Regret, shame, loss, anger, guilt, despair, all of it pouring out from him. And when eventually his body ceased to convulse and his tears refrained from flooding his face, he slowed to a whimper. All the while, Avorra kept her hand on his shoulder. What he could not see, was that her eyes were closed in prayer and that the other angels in the Council above, were all praying with her. "Jake we have to go, to leave Amy. We have little time."

As Jake composed himself, drying his eyes and wiping his face, he stood up and brushed himself down, then turned to face Avorra. There was something in her voice that concerned him. Her tone had changed. She seemed more serious. "Why?" he asked.

"We have to leave Amy now and go to your work place.

There have been developments that have changed things slightly."

"Changed things?" Jake repeated sensing her concern. "What type of things?"

"I'll show you, but first you need to send a message saying you are not coming into work today. It's Friday and they are expecting you to be in."

"What should I say?" he asked reaching for his phone.

"That you feel poorly. Send it to Cynthia and ask her to make the correct excuses for you. Oh and Jake, ask her to arrange a cake for your mother's birthday too." she said with a wink. He sent the message and then looked up just as she reached for his arm. Before they left, he managed to glance back at Amy. His reaction to her had changed. No longer did he feel so inclined to put all the blame at her door. Nothing could bring their daughter back to them, but continuing the pain and not forgiving was destroying more than just one life. *Perhaps,* he assessed *it was time to let go and start to heal?* As he was leaving, this thought remained with him.

They arrived at the back of a large wooden panelled room. The carpet under their feet was a lush deep red. Thicker than most office carpeting, imported specifically from a Persian company that also supplied to members of the Saudi Royal Family. He had only been invited into this room once. Then, he was poured a glass of the finest grade aged whisky, served in French cut glass crystal glasses and offered a Montecristo Cuban cigar imported from the finest cigar makers in Havana. The best of everything for Edward the CEO of TecTT.

The room was empty. Curious, Jake looked questioningly at Avorra. *Why are we here?* He asked without speaking. Avorra ignored him and instead led him to Edward's desk. Her eyes indicated that he should look at the document on the top of the desk. Jake furrowed his brow and did as instructed. He walked around the desk so that he stood behind the green leather chair, pulled back as though someone had recently been seated there. He squinted as he read the contents of the document. He noticed that they were stamped TOP SECRET in red across the top. Since he normally wore glasses to correct his long sightedness, it took a little while for his eyes to adjust. What he read chilled his blood.

The first page of the document was a list of everyone involved in the research and development of PROJECT IMMERSE. Jake's eyes scanned the page and the next page and the one after that. Despite five years worth of dedication to this project, *his* project, his name was missing from the list. Confused, he looked up at Avorra. "I don't understand," he questioned aloud as he kept re-scanning the pages, "my name isn't on here. Why is my name not on here?"

He scanned the page he was reading further. It was a cost analysis proposal and breakdown of bonus payments to specific staff on completion of the project. It was written as though the deal had already been done. Yet his name was not mentioned. It was as if he did not exist. Just as he was about to quiz Avorra further, Edward came into the room from the bathroom. Jake and Avorra swiftly moved to the left corner of the room. Neither took their eyes off the large man hobbling towards the desk and falling heavily into his chair. He pulled himself close via the swivel wheels and sighed deeply as he glanced at the document on his desk. He hesitated and looked around him suspiciously, before pressing the intercom on his desk.

"Margaret, has anyone entered my room in the last few minutes?"

"No sir. I have been here all morning. No one has come by your office."

"Good. Okay, can you let Henry know I am ready to see him now please. Oh and bring us some coffee and cake will you. Not those nasty pastries the rest of the company gets. I want macaroons. And maybe some carrot cake from that place down the street."

"Yes sir. I'll sort it straight away.'

'Good. Thank you Margaret. And one more thing..."

"Yes sir?"

"Did you get me the details on Jacob Hayden Bridges that I requested?"

"I put them on your desk sir, in the black folder as discussed."

"Good. Good. Okay that's all." Edward reached for the unmarked black folder on the right hand side of the desk and opened it. He gave it a quick scan over, nodded with satisfaction, then replaced it back where it was. He then returned to looking over the document in front of him.

Why does he have a document with my name on? He shot a perplexed glance at Avorra. *What's going on?* he queried silently. Avorra indicated for him to listen.

"Sir, there's a call for you. From a Mr Black?" Margaret's curious voice buzzed over the intercom.

"Put it through and get Henry to wait until the call is finished. Then leave us in privacy okay?"

"Yes sir. Understood."

The call was put through but instead of having it on speaker, despite there being nobody in the room, Edward placed the receiver to his ear.

"All dead lines are being cut off as instructed... Yes... Only myself and Henry... Of course he can be trusted, but as you say, nobody is ever really fool proof in matters of this type of business. I have him by the balls... Tight leash. Hah... Yes indeed, everything is under control and set to go...Good. Oh and one more thing...the wire is set up to that account right?..Let's say that there are things I prefer my wife not to know. How many designer handbags does a woman need right?...Hah! Indeed!.."

He replaced the receiver and picked up his phone. Jake walked up behind him to see who he was messaging. *Who is Helena? That's not his wife!* He was arranging to celebrate a big deal with that woman this weekend. *Another last minute 'work trip' scheduled,* Jake thought, knowing how many of these men chose to live their lives. Then he recoiled as he saw two naked photos of this Helena in explicit poses. She looked to be no older than late twenties. He was at least seventy-two. *Gross* thought Jake as he walked backwards away from the man he disliked more and more with each passing moment. He looked at Avorra and shot out his tongue in a mock vomit face. Avorra raised her brows and shook her head. He could feel from her energy that she also felt repulsion towards this man. *Can angels get angry?* Jake pondered, before glancing at her and realising she could read his every thought.

She did not reply, but instead nodded towards the door. Henry was about to enter.

"Let him in Margaret." Edward informed his secretary. He straightened the documents on his desk and sat back into his chair. The door opened and Jake's boss glided in with a welcoming smile and over the top exuberance. He wore a navy blue, feint lined suit and a light blue shirt and a tie with pink and white stripes. He looked smart and polished and ready to move up a financial rung on his ever expanding ladder.

"Edward! Lovely to see you on this gorgeous Friday

morning. I must say Edward, that you are looking very fine today." the younger man squealed. Henry did sycophancy like he wore aftershave, to excess.

"Indeed I am Henry my boy, indeed I am. It's a very fine day indeed. Sit down, sit down. Coffee is coming." the older man announced as they shook hands and patted each other congratulatory on each other's shoulder. They both sat back in their chairs and then Edward, without a word, slid the black folder containing Jake's name, towards the other man. "You have people?" he asked raising a brow.

Henry opened the folder to the front page of the document, scanned it for a moment, furrowed his brow and nodded slowly. "Is it entirely necessary? I like him."

"It's been requested. There is no choice, so yes it is necessary. I need to know if you can sort this or I shall have to consider using someone else." the older man said. His tone had a suggestion of threat to it. He wasn't a man to be refused.

"It can be done for Tuesday. We need him to sign off some important documents first, and more importantly of course, hand over the files and data for the chip. Without that information, the project is useless." Henry conceded.

"And he is the only one who has access to this?" Edward asked with incredulity.

"Yes. It was put in place as a security option."

"Have you ever wondered if he has made copies or, God forbid, has been corrupted by an outside interest?" Edward asked furrowing his brow.

"No. It isn't possible, not with Jake. Let's just say, that he is tied to his work." Henry said with a knowing raise of his brow.

"Ah yes, the *accident*." Edward said leaving the word hanging. *What the hell does that mean? Why did he say it like that, like it's questionable? What the f...?* Jake's thoughts were interrupted by a knock on the door.

"Enter!" Edward replied. Henry drew the black file close and Edward turned his document over so that it was positioned face down. An attractive woman in her late forties arrived with a tray on a trolley. The tray was loaded with a polished silver coffee set, cakes of a varying assortment, plates, cutlery and napkins. She did not say a word, nor make eye contact. And the two men said not a word either, but their eyes scrutinised her. She poured the men coffee and moved the trolley with the tray to the right of the table. When she had finished and left the room, closing the door behind her, Henry raised his brow and nodded at the older man. He in turn, smiled.

"Let's just say that the new wife didn't want another 'would-be Mrs Hilliard' taking her place. She picked her! You know that given the chance, I would have had some young filly pouring milk into my coffee." he said with a guffaw and a wink. Henry faked a laugh and wrinkled his nose in disgust when the old man wasn't watching.

They helped themselves to cakes, added milk to their coffees and then sat back and regarded each other. Edward spoke first.

"By Tuesday. He has to be gone by then." he stated then bit into a green macaroon. "Mmm. Delicious."

"It'll be sorted. Shame. I liked him." Henry added trying to avert his eyes away from the crumbs falling out of the side of his boss's mouth. He despised the creature, yet was playing the game and biding his time. Two more years and he was ripe to take over the company. It was promised.

"How will you do it?"

"You leave the details to me Edward. The least you know, the better." Henry declared with a wave of his hand.

Jake shot a glance at Avorra. He was in shock. *Are they talking about me? Are they going to fire me or get RID of me?* She did not answer, but simply continued to watch the men. She looked lost in her own thoughts. Perhaps she was communicating telepathically again with the Council above he wondered. *How can this be happening to me? I...I don't get it. I poured myself into this project, this company. Damn, I am this project!*

He sat and listened as they spoke about future projects and the logistics of how the project will be moved forward once the details are in place and everything signed off. And when 'all loose ends are tied up.' Those words sent shivers down his spine. *Spineless bastards* he growled to himself.

It was when the conversation had moved to the nitty gritty of the chip and the IMMERSE project, that Jake really started to worry. Since when were the military and the heads of the national security agencies involved? That was never discussed. Surely the chip was for improving humanity? After all, hadn't he sat in on all those meetings with the varying medical institutions? They never once discussed considering the use of the chip for military, security or control purposes.

An anxious knot started to twist in his stomach. He moved closer, hoping to read the document over Edward's shoulder, but despite turning it back over to face the right way up, he had not re-opened it. *Damn* thought Jake. *What was in the rest of that document?*

"So as soon as the project is signed off and the money deposited, it is out of our hands. Correct?" Henry asked.

"That's right." the older man said leaning back in his chair. "Once signed, our job is done. Signed, sealed and delivered. And once Jake is out of the way, then no one will be able to trace it back to this company. Our hands will be clean. We will be on our yachts in the Caribbean, soaking up the sun and smoking more of these babies." Edward smiled appreciatively as he studied his cigar and offered a Montecristo to Henry. "Ah, life is good."

Just before Jake ran at the men with his fists clenched, Avorra had grabbed his arm and transported him back to his mother's garden. This time, no children sat giggling and making daisy chains on a picnic blanket. There were just the two of them in the late morning Spring sunshine. Jake could not speak. He was incensed with anger and outrage. *How dare they*, he thought over and over. *How dare they*. His mind kept running over the conversation between the two men and the way they were so self congratulating about what they had done and the devious things they planned to do. Then a thought struck his mind.

"What day is it today?" he asked her.

'Friday.' she watched his mind working, listening to his thought processes.

"I'm confused. One minute I am somewhere on one day, then another place the day before. That's what makes me think this is just some weird fucked up hallucination or something. None of it makes sense."

"Timelines only exist because you think they do." she added as a way of explanation.

"What the heck does that mean?" Jake asked in exasperation.

"Jake, we don't have time to go into deep explorations of timelines and quantum theories. You will simply have to trust me that this is all real and that your life, as well as everybody's life on this planet, is in jeopardy. And besides," she added in a matter-of-fact manner, "if we don't do something very soon to stop all this, you aren't surviving past Tuesday anyway!'

Jake was shocked into silence. He didn't expect such a callous comment from an angel, even if she was blue and sent down to kick his arse. Yet despite feeling affronted, he knew that something had to be done to prevent both the project moving forward and his proposed murder. He couldn't help but wonder how they would do it? Would he be bundled into a car and thrown off a cliff or tied up in chains and sunk to the bottom of the river mafia style? Or perhaps an arranged suicide? Or maybe an accident? Yes, that seemed more likely he thought; far more believable. Though he had been suicidal, so that was a bummer if they chose that route, he pondered.

Meanwhile, Avorra stood by and watched him as he walked around in circles with these thoughts. He was definitely out of the suicidal pathway for himself and he was suitably unnerved by the nefarious plans of his company leadership, but she noted, that he missed something important about the meeting; something that had been mentioned. She waited for him to recall it, but as the moments passed and his thoughts constructed a plan, she knew that its relevance had by-passed him. She sighed inward, as she realised that people usually only ever saw just a small piece of the bigger picture.

"So then, it seems I have just four days, perhaps less, to come up with a plan. If I don't, I'm buggered." he added frowning.

"I guess you want to live now?" Avorra said stating the obvious. Jake was taken aback. She was right. Throughout that meeting, all he could think about was how to avoid being killed off.

"Yeah. I guess." he agreed with a small shrug. Avorra smiled to herself. That was half of her mission accomplished. She wondered if she would have achieved that quite as easily if not for the late development of his planned demise? When the Council informed her of the existence of the document, she was saddened. However, despite taking a risk to expose him to the men's plan, she also saw it as an opportunity to change his mind. She was grateful that it worked. It could so easily have gone the other way. Her mind meandered back to when she was propositioned for the mission.

It was never going to be easy. Not for Jake, nor for her.

"So what are we going to do?" Jake asked in desperation. Avorra brought her attention back to him. This was bigger than her. She required the help of the Council.

"To provide you with the answer you require, I will need a little while alone. My elders at the Council will have a better understanding of these matters than me. For that reason, I am going to take you back to your apartment Jake. I suggest you have a rest, maybe shower and eat. We have a long weekend ahead of us. There is so much you have yet to see, before you can truly understand why I am here."

He opened his mouth to speak, but she had already touched his arm. The next thing he knew, he was lying on his bed again, looking at the ceiling.

3

THE COUNCIL OF BEINGS

Azera was neither a planet nor a definitive place. It existed simply because the Council chose it to exist. It was unaffiliated to any planet, solar system or Universe. Thus it was deemed a safe and objective space for the members of the Council of Beings. There existed on Azera, other member bodies, including, though not restricted to, the Council of Angels. It had no lists, no grading or hierarchical systems in place. It was simply a space for higher souls to share wisdom, teachings and understanding. As the name of the Council suggested, it existed for the conference of angelic beings and these came from planets past and present that existed within the Multiverse.

Avorra returned to Azera to confer with the higher souls in the Council of Angels. Although an old soul herself, who had transmuted to the angelic realm and this was her first planetary mission and probably one of the most important given to a lower angelic being for centuries. Though time was usually of no relevance on Azera, time was running out for Earth and its inhabitants and the consequences on the rest of the Multiverse was still unknown. With the imminent threat on Jake's life and his project due to be taken over by the darker side of the human race, her mission to save Jake from ending his life and going on to destroy his work, had taken a sharp turn into deeper and more complex territory. The steps she took next, were crucial.

She was welcomed into the Council Chambers immediately. Despite no words or ceremony, the love that enveloped her and permeated through her soul, provided energetic revitalisation. It was an intensely beautiful feeling of peace and oneness; a sensation that no one word could ever entirely describe.

She closed her eyes and disseminated her thoughts. They listened in silence. When finished, she stood without motion, weightless, empty of mind and full in heart. She felt them before she heard their whispers. They were all as one. A decision had been made and agreed upon. It was time for her to return to Earth; to Jake and to continue the mission that she had been chosen for.

JAKE LAY on his bed for the longest time staring up at the Artex paint patterning on his ceiling. It was crackled and yellowing in places, with stringy, grey cobwebs slouching lazily in each corner. He still had not managed to replace the broken light shade from months ago, so a dusty bulb hang limply from the centre of the ceiling.

He chose to glance around him. Books haphazardly piled, letters and half written notepads fought a lamp and some dust layered toiletries for space on the top of the low laying chest of drawers.

He employed a cleaner, but he kept cancelling her out of shame. He always intended to clean up before the day she was due to arrive, but he never did. Everything in his life was in survival mode, including this flat. He had always been cautious with his money and rarely over spent, preferring instead to save. After his divorce settlement, he bought a small house in which he later shared with Amy and Eloise. They were ploughing all their spare money into a wedding fund. After the accident, he never returned to their home and rented this tiny flat in a busy London suburb, from a friend.

He recalled the moment he and Amy met. A friend's summer house party overlooking the River Thames an hour's drive away. It was a truly beautiful and warm evening in late June. Shorts and funky shirt weather. He had a low alcohol can in his hand and a paper plate with barbecue food in the other. He spotted the only one, unoccupied chair on the outside decking and hastened his way towards it. However, the rush to get there before the salad and coleslaw slid off his too papery, paper plate, meant that his mind was focused entirely on the task at hand. He didn't see the other contender for the chair until it was too late. She was talking on her phone and casually striding with her drink in her other hand, towards the only outside seating space unoccupied. Laughing, with the phone to her ear, she slid onto the chair and looked up just as a dollop of coleslaw landed with a plop onto her light blue summer dress.

"OH SHIT!" Jake exclaimed as the salad and the sausage rolled off his plate and followed suit. He watched with both horror and bemusement as the receiver of his lunch, screamed out, threw her drink over the back of the man to her right and looked up into the face of her food assailant, a look of bewildered shock on her face. "Oh Lordy, I am so sorry." Jake mumbled. He bent down to try to retrieve his lunch off its new home, but didn't know what to pick up first, so he retrieved the fat sausage that sat squarely in the middle of a salad and coleslaw mush.

"I GUESS that's what you call a sausage roll!" he said without thinking. It could have gone either way, but Amy saw the funny side. Luckily her friend who lived in the house with her husband, lent her a new outfit. And that's how they began a six month relationship before they conceived Eloise during an early Autumn, cold and wet camping trip to the Brecon Beacons. It was freezing, they got drunk and no precautions were considered. Hey presto! One unplanned for little girl was on the way.

As Jake sat back and reflected on those early courting days with Amy and the subsequent months of pregnancy that ensued, he wondered if he and Amy would have made it if she hadn't conceived? There was so much he loved about her, but was there enough for the relationship to have made it without the gift of Eloise? She was an accident yes, but she was also a beautiful gift. Did he wish he hadn't met Amy that day? *No,* he decided. Did he wish they hadn't conceived a child together? He pondered on this for the longest time. Then he remembered his little girl's sparkling blue eyes and infectious smile, framed by the cutest dark curls. *No. I do not regret meeting Amy or having Eloise.* He declared to himself with assurance. *Perhaps it is time to get my house in order, since time is something I may not have much left of,* he decided as he got up off the bed and started to tidy up his bedroom.

By the time Avorra returned, it was late afternoon and

the sky was starting to darken with the threat of rain. Jake felt her presence before he saw her.

"You've been productive I see." she said as she looked around the flat. Discarded dishes from all over the flat, were in the dishwasher and running a cycle. The overflowing washing basket was just a quarter full and clean clothes hung drying in an airer in the spare bedroom. The bathroom had been sprayed and wiped over and bleach placed in the toilet bowl. The bed had clean sheets on, books and papers were neatly piled on dusted surfaces and the cobwebs had disappeared. "I'm impressed." she added with a smile.

"I guess knowing your life is about to end, kinda puts a firecracker up your ass!" Jake replied with a smirk. He had started to walk towards the kitchen to make himself a much earned cup of tea, but then Avorra did something that made him stop in his tracks. She laughed. Yet it was not just a laugh; she giggled like a child. He swung himself round to meet her head on. The sound she made had reminded him of his lost little girl.

"Tea?" Avorra said as she swept on past him. He noticed that despite fixing her face into a serious expression, there remained a flickering twinkle in her eyes and a slight raise of the right hand corner of her mouth. Amy also did that. As the blue angel disappeared into the kitchen, his mind was considering endless and impossible possibilities. He had so many questions.

. . .

"So how did the meeting go up there?" Jake asked fixing his eyes upward and breaking the awkward silence between them. "Did you figure out a way to save my sorry ass?" She did not answer. Jake squirmed a little in his seat. *Perhaps she thinks I am taking this too lightly?* he pondered. She sat opposite him and seemed to compose herself and her thoughts before speaking.

"Tell me Jake," she asked meeting his eyes, "what have been your thoughts on the past twenty four hours?"

Jake was taken aback by the directness of the question. He was confused. Surely she knew his thoughts since she read them all the time? "Do you mean tell you aloud? Like not in my head?" She nodded. Her face took on an open, yet serious expression, as though he were at an interview. Then he realised something that blew his mind – they were all watching him; not just Avorra. He squirmed a little more and felt himself sinking into the chair.

"Part of me thinks I am on a weird mind trip. Like as though I have been kidnapped, strapped into a chair and force fed some kind of hallucinogenic drug. But then, another part of me believes that what I am experiencing is real." Avorra nodded for him to continue.

"It's like I get another chance at life." he said glancing at her then down at his feet. He continued. "You know I was planning to end my life after this deal don't you?" Saying it aloud made it finally real, though he felt shame and guilt creep into his heart, which no longer felt so broken and pained. "Well," he mumbled looking first to his hands which he twisted in and out of themselves, and then up to meet the beautiful, open and comforting face of his blue companion, "I guess I no longer feel that way. In fact," he added with a resigned smile, "I'm ready to fight to stay alive."

AVORRA SMILED. She felt the assurance of the Council above her as they too shared her joy. "And what of your work?"

A SHADOW FELL across Jake's face as he masticated on all the knowledge he had acquired in the past day. The way his family were broken and each suffering in one form or another. Except perhaps for Mia, though he knew that her propensity to suffer with anxiety, was being triggered with the weight of others' struggles. How the loss of Eloise had wounded each person and that he was the only ointment that could heal those wounds, save for bringing her back. And he already knew that possibility was never going to be an option.

A thought crossed his mind and his face lightened with the idea. He glanced back at Avorra. She could read his thoughts. However, a look of sympathy crossed over her face as she shook her head slowly. She wasn't coming back. Jake sighed.

"I THOUGHT my work was so important, you know? My way of helping people." he said with resignation. "During my research, I visited hospitals and hospices and watched the old and young alike, die horrible deaths from diseases like cancer. When I watched a child not much older than Eloise pass from neuroblastoma and saw how broken the family were, I resigned myself to finding a way to beat this disease.

We spent years working with doctors and scientists and researchers, to find a way to stop normal cells from transmuting to become killer cells that would go on to destroy the body. I spoke to psychologists, philosophers and even deeply spiritual people, to explore ways of convincing the body not to encourage the negative advancement of these cells. But it was all fruitless. The diseases continued no matter what we tried. I lost my marriage to this work. Sarah was my best friend and I neglected her. In reality, I forced her to look for love elsewhere, because I was already deeply engaged in my own affair with my work."

AVORRA SMILED and lightly touched the tip of his knuckle of his left hand which lay rested on the table. He was transported to an image. They were in Sarah's house. It was night time, he could sense the darkness outside and that end of day feeling of relaxation and exhaustion. Sarah and her husband David, were on the sofa, glass of red wine each in their hands. She had her head on his right shoulder and her feet curled up beside her as she always did when snuggling on the sofa in the evening. They looked at peace together. In fact, he could feel an energy of balance and harmony they emitted as a couple. They were talking. He couldn't hear their words but he felt the depth of their relationship - the love, the respect, the friendship. And then he knew. She was happy, he was happy. And that was all that mattered. He could finally release that heavy stone of regret that prevented him from truly letting go of the guilt of destroying their marriage. She chose to leave and made the best choice for her. Avorra removed her hand and held his gaze. She saw something new in his face that wasn't there when she first met him; resolve.

Jake sighed and sat back in his chair, reflecting on all he had learned. "So," he stated matter-of-factly, "I lost my wife to my job, I lost my daughter to an accident, my family is a mess, my life's work is apparently going to destroy the human race and my bosses are planning to kill me in what...?" he said looking at his watch. "Roughly three days?" He sighed. "I'm doing well aren't I?" He shook his head and looked upwards. A thought struck him. "Why can't you guys step in? You know, take out the bad guys? Then the rest of world could carry on living their lives as they see fit. Or mucking their lives up if you look at mine." he added rolling his eyes.

"Freewill Jake remember?" Avorra reminded him.

"Ah yes. Freewill." he added blowing out his cheeks with a sigh, "So, what's the plan?"

"You destroy the chip, the data and all information relating to the chip."

Jake laughed and threw his head back, leaning into the chair. "You make it sound so easy.
And how do you propose I do that? Assuming I want to that is..."

. . .

"You still don't see do you Jake?"

"See what? What am I supposed to see exactly? You say this chip will destroy the human race, but all I see is a technological advancement that would enable people to live longer, happier lives free from devastating and crippling diseases. And that's just one aspect of it. What if we could do away with crime, or mental illnesses like paranoia and schizophrenia? Or severe depression that often leads to addiction, harm to another, or even suicide. What if we found a way to cure all that? How many millions of people could be helped and saved worldwide? Don't you think *that* is worth exploring?" Jake implored with passion. His voice was animated, pleading and perhaps to another human being, convincing. However, Avorra was no human being.

"It is time to show you Jake. It is what the Council decided. It is time to show you the future. The future that *will* exist if the chip is implemented. You see Jake, whilst your intentions to help humanity are benevolent, there is an opposite, malevolent viewpoint held by a small number of men and women whose priorities are not for the good of mankind. Indeed, as you will see, it is very much the opposite."

4

OPERATION END GAME

'Who controls the past controls the future and who controls the present controls the past'
~ George Orwell

THEY WATCHED the numerous black SUVs circle around the forecourt, until they reached the entrance doorway, where they would stop to deposit their passengers. Doors were opened and held open for officially suited men and women to exit and then proceed to through the doorway to the building. Some of the passengers were not suited, but instead wore the clothes of their country, such as those from wealthy Arab, Asian and African countries. Each guest was greeted by someone in a suit and checked off with a clipboard. Jake noticed the line of strong bodied, suited men. Jake regarded these men. Short crew cuts, wide shoulders, earpieces attached to ears, black sunglasses and when they weren't holding a hand to their earpiece, they were clasped out in front of them. Security he guessed with a raise of his brow. Avorra hadn't told him where they were heading, so he was trying to take in as much detail as possible. He wanted to figure it out before being informed.

He noticed that every one of the guests who entered the building, had with them a metallic black suitcase. That lifted his curiosity. *Who are these people?* he pondered.

"Elites. Well," added Avorra with slight contempt "they call themselves that." Jake regarded her with curiosity for a moment and again so many questions rose to the surface. She met his gaze squarely. "We don't have time for questions Jake. We are here to observe."

"Observe?" Jake asked perplexed. Avorra nodded. When the line of cars had expired and the forecourt was empty except for some of the security men, Jake took a moment to reflect on their environment. He studied the building. It looked like a mansion of some kind, but with so many dignitaries amassing in one place, he counted around a hundred at least, he couldn't help but wonder what type of person owned a place like this? He considered the possibility of it being a conference or business centre, disguised to resemble someone's private residence? So many questions.

"Shall we go in?" Avorra cut into his thought process. Jake nodded. His curiosity was piqued. She touched his arm and they found themselves standing at the back of a very large room. The people he saw enter the building were now seated in a large circle. In front of each person, was an open laptop. *Hence the suitcase*, Jake thought.

A buzz of excited conversation filled the room. It was a

beautiful, grand room, with gold ornate trimmings on elaborate architraves and tall, wide windows extravagantly dressed in heavy drapes. A huge chandelier dominated the centre of a rose ceiling above them. Large, gold framed paintings of various landscapes and people from the past, filled the vast wall spaces. He guessed that the room once probably served as a ballroom. His mind wandered to curious thoughts of a past history full of grandeur, dancing, eloquently dressed ladies in beautiful ballgowns and men in sharp black tuxedos. Music playing, dancing, champagne, fine dining. The stories of the room's past lives flashed before him in seconds.

His train of thought was sharply derailed by the commanding voice calling for everyone's attention. The man who was the only one standing among the guests, was situated to the top left of the circle, He welcomed the attendees and thanked them for their presence at 'this most important meeting.' He then went on to quote someone Jake had never heard of. Something about power being in the hands of a chosen few. Then he said something that chilled him to the bone.

'YOU HERE TODAY, you...are the Chosen Few.'

JAKE SHOT A GLANCE AT AVORRA. *Chosen Few. Chosen to do what?* He questioned silently. Avorra ignored the question and returned her gaze to those in the room. Jake followed suit. The man who spoke, then introduced the person seated to the left of him. Everyone stood and applauded this new speaker. Jake regarded him. He was definitely familiar but who he was, Jake couldn't recall.

For the next few hours, they watched as speaker after speaker disclosed their plans for the future of the human race. Jake lost count of the amount of times his jaw dropped in disbelief and shock. He noticed that Avorra watched him intently, watching his reactions as disclosure after disclosure was divulged. Each plan seemed more devious, unbelievable and nefarious than the previous. After approximately forty-five minutes, one man stood up and the room went silent. He was a serious looking, military type with wide shoulders and a strut that hinted of a long serving military career. Jake noted that he had a ruthless air about him, not helped by the cold, steel grey eyes in a pinched, action man chiselled face that rarely cracked a smile.

He was joined in his presentation by a shorter, slimmer man who pulled out his chair and checked the overhead projector which until that moment, Jake failed to notice. *Who are these people and what are they doing here?* he thought as he waited with baited breath to hear what he had to say.

'Ladies and gentlemen, esteemed guests,' he announced to the room, 'welcome to Operation End Game.' The room erupted with clapping and a buzz of excitement. 'Thank you. Yes, these are indeed exciting times for us.' He nodded to the smaller man who obviously was responsible for the projector. 'We have the chip!' Again the room erupted and this time a self congratulatory smile cracked across his stony features. He placed a hand up to command the room for silence. A slide appeared above him on the projector. The same slide also appeared on each laptop. 'This...' he said, pointing above him, 'is the future. Is *our* future.'

. . .

"Is that my chip?" Jake asked Avorra. Confusion and incredulity choked his voice. *That's my chip!* he screamed in his head. Avorra nodded.

"This is what will happen if the chip is not destroyed. In fact, this is already in place. The only thing they are missing is the chip and the data. And the only reason they don't yet have it, is because you are still alive to protect it. Tell me Jake," she asked with genuine curiosity, "why did you not share your information with anyone else?"

Jake thought for a moment before answering. What a curious question. And truthfully, one he had never contemplated before. The answer was simple, yet from a business and corporate perspective, made no sense. "I just knew I shouldn't," he shrugged and left the answer hanging between them. Avorra made a curious face as she digested the answer. Then nodded to herself and smiled. Their conversation was interrupted by the voice of the military guy. Jake noticed for the first time, that his accent was not British. He was American. Then he properly took a closer look at the people in the room. There were many different nationalities represented between them. *Curious. A global group of elites.*

'With this technology, we can hack the human brain and create a new human consciousness. One that can be controlled; be manipulated and be entirely directed, not by freewill, but by *our* will.'

. . .

"What the f...?" Jake mouthed to Avorra. He was in shock. "How can they think like that? What type of human would want to do that to another, let alone to their entire human race?" He asked as he listened further.

"The kind that would kill you for being in the way," Avorra stated raising her right brow. Jake shuddered.

'I know you will have many questions, so I am going to introduce to the front, esteemed scientist and award winning medical Doctor...,' said the man as Jake gasped. He knew that guy. He studied and followed his work. He even consulted him once on the possible implications for the human brain, if a foreign substance was inserted into the brain fluid. This man was a scientific hero of his. How could he sell out to the bad guys?

"Money Jake," Avorra cut into his thoughts, "Isn't it always about money? Isn't that what makes the world go round for you humans? How much money, things and power you have over another?" she looked directly at him, no, into him, as she spoke. He felt exposed, seen and ashamed.

Jake returned his attention back to the presentation. He listened as the Doctor described the process of how the chip would enter the brain fluid and release EMF pulses to the part of the brain requiring functionality. The nanotechnology was so minute, that it could only be seen through a microscope.

He explained how this nanotechnology was connected to a main 'Mother' main frame computer, which initiated all the commands to the brain. Then he explained in layman's terms, what nanotechnology was and why it was a crucial element in the process.

'With this nanotech inserted, undetected, into the body, or the brain in this aspect,' he said pointing to the slide above him, 'we can have full control of the human mind and the human would have no clue that their brain had been hacked,' he said in triumph. A buzz of conversation filled the room.

Jake felt nauseous. "I think I am going to throw up," he said as the blood drained from his face. Avorra touched his arm and they were outside in an instant, with just enough time for Jake to turn his back and vomit. When he was finished, he found a wall and leaned his back and head against it. "I did that. I created that...that...thing."

Avorra sighed. She could not lie. It wasn't her nature. In fact, it was impossible for her to tell an untruth. "Yes you did Jake. But there is still time to change this. The future doesn't have to be this way. There is still time."

"Show me how? I'll do it now. Right now." Avorra did not speak, instead remained silent and looked up with her eyes closed. She was in communication with the Council. Jake looked away despite his curiosity. It seemed so private; so beautiful. Unlike me, he thought to himself as he devoured the realisation that he had inadvertently created the greatest weapon man could use against man.

"It has been decided," she announced standing before him, "that it is better for you to see all of the future in its darkest conclusions."

"So we are not going to destroy the chip now? But I don't understand. You heard what that Doctor guy was saying – they are going to insert nanotech inside every human brain and control them. What was the word he used? Hacking. That's right, they are going to *hack* the human brain! We have to stop them!"

Avorra smiled. "Patience Jake. Everything will work out according to the right time. It is good you now see the reasons for me being here, but first, you have to know what could happen, just in case."

"Just in case?" he questioned raising his voice, "just in case of what?"

"You decide to do it all again." Then she touched his arm and they were back in the room.

. . .

'So how will we get this new type of technology into peoples' brains you may ask?' the Doctor said. Then he put a slide up that curdled Jake's blood. The Doctor held a tiny object in his hand. 'This,' he declared holding a small white pill in between his thumb and his forefinger, 'is the future of the New Human.'

Another buzz filled the room, as each person picked up a small, clear white plastic bag with one white pill. Some of the attendees studied the content of the bag, others took the pill out to regard it more closely. It was the size of a normal coated pill, but each one had a blue mark on. Jake couldn't see what the mark was, but it looked like a logo of some type. They were showing them to each other and were deep in discussion until the military guy stepped up and commanded silence again. Nobody argued with the military guy. Silence filled the room once again.

'Each 500mg tablet contains a nanotech substance designed to enter three areas of the brain. Now, for basic understanding, we are going to break these three areas into memorable sections for you, since not everyone here is a brain surgeon right?' he laughed, lifting the mood of the room. Jake noticed how intently the attendees were listening. 'So we will call these areas of the brain, forebrain, midbrain and hindbrain.' A slide came up above him and on their laptops explaining these areas and the functionality of each area.

'As you will see, each of these three areas are responsible for different functions of the brain and the body. Now,' he stated with enthusiasm, 'imagine that we had technology in place that could control these functionalities? That we could control how a person thinks, how they move and what they could do. Imagine,' he said in a low, but commanding tone, 'what we could do if we had total control over a person's mind and body? Just imagine, ladies and gentleman, that we discovered a way to eradicate freewill and free thought from the human mind. With this technology, ' he said holding up the pill, 'this is all possible. Indeed, with this level of control, the possibilities are endless.'

The room erupted in discussion and Jake looked down at his feet. The speaker then explained to the attendees the science behind the pill and the process of how the technology would reach its destination- the brain fluid. There it would sit awaiting commands from the Mother computer. He explained that its first instruction, would be to shut down the area of the brain responsible for free thought and critical thinking. Denying the existence of an external spiritual God-like presence, would be the second instruction. 'After that ladies and gentleman,' he continued, 'that human is a totally malleable being, which we can control and manipulate to suit our own agendas. It's perfect.'

"I HAVE CREATED A MONSTER," he said with regret and shame. "What have I done?"

"YOUR INTENTION WAS for good Jake. You are not like these people. Their intention is not for the good of humanity. You," she said with tenderness in her voice, "only wanted to help humanity."

. . .

He sighed. Part of him wished he had gone through with suicide the day after he found out about the accident and Eloise's death. The intention was so strong in him then. The will to leave so overpowering, yet his rational was that he could not leave those whom he loved. The push and pull of those emotions almost destroyed him. It was then that he poured himself into his work. He was given unlimited funding. Then a thought struck him. *Why was I so encouraged to dedicate myself to this project instead of taking time off to heal?* He thought back to the conversations he had with Henry after the accident. He desperately wanted to take a sabbatical. Or at least a couple of months off. Yet Henry poured attention on him, suffocated him with false friendship and ultimately convinced him that dedication to the project would be a suitable distraction for his pain.

The bastard! Jake thought clenching his jaw and his fist. *He had this planned all along. He was always a part of this. Yet he wasn't in the room?* He glanced questioningly at Avorra.

"Henry is simply a manager. He is as expendable as you," she said as way of explanation. 'These are the self proclaimed elites. They believe they are better than the rest of humanity. Don't worry, you will soon see."

Then another thought memory caught hold of him. One that threatened to crush his soul. "I remember now," he said in astonishment, "I was going to quit the project because I had concerns."

. . .

"And what else do you remember?" Avorra said. Jake couldn't see, but her face had alighted in wonder.

"A meeting. I informed Henry that the project could not work because of concerns I had about the technology getting into the wrong hands."

"And his response?" Avorra asked with piqued interest. Jake reflected for a moment before replying.

"He told me not to worry as he would ensure that I was the only person to have access to the project until I felt ready to present it out."

"And then what happened? Do you remember your response?"

"Yes," said Jake in a serious voice, "I told him that I did not want to continue with the project and that I was going to destroy the chip."

"Do you recall why you were concerned about the chip Jake?" Avorra was searching. He could feel it.

"Because, because..." he replied probing his memories for the correct answer, "because I was worried that it gave too much power to AI over the human brain. And also, what could happen if this new technology got into the wrong hands."

AVORRA SMILED. Jake stared at her with incredulity. He knew all along that the chip had the ability to be used malevolently. *So what happened?* He thought. *Why did I continue with the project knowing this?*

"I'LL TAKE you back to that place soon Jake." she said responding to his thoughts. "For now, let's return to the room. It's important for you to know their plans."

FOR THE NEXT hour or so before the attendees enjoyed a lavish lunch, they watched a presentation on how this nanotechnology had the capability to be controlled through instructions sent by signals initiated from a main computer. The Doctor guy described the functions of the brain and how each functionality currently operated, then compared them to how the nanotechnology could manipulate different instructions to the brain by diverting and controlling current brainwaves via EMF pulse activity. This would be carried out on a microscopic level, so that the person would be unaware of any changes occurring in their brain.

'WITHOUT THE PERSON feeling any change, or being aware of any difference in their brain activity, they will then become completely compliant to the instructions fed into their brain from the Mother computer. They won't know it, but they will become a new type of human, whom we are calling the New Human.'

JAKE GASPED. His mind raced around trying to figure out if there was a way for this evil project to fail, but he couldn't come up with a lifeline. If indeed this nanotech made it's way into the brain, then it would indeed be capable of both receiving and sending signals. It was fool proof. Exactly as he envisaged it, minus the nefarious end game.

'AVORRA, If this goes live, humanity as we know it, will be destroyed!' The blue angel simply nodded solemnly, continuing to watch the room.

THEY ENDED the meeting for lunch. When the room was completely empty except for the security guards that acted as sentries at each doorway, Jake walked towards the desks. He looked at the pills. He couldn't hold them since the guards in the room might have seen the packets move. He could not alert them to his presence, albeit as an observant ghost. He was wracking his brain again, trying to recall information that might figure out an opportunity for their project to fail, but his mind was blank. He knew, within the deepest part of him, that the only solution to preventing this from happening, was to destroy the evidence, or go back in time to prevent the conception of the chip.

"SOMEONE ELSE WOULD HAVE COME up with it Jake, you know that. How many companies do you think were in the running for this project? How many decades have scientists spent trying to conceive a workable chip? The amount of animals and even humans that have been sacrificed in the name of scientific advancement..." her voice trailed off as she watched him lean against a wall in shock and anger, holding his head in his hands.

"Until I figured it out, right?" he said shaking his head. He was both a genius and the father of the end of the human race as they knew it. "Fuck! Fucketty fuck!" He glanced at Avorra who had raised both her brows in surprise. "Sorry," he apologised, "but I did just find out that I killed freewill!"

"It's okay. I understand this has come as quite a shock to you." she replied gently.

"I have a question?" he asked, meeting her eyes, "how are they going to get billions of people to take this pill?"

"I'm glad you asked Jake." she said with a knowing smile before placing her hand on his arm.

They landed in a factory in the middle of a desert. He guessed they might be in a US state, given the accents of the men driving trucks and shouting instructions to the workers below them, who were handling large wooden box containers. Jake glanced over at Avorra. *Where are we?* Avorra indicated to keep watching the scene ahead.

He counted at least five large transporter trucks. Their tailgates were all lowered and pallets containing numerous crates of these plain wooden boxes were being loaded on. There was a hub of activity emerging from the opened factory doors, as crate after crate was placed on the trucks, landing with a thump. *Whatever is in those crates, hold some weight* thought Jake. He noticed that many of the men on the ground had a darker skin colouring and spoke with a Spanish dialect, though it could easily have been Latin American. He wondered if they could be near the Mexico border, or even in South America.

"What are they doing?" he finally asked.

"Loading the pills." she said. He shot a surprised glance at Avorra. A few moments ago, they were listening to men only introducing the idea of the pill and yet now here they were, watching them about to be shipped out.

"Where are they taking them?"

"To secure warehouses across the world." she answered matter-of-factly. "The process is about to begin." she added meeting his eyes and holding his gaze. There was something about her eyes that he couldn't shake off; a slither of a vague memory, a scent of something past. He shut off that door in his mind and focused back on the scene unfolding before him. He felt as though he were watching a film. *Where are the good guys?* He pondered watching in disbelief as crate after crate of wooden boxes containing these destructive nano weapons, were loaded onto waiting trucks.

"You Jake, are the only good guy the world needs right now." she replied with such seriousness that Jake slid inside himself trying to find a dark hole in which to hibernate. That was some responsibility on his shoulders.

"So what happens when they get there? To these warehouses and places?"

"They wait."

"Who waits? What are they waiting for?" sometimes he wished Avorra would tell him everything all at once so he wasn't being thrown titbits of information to figure things out.

"Your brain wouldn't be able to comprehend everything if I showed you all at once." she replied to his thoughts.

Damn he thought as he realised she could hear everything he was thinking, then *damn* another twice as he remembered that she could hear literally everything he was thinking. Instead, he tried to focus on what he did know. That truckloads of those evil pills stuffed with mind control nanotech, were heading all over the world, to holding facilities awaiting instructions to release them to the unsuspecting populations of those countries. Then a thought occurred to him.

"How are they going to convince the world to take these pills?" he asked. "I mean, that's a pretty big ask right there. People aren't stupid. They aren't just going to take something without first wanting to know what it is, what's in it and how safe it's going to be. They are going to want to ask questions for sure!"

"How were *you* going to get the technology into the brain Jake?"

"By direct injection. My team and I worked with the best brain surgeons to devise a way of inserting this technology directly into the brain fluid near the base of the head. It was fairly painless since the needles are tiny enough to allow these minute nano microbes to enter into the fluid without causing harm either superficially to the external skin or to the brain matter functionality. However, we had agreed to trial under general anaesthetic to begin with, just to be sure."

He glanced over at Avorra. He couldn't read *her* thoughts, but he could tell that she had many questions of her own. "It was safe. On all the animals we trialled, none were adversely affected by the insertion."

. . .

"And the humans?" Avorra asked meeting his gaze. "How did they respond?"

Jake bit his lip. "We hadn't begun the trials on human subjects yet."

"And why not?"

"Funding, time, the usual constraints. And to be honest, previous trials conducted by other scientists and researchers on their human subjects did not bode well for the subjects."

"Yet," Avorra added in a serious tone, "you planned to sign this off on Monday as a workable chip to insert into a human being." He detected sarcasm and anger in her voice.

"Yes. I guess," he replied with hesitation, "but to be fair, they did tell me it was going to be handled by the government and the medical institutions after that."

"And that is why I am here Jake."

"What?" he asked confused. "You're here to stop me signing the contract right?"

. . .

"Yes and no. I am here because your intentions were in the right place. However, your reasoning wasn't. You are naively trusting of those in authority. You always have been. And that Jake, is your biggest weakness."

She was right of course. About all of it. He had always been naive and trusting. And despite his father being a drunk and a bully, when he was sober, he was a great father to his children. He realised at that moment, just how much he hated his behaviour, but also loved him. And this meant that he forgave him so easily and thus allowed him to continue his behaviour, by justifying it. Then the realisation, hit him like a hurricane- this had been his response to everything his entire life. He saw, but chose not to see. He knew that this technology ran a risk of being manipulated for less benevolent purposes than his own, but he chose to ignore the doubts. The question he was asking himself at that moment, was why? Why did he turn a blind eye to the risk?

The answer came like a punch to his stomach. Ego. He ignored his inner warnings and intuitive insight, because he was driven to achieve through the desires of his researcher's ego. The realisation that he wanted this project to succeed, despite the warnings, stopped him in his tracks. A tsunami of guilt and shame floored him. "I...I...I'm sorry." he admitted. "I'm truly sorry."

"I know." Then she put the palm of her hand to the left side of his face and looked at him with deep love. In that moment, there existed an energy, like an umbilical connection of pure love, running through her and into him. He looked into the face of his blue messenger and felt something wash over and through him. A calmness, a peace, a feeling of something leaving. And what remained, was an inexplainable feeling of forgiveness.

"It is time we moved on. You wanted to know how they are going to get the people to accept this pill?" Jake nodded. "You're going to love this." she added with a wry smile as she touched his arm and sent him transporting again.

They were inside this time. In a room with just five men. The room had no windows and just one exit, a closed, grey metal door. The five were seated on wooden chairs around a wooden table. Each had in front of them a document, a pen, a clear notepad and a glass of water. There was a knock on the door.

'Come in!' cried out one of the men in an American accent. A man entered with a tray. On this tray was a decanter of whisky, five glasses, ice, napkins and a plate of shortbread. He placed the tray down in the centre of the table and left, closing the door firmly behind him.

'Gentleman?' asked the same man who spoke, indicating the whisky. The other men nodded. He poured each a drink. 'To Operation End Game.' he announced and raised his glass. The men repeated the same words and took a drink from their glasses.

. . .

'Let's proceed.' he said placing his half drained glass in front of him. He looked around him. He gave the nod and opened the first page of the document in front of him. 'As you know,' he said, 'we have been trialling the pill on human subjects for the past six months. The results have been mixed. The coating on the first batch leaked the contents into the blood circulation system before the nanotech could reach the brain. This resulted in both failure and loss of subject.'

'How did the subjects die?' One of the other men interrupted.

'They were eliminated of course. We cover our tracks always sir.' the first man stated.

Jake shivered and tried to hide against the wall, despite being invisible. *These are not good people* he thought. He sensed Avorra gesturing him to remain calm.

'So what is the current progress of the pill? Have we successfully formulated the coating to remain intact for the tech to reach its destination?'

'Yes sir. The project is live.'

. . .

Jake shot Avorra a glance. *We're too late*, he cried out in his mind. *They are already starting to roll it out.*

"Relax Jake. This is the future remember?" she said in tone that calmed him. They were so close to the men in that small room, that he felt sure he could be seen and heard.

They listened as the men discussed the logistics of the roll out. They were talking in the present moment and not some future event. It was as thought the pill was already in the process of being accepted by the people. Avorra was reading his thoughts and indicated for him to listen to the conversation in the room.

'Now the pill is ready to go live, we need to convince the people to take it. Gentleman,' said the man who had been doing most of the talking and was obviously leading the meeting, 'the document before you is a plan of what happens next. I don't need to remind you, that this is top secret and cannot be discussed outside of this room other than to your sub divisions and only then as much as they are required to know. Do you understand?' The other men nodded. 'Not even the Heads of State, including the President, gets to hear about this. Is that understood?'

'Yes sir.' they all agreed in unison.

'Good. Now here is the plan...'

. . .

THE MAN EXPLAINED to the others in the room, that there would be a threefold approach to the global community. Firstly, they would announce to the world a potential global disaster. A new parasite had been discovered in a water system in the Amazon rainforest. It was reported to have made hundreds of people sick, with many deaths. Whilst there was no cause for alarm yet, people were being treated with existing anti-parasitic medication and the authorities were keeping a close eye on the situation. This would plant the seed in peoples' consciousness that danger lurked, but that they were safe in the hands of the authorities and the leaders. Install a hint of fear, but reassure them that authority was in control.

The second phase, was to spread the news that none of the existing drugs were effective in treating the parasite. More people were dying after getting ill. Then, new outbreaks would be introduced to other parts of the world. Whilst the Amazon is known, it is remote and thus not of direct significance to the rest of the world. Place danger on the doorstep of those living in the West and the story changes. New York for example, or Paris or London. Fear mutates and people start to panic. This is where the positioning of propaganda is key. The media would be brought in to lockstep the message. Danger, fear, death, panic. By the time the fear had been ramped up, the people would be begging the authorities to help them.

Lastly, the third stage would be a cure. Since this was a new and unknown parasite, it was not responding well to existing anti-parasitic drugs. People were starting to die and the authorities were demanding a cure. Thankfully a laboratory in Argentina had been working on a new anti-parasitic drug. When trialled on some of the patients suffering from the parasitic water contamination, early reports indicated that it was curing people from the sickness. Thus a miracle cure had been discovered. Every government in the world would order millions of this wonder drug and designated centres would be set up in every town and village to administer the pill.

There were no known side affects and the drug was hailed as a miracle. The media would promote it as such and continually inform the people that unless they took this drug, then the likelihood is that they would get sick and possibly die. And the consequences for not taking it, could have an impact on the rest of humanity, since it was the right thing to do. He explained how they would ramp up the level of fear, so that the people would literally be begging for the medication.

'WE CREATE both the problem and then the solution to the problem. People will be so blinded by the propaganda that they would eat out of our hands if we asked them.'

JAKE WAS HORRIFIED. Their proposed plan was so simple, as to be transparent. Surely the people would not fall for it? "There's no way this would work." he affirmed confidently to Avorra, "People aren't that stupid." Avorra raised her brows and shrugged her shoulders. "Really?" he replied in shock. He couldn't see how this could work; it made no sense to him.

'YOU SEE GENTLEMAN, people like to follow instructions. They like being told what to do. They are so used to being brainwashed by a system designed to keep them in check, that if the authorities told them to jump, they would respond 'how high?" The men in the room chuckled. 'You laugh because you know it is true. And because we have showed it to be the truth time and time again. We have always controlled them to an extent, but this is our opportunity to truly chain them to our command. No more freewill or free thought. No more dissension, or political unrest. No protests, no crime, no unnecessary individuality or wild creativity. In fact no creativity whatsoever. No gentlemen, the future of humanity will be in our hands. We will tell them what to say, what to think and what to do. And if we choose to, we will shut them off too, because we will hold the kill switch. Just imagine, a world where the elites own everything and everyone. It will be like heaven on earth and we will be the kings of our own kingdoms.'

"THE GUY IS A FUCKING LOONY TUNE!" Jake declared rolling his index finger in a circle around the side of his head. "Evil fucking monster!"

"JAKE! Please contain your language. Remember whose presence you are in." Avorra scolded him and lifted her eyes to indicate upwards.

"OOPS, SORRY." he grimaced apologetically. "But seriously Avorra, this is some crazy stuff right? You've got to admit that these guys are on another planet! Oops," he added apologetically, "sorry, no offence." Avorra turned away and hid a giggle from him. She couldn't help but like Jake, despite the reasons why she was there.

"So," he continued, "what's the plan? How do we stop this from happening? I'm ready. Tell me what to do and I'll do it. Just say the word!" An anger was intensifying within him with each word he heard in that room. He still could not believe that people like this existed at the top of the food chain. It incensed him to think how arrogant they were when speaking about the normal person on the street. They were simply fodder to them, or as his father used to say 'shit on my shoe.' *How dare they* he kept thinking over and over. *How fucking dare they!*

"You need to hear a little more before we move on. It's important that you fully understand how it all begins." Avorra said calming him down.

"How it all begins?" he repeated with concern. Avorra nodded. The main guy started to speak again. He was responding to a question posed by one of the other men.

'There is no new parasite, no. However, we will ensure that there will be some level of controlled contamination in some of the water systems. That will be real. Of course there will be many casualties, but everything will be contained. Whilst there is no real danger to the global public, the simple fact that a danger exists will be enough to inject fear into every person on the planet. Everyone needs water and without fresh and safe water, people have no hope of surviving. We play with that. The threat will be real and fear will do the work for us. It's a win win for us all.' he said with a smile. 'Except for the people of course.' he added with a wink and laughed. And everyone except Jake and Avorra laughed along with him.

Avorra took him back to his flat. Once again, she conjured up a meal out of magic ingredients in a near empty fridge. His cupboards were similar, though he did own some microwave rice, a bag or two of pasta and a few tins and sauces. And there was always teabags, of which Avorra made good use of.

"Blimey. What a mess!" Jake said as he cradled the steaming mug of tea. "I can't believe there are people like that out there. Devious little sh…," he caught himself in time, "sorry." he added with a grimace. He hadn't realised how crass his language had become, until he acquired the constant presence of a blue angel! "It's really weird you know," he said looking intently at her, "but I feel like I know you; like I've always known you."

"Maybe there's a little bit of me that reminds me of you." she replied ambiguously.

"I haven't a clue what that means." he answered rubbing his face with the palms of his hands. He suddenly felt exhausted. He yawned and stretched. He could sleep for years at that point.

. . .

"You should get some rest. I will come back in a few hours. We have much yet to see."

"Can't we go straight to the office and destroy my files etcetera now?" he just wanted this all to end and for the future that he witnessed, never to happen.

"No. It isn't possible. Earlier today, they placed extra security inside your office building. There is no way of you entering the building this weekend without raising suspicion. It has to be on Monday morning."

"Monday? But I'm due to get whacked by Tuesday!" Jake declared. Exhaustion was causing hysteria to edge his voice.

"They expect you to sign the contract after lunch. I suspect they will make an attempt on your life either later that day or Tuesday morning." she offered pragmatically.

"Er...it may have escaped you, but this is *my* life that we are discussing here. And yes, I know a few days ago I was ready to check out, but right now, I am ready to fight to stay alive. If those bastards think they are going to take away my right to kill myself, then they have another thing coming!" he blurted out and sat back in his chair with a resolute look on his face and his arms folded. Avorra laughed.

"Are you laughing at me?" he asked with incredulity. Avorra covered her face with her hand but couldn't stop herself from laughing aloud. Jake was so taken back by her unexpected and surprising response that he found himself smiling, then chuckling, until he too was wracking with hysterical laughter. Every time he tried to stop, he thought of Avorra's face in joyous laughter and he broke out into laughter again. It was moments, but if felt much longer and it felt so good to release all the pent up emotion he had been feeling and all the disbelief about both his current position and the proposed future ahead of them.

"Sleep now Jake. I shall come back for you." Avorra said as the laughing subsided. Jake was so exhausted, he fell asleep fully clothed on his bed.

5

THE COMING

His dreams were filled with chaos. People running wild, screams, children crying. Armoured trucks, soldiers, police with batons and plastic shields, smoke, gun shots. He awoke with a jolt and felt the hand of fear grasping at his heart. He sighed in relief as he glanced around him to the familiar surroundings of his room. He breathed in deeply, his anxiety crawling away. *Just a dream*, he reminded himself. *Just a goddamn dream.*

He walked into the kitchen half expecting Avorra at the stove. No breakfast awaited him, no hot mug of tea steaming on the table. He checked the clock on the wall. 10.25am. Saturday morning. He must have slept for at least ten hours. *Why did she leave me sleep for such a long time?* he wondered. He filled the kettle, yawned and went to the bathroom for a shower. He stood under the rose shower head for much longer than usual. He had an urge to wash away all of the badness and the evil and deception in the world. *If only the water could cleanse deep inside my head* he prayed.

Then he remembered the meeting from the day before; the water, the parasite, the nefarious plan to rule the world.

He looked at the water that fell on and around him and suddenly felt a desire to leave the shower and get out. Then the realisation hit him; even the made-up story of the parasite had impregnated a seed of fear within him. He heard the questioning words, 'what if?' ring out in his head. And in that moment, he saw just how simple and affective their evil plan was. A quote he once remembered from the stoic philosopher Seneca sprung to mind,

'WE ARE MORE OFTEN FRIGHTENED *than hurt; and we suffer more from imagination than reality'*

HE MUSED on that quote and thought how powerful the state of fear was to the human mind. He was reminded that during his years of research for the project, of all the conversations he had with researchers, philosophers and psychologists. He knew more than anyone how fear was one of the biggest contributors to disabling people; whether it be their physical or mental states of being, or whether it prevented them from living the life they desired. Fear could be more devastating in controlling the human psyche than any other emotion. Only the emotion and feeling of love was as, if not more, powerful than fear.

These thoughts were interrupted by a calamity from the streets below. He wrapped a towel around him and lifted up the sash window of his first floor Victorian flat and stuck out his head to take a look.

"WHAT THE...' he said to himself in shock. In the street, his normally quiet street, people were fighting and clashing with police. He looked at the agitators and gasped. These weren't thugs or hooligans, but normal looking men, women and children. He saw a young girl no more than eleven or twelve, throwing an empty can at the shield of a policeman. She turned to run, but he grabbed her shoulder and swung her with incredible force, against a parked car as though she were a cat. Her body smashed against the metal with a thud and she landed to the floor in a heap. One man broke free from the group and rushed to her aide. The policeman who threw the girl started to hit him with a metal baton. Despite the blows raining down on him, he tried to lift up the girl and remove her. Then another policeman joined the baton attack and suddenly there were three hitting, kicking and punching him. The other people who were in the crowd, were being chased by police and retreating. He daren't look back to view the fate of the man and the girl.

He pulled his head back and quickly closed the window. He slid down to the floor and shook. *What the hell just happened?* he asked himself. He tried not to think about the man or the girl, but the image was imprinted and refused to be erased. He noticed that the uniform that the police wore, was not like the uniform of the regular British police. They were still black, but the writing of POLICE was in gold and they wore black balaclava masks. And there was something else that disturbed him – their eyes. They were cold, unseeing and devoid of emotion. *Like human robots* he thought.

Confused and in shock, he rushed to get dressed. "Avorra, Avorra!" he cried out. No response. "What the fuck is going on?" He rushed to check his phone. It wouldn't turn on no matter how many times he pressed the buttons. It was dead. He searched for a calendar, then realised that it could be any day of the week since he didn't possess one. Every date, diary entrance; anything to do with time or his life, was in that phone. He hadn't realised how much he relied on it until that moment. "Where are you Avorra?"

He thought of his mother and how she would be panicking if she heard something on the news. *The news!* He rushed over to the TV set and switched it on. There was nothing about rioting or police clashes. What he saw instead, were the same dead eyes staring back at him. The newsreader's voice was monotone and repeating what could only be described as official narrative propaganda. *Lily and Mia!* He quickly dressed, grabbed his keys and was about to leave when he had a thought. He rushed back into the flat and found a baseball cap and scarf.

By the time he walked onto the street, it was clear. The police had left, though he could see police activity further down the road to his left. The protesting people had dispersed. All that remained, was the can thrown by the young girl and the blood splatters that would stain the tarmac until the rain came.

Jake walked up the road in the opposite direction of the police and headed towards where he his car was parked. He looked around him. This wasn't the street he knew. Once beautifully painted doors were battered and splintered, and most with paint peeling. Most of the windows were broken and ragged curtains hung out like limp pieces of torn flesh. Cars were smashed and dented or spray painted. Most were rusting and looked like they had been neglected for years. Some of the houses adorned red writing. He squinted to read the repeated word in graffiti scrawl. It looked like 'FREEDOM.' Jake's heart began to sink. Before he had located his car, which wasn't where he left it, he already knew its fate.

With no transport, he had no choice but to walk. As he

made his way through the streets towards the main drag, he noticed how similar the streets were – broken, ripped apart and full of the same graffiti writing. Other words like RESIST and WE WILL NOT COMPLY decorated walls, cars and rubbish strewn pavements.

"What the f...?" he whispered to himself as he walked through streets he should know, but instead resembled something from a scene in the war torn Middle East. *Where is Avorra? Why isn't she here?* He thought over and over in his head. If this was a fast forward to the future, he wanted to escape it. The eerie silence of the streets, the intermittent wails of a siren, shouting in the distance and the desolation around him, were reminiscent of apocalyptic scenes from films.

He approached the main street of his town. No cars drove past. No shops were open for business. In fact, all were boarded up or wrecked by vandalism and again, covered in graffiti, including the red writing. Most importantly, there were no people. *Where is everyone?* He decided to head towards the Underground. He deduced that if driving wasn't an option, then he would try the public transport. A sound rang out above and all around him. A shrill noise that made him cover his ears with his hands. He looked around him in an attempt to find the source of the noise. It seemed to come from above, but he couldn't see from where. Fear and anxiety rose up within him. Something wasn't right. He sensed the danger before he saw it.

Police cars were heading his way. He looked around him and desperately searched for a place to hide. But there was nowhere. All the buildings were locked and boarded. Doors were shut. There were no cars to hide behind. He was totally exposed. He recalled the way the batons rained down on that man's head and shoulders and the little girl lying lifeless in a heap. Suddenly, panic electrified his body.

"Oi, over here...quick!" he looked towards the direction of a voice calling out to him. A door was held slightly ajar and a hand was seen beckoning him over. "Hurry before they see you!" Jake ran as fast as he could and as soon as he rounded the side of the door, two arms pulled him in and closed the door shut. He was in near darkness. He counted at least three bolts being slid across as well as keys in a lock. "This way, hurry!" the voice commanded. A lighter flicked on in front of him and he found himself following the back of a man down a hallway, then through a door, through a room, another door, another room, until a hand was placed in front of his chest indicating that he stop. "Ssh!" the man whispered and they waited. Jake was sure he could hear his drumming heartbeat bouncing loudly off the walls, like a teenager's stereo. "Okay, quick. Move!"

Another two locks were opened and suddenly they were out into the open and in the fresh air. It was a back yard garden and full of discarded furniture, corrugated roof tiling and huge pieces of cardboard. A tunnel had been created in the middle of this rubbish, which led towards another door. The man, whose face and head was completely covered with a metal meshing balaclava, placed a finger to his mouth. Jake held his breath as well as his desire to speak. Three raps of his knuckles on the door, a short gap, then two more. They waited a few moments, no more than ten seconds, but it felt like forever. The man kept looking nervously upwards beyond Jake's head. Jake daren't look out of fear, but he sensed danger. And then he heard the sound. A low humming coming from beyond the building they had just vacated. Curiosity was about to get him to turn around, but he was yanked through the door by two pairs of hands on his arm. They pulled so fast and hard, that he landed back first against the wall. A finger was placed on his mouth as his eyes met the desperate brown eyes of his rescuer.

The three men waited. Their hearts beating and breath held at the back of their throats. The humming hovered outside for a moment or two and the eyes of the man holding him darted over to the other man. Nobody breathed. Then the humming grew distant until silence outside once again prevailed. The man let go of Jake, breathed out hard and indicated for him to follow. Jake looked around him. The walls and ceilings were covered in foil insulation. Windows were blacked out and covered in the same metallic meshing the man who originally pulled him off the street wore.

Jake was escorted through a rabbit warren of similar rooms, until he entered one with a trapdoor. "Wait here." the lead man said. Jake noticed with intrigue that he had a Spanish accent, which shouldn't have surprised him since he lived in a multicultural area of London. The man did the same rap on the trapdoor and waited. An older man with a dour face opened it and regarded the three men. He took a long look at Jake before grunting and indicating they could enter. "Come on." the man with the Spanish accent said as he started to disappear underground through the door.

What he saw when he stepped off the last of the steps took Jake's breath away. Dozens of people congregated in what was essentially a basement. He tried to look around to take in the environment, but he noticed everyone was staring at him. *Why?* He thought to himself.

. . .

"Bring the machine." the older man who opened the trapdoor piped up. Jake looked around him and fear crept up into his tummy. The man who rescued him, nudged Jake to move forward. He noticed that women with haunted faces hugged their children tight as he passed. An old lady coughed, someone groaned on a makeshift bed, but otherwise, everyone in the room watched in fearful silence as he made his way towards what looked like a radio machine. "Here, put your face close. Then look into the lens." the trapdoor man instructed.

Jake did as he was asked. He recognised this machine. He had seen them in presentations when researching the chip, but this had additions and was rather battered. It looked like it had seen better days, yet that was impossible; this facial recognition technology had not yet been invented for public use. He tried to ask a question, but the man behind nudged him to do as he was told. He complied and placed his head forward.

The trapdoor man placed the machine to his eyes and held it. Jake fought the temptation to close his eyes as he was forced to look into the light emitted from the laser. For a split second, he wondered if they were going to blind him. He had no idea who these people were, but he also knew that he was probably safer down in the basement with them than he was out on the streets with a robotic and ruthless police force.

"He's clear. He's one of us."

Jake felt the fear lift from the room as the people around him relaxed. Sighs were audible, as previous conversations returned and they continued doing whatever they were doing before he arrived on the scene. A few men and one woman gathered around him. The man who pulled him in originally, removed the mesh balaclava from his head and spoke.

"So what's your story?" he said.

"Where did you come from? How come you are dressed like that?" the woman said looking at him suspiciously.

"Come on, who are you? And how come you were out there on your own. No one travels alone these days. Even the protesters never travel alone."

He searched inside him for answers. They were right. He wasn't dressed like them. His clothes were smart. He wore clean denim jeans, an ironed blue shirt and a grey designer sweater. A fairly new pair of white Nike trainers adorned his feet and the baseball cap on his head was a present from Mia that he hardly ever wore since he spent his time either sporting office wear, or slouching around at home in pyjama bottoms and tee shirt.

In comparison, without exception, every single person in that room wore drab, well worn clothes that had not seen a wash in a very long time. Hair was wild and unkempt and in most cases, obviously unclean. Dirt streaked faces and hands and arms. He stood out like the proverbial sore thumb.

. . .

"I LITERALLY HAVE no idea what the fuck is going on." he finally blurted.

"WHAT DO YOU MEAN? 'What the fuck is going on?' What the hell does that mean?" the second man he met moved into his personal space. "Look at you! What the fuck are you even wearing anyway? What, did you rob an antique clothing store or something?" he almost spat out the words as he spoke them.

JAKE LOOKED DOWN at his clothes then at those of the man confronting him. He wore a grey tunic style top over brown trousers. A black belt hang across the middle, with pouches filled with ammunition and weapons. Black army type boots, scuffed and worn on his feet. The other men wore similar clothes. The women and children around him had similar, but wore cardigans or jumpers hanging loosely over their tunics. He thought quickly. He knew that he had to be accepted by this group of people, so a realistic explanation was required.

"YES I DID. I was chased and beaten by a gang and ended up in an abandoned house. My clothes were torn and covered in mud, so I raided a trunk. This is what I found in there. There was a pretty pink dress, but it wasn't in my size." he said offering a smile.

A woman behind him giggled. He turned around to see a woman similar to his sister Suzannah smile and then look shyly at her feet. He winced as he thought of the women in his life. *Where are they and what are they doing? God, please let them be safe,* he silently prayed.

"Harrumph!" the dour faced man commented from the back of the group that surrounded him. "Strange story. And what, did you manage to grab a shower while you were there?" That raised the attention of the others. Jake felt as though he were about to be closed in on, until a voice from the back left of the room called out.

"Leave him be. He's clean. He's one of us." The trapdoor man grumbled but relented, nudging past Jake, banging him on the shoulder in the process.

"Ignore him. He's just angry that's all." said a man with a kindly face and a welcoming smile. From his accent, he guessed he was American. He stuck out his hand in greeting. "Tom." he said with a smile.

"I'm Jake." They shook hands without leaving eye contact.

"Hey Jake, come over and meet the family."

He followed Tom to a 'family unit' area at the back of the room. It was partitioned only by a linen cloth makeshift curtain that ran on a string from a wall to the bunk bedpost. There was very little privacy.

Tom introduced him to his wife Bettina and a boy of around twelve called Will. Jake smiled at the boy but the boy simply stared. "You'll have to forgive my boy. He turned mute after The Coming. He hasn't spoken in five years." Jake smiled again at the boy, who had grown weary of the newcomer already and returned to his bunk. "Take a seat Jake." Tom said gesturing to an empty metal chair. "You want some coffee?"

"Coffee? Yes please." he said with smile. It was the best question he had been asked since waking that morning. He watched as Tom took a large container from a chest under the bed. He also brought out three cups. One for each of them. He poured dark black liquid into the cups then handed a cup to his wife and one to Jake. Bettina thanked her husband and joined some of the other women in another section of the room. He noticed a slight Germanic accent, but did not comment.

Even before he tried it, he knew it wasn't going to be like any coffee he had tasted before. He took a sip and fought not to let his mouth spit it back into the cup.

"Hah!" Tom declared as he watched with growing curiosity. "You've not had this coffee before have you?" Jake shook his head. The liquid was bitter and thick and gritty. "Just so you know," Tom said leaning in so Bettina and Will couldn't hear, "I don't buy your story Jake."

. . .

Jake felt suddenly exposed. What should he say? Was it worth developing the lie further? What would happen if Tom informed the others that he hadn't told the truth? Would they grill him? Torture him? *Kill* him? "I...I..."

"Relax man. I could tell as soon as you walked in that you don't come from round here. I ain't gonna tell anyone anything trust me. I'm a lone wolf and if it wasn't for these two," he said indicating his wife and son, "I would have left this place a long time ago." he moved in a bit closer to Jake. 'So, what's the real story?'

"Trust me, if I told you the truth, you wouldn't believe me." Jake replied with a wry look.

"Try me." Tom replied. "I used to be high military intelligence, until just before The Coming began. I was all in, following orders from above you know?" Jake nodded thinking back to Edward and Henry at his company and IMMERSE. "Then one day, I came across a man in a hospital, who was unlike any other man I had met. Well, when I say man, I mean he looked like a man, walked like a man, dressed like a man, but..." and he lowered his voice to a whisper, "the man he once was, had left him. He was like a robot in the shell of a man." Tom leaned back to allow Jake time to absorb what he had heard. It correlated with what he saw in the policeman in the street and the newsreader on the TV. He nodded to himself.

. . .

"WHAT HAPPENED TO HIM? This man you saw? Why was he like that?"

"THE PILL OF COURSE! It's what it does. It lobotomises you." Tom's words strangled the air around Jake. He couldn't breathe. "You okay man?" Tom asked reaching out and touching his arm the way Avorra did. *Where is Avorra?* He wondered as he recovered his focus. He had so many questions.

"HOW MUCH DO YOU KNOW?" Jake asked recovering. He was now curious.

"WELL," started Tom reflecting, "it was around ten years ago. Well before The Coming. We had all been sectioned into these grid cities..."

"GRID CITIES?" Jake interrupted.

"OKAY YOU'RE SCARING me now. Where have you been? Before I continue, I want to know why you don't know any of this and why you are dressed like that." Jake felt the stress emulating from Tom so he made the decision to be as honest as he could without freaking him out. He had to think quickly. He decided to make up a plausible story to avoid further questioning.

. . .

"Okay, okay." Jake relented. He took a deep breath and leaned forward in his chair and indicated that Tom did the same. Like conspirators, they huddled close as Jake explained that he had awoken from a coma in an abandoned private hospital a few miles away. There was no one around and since his room was in an underground chamber area, he had obviously been forgotten about. He had no idea how long he had been there and no idea of the time, day or even what year it was. He found those clothes in a locker in a bag in his room. He showered and shaved since his bag also contained those items. Then he left the hospital to make his way to his flat which was a few streets away. He explained that everything he once knew had gone. His flat was abandoned and he managed to hang out there for a while, but he soon ran out of provisions and that's when he started wandering the streets. He heard the siren and was saved by those men and brought into the basement space. When he finished he sat back in his chair and shrugged his shoulders as way of explanation.

"So how did you get here? How did you escape being detected by the drones?" Tom asked still suspicious. "Nobody escapes the drones."

"I...I don't know. Truthfully, I just did. I've been freaked out since the time I came round. What I do remember though, was that coffee tasted so much better before!" he added with a laugh. Tom laughed also. It broke the line of questioning he was getting from Tom. "I guess I've missed a lot. And I have a hell of a lot of questions!" Jake added.

. . .

"I can imagine! Okay, what do you want to know?" Tom asked relaxing.

"Firstly, what is this 'Coming' I've heard mentioned a couple of times?"

"Oh boy." Tom said looking over his shoulder at his son. "We try not to say that word too loud around Will." he whispered with a nod to his boy who was reading. Jake nodded and mouthed an apology. Tom moved close again. "The Coming was when they brought in the drones."

"What drones?" Jake asked remembering Tom mentioned them earlier in the conversation.

"How much do you know?" Tom asked furrowing his brow. "Were you around when they brought in the pill?"

OMG the bloody pill he thought in horror. *It actually happened?* "Remind me Tom. My memory is still so fuzzy from being out of it for so long. The coma, you know?"

"Sure, of course. Well, around 2028 there was an outbreak of a deadly parasite. It affected the water and was making people sick. It started someplace in Africa or South America, I can't remember, but it soon spread to the rest of the world. It went on for a couple of years with many people dying. There was so much fear and nobody wanted to drink water from taps, only drink from bottled water, which became so expensive that water became like gold. Swimming pools closed, people refused to bathe and even things like ice cubes and ice lollies were shunned. Think about it, everything to do with water was a no go. You can imagine the paranoia."

JAKE THOUGHT back to the meeting in that room with those men. Bastards he thought as he recalled their words.

'WE CREATE *both the problem and then the solution to the problem. And the people will be so blinded by the propaganda that they would eat out of our hands if we asked them.*'

"SO WHAT HAPPENED NEXT? Tell me about the drones." he asked.

"WELL THEY CAME in a few years after the introduction of the pill. It had another more scientific name, but that's what everyone called it. They told us it was a miracle cure. So you can imagine, that given how much fear there was about the water, pretty much everyone was desperate to take it."

"EVERYONE? DID YOU TAKE IT?" Jake asked wondering why there were people living underground in basements. His thoughts were full of questions. *How many more groups of people lived this way? And what are they hiding from?*

. . .

"No, not everyone. At first, it was just for the elderly and vulnerable. They were the ones mainly getting sick and dying. But there was so much paranoia and fear around, that soon everyone was literally begging to get this pill. It was crazy!" Tom said shaking his head at the memory. "And no, I didn't take it. After I saw that guy in the hospital I just knew something wasn't right. It wasn't just one guy either. Soon I started to see more people like him. Men and women, all with that vacant stare. You wouldn't know from a distance that they were like that, until you came up close. It was so weird."

"And you think it's because of this pill; their odd behaviour?" Jake asked with intrigue.

"Without a doubt. Like I said, it lobotomises you. And that's a fact."

Jake sat back and thought about what he had just heard. The events came as no surprise to him since he had already heard it first hand from the constructors of the plan, but for the subjects of the experiment to be called *lobotomised*, took things to a whole new level.

"Not everyone took the pill. Many like me, were suspicious. Then of course, you had the conspiracy theorists who were having a field day on this. It was like all their

Christmases had come at once to begin with. Finally, all of their research and so-called collated evidence and proof of a military intelligence colluding with a bunch of corporate elites, proved to be more than just a theory. It gave them an opportunity to attempt to dissuade others from taking it. Videos were posted, data and letters leaked, but since the media were also in on the deceit, they were used to ridicule these rebels and made to look like tin foil hat wearing nut jobs. Trying to stop their plan was impossible. Cognitive dissonance, fuelled by continual propaganda, had created a form of mass formation psychosis on the people. I guess people will want to believe whatever the loudest voice tells them to. And the voice of the narrative at that time was deafening." Tom sighed and looked resigned.

"So let me see if I understand this. A dangerous new parasite was discovered in the water that made people sick and caused some to die?" Tom nodded. "Okay, then they rolled out this pill as a type of wonder drug that was going to combat and neutralise the danger, am I right?" Again Tom nodded in agreement. "Right. Except the sting in the tail is that this pill does something to the person's brain that renders them almost robot-like. Have I got that correct?" he asked as he remembered the empty looking, cold eyes of the policeman with the baton earlier.

"Yes. And we have proof." Tom replied with renewed enthusiasm. "Someone in the military posted out information on what this pill did to the brain. Apparently, the pill contains some kind of technology that acts like a transmitter to send and receive signals. I'm not technical, so I don't really get this shit, but I do know that within a few weeks of taking this pill a couple of times a day, over the proposed period of five days, then the person changes. Literally. They lose all sense of self. They have no original thoughts or the ability to critically think for themselves. They no longer drink, smoke or have any bad habits like eating junk food or drinking fizzy soda. They refuse touch or connection, so the family unit falls apart, and the very worse thing – they spy on you!"

"Spy on you?" Jake repeated in astonishment.

"Yup! They become walking spy monitors. It's flipping freaky I tell ya. When you're around one of them and you haven't taken the pill, then you have to watch your back, because any minute they could report you to the authorities on you and you get taken away."

"Wow! What happens to them; the people who get taken away?"

Tom shrugged. "Killed or lobotomised I guess".

It was a lot to take in. How could he tell Tom, Bettina, Will or any of the others existing in that dank, dark basement, that he was responsible for the state of the world they were trying to survive in? Shame flooded his veins. He closed his eyes and prayed silently. *Avorra where the hell are you? Take me back please? I promise I will destroy the bloody chip!!!*

"I'm sorry." he said with sincerity.

"Hey, it's not your fault. It's not like you invented the bloody pill or anything." Tom said reassuring him with a friendly pat on the knee. "No, those bastards have a lot to answer to. Hell won't come soon enough for those evil pigs."

"You didn't tell me about the drones or The Coming," Jake said diverting the conversation away from possible retribution.

"Oh yeah. Hell, things got scary after the pill started to turn people into living robots. But nothing was as bad as the drones. They arrived one Monday morning in every town and city. The mainstream media with its narrative in lockstep, declared across all of its platforms, that since the roll out of the pill, deaths had been reduced and the outbreak was now under control. Cleansing of the water systems now resumed since the water was being treated at source. However, to ensure any rogue outbreaks didn't go unnoticed, a new form of surveillance was being brought in globally. This is when they brought in the drones. They came in their millions and scattered across the globe, across all countries and continents. We call this day The Coming."

. . .

"And what do they do, these drones? I'm sorry for all the questions, it's just bloody scary stuff you know?" Jake stated. He was horrified, yet also intrigued. He felt like he wasn't just watching a scary movie, but somehow fallen into it. And without Avorra, he had no way of getting out.

"Rumour has it that the stuff they put in your brain, has some kind of tracking device to it."

"So they always know where you are and can track your movement." Jake interjected. He had witnessed this type of bodily surveillance being researched at development stage. He always raised the objection of ensuring personal, mental and bodily autonomy when confronted with this idea. It was once mentioned by Henry in one of their meetings, but Jake closed the conversation down. He despised the idea despite the work he developed. His work was to help people. That suggestion was to control them.

"Yes exactly." Tom agreed. "And not just that," he said leaning forward, "they can literally shut off your brain anytime they want."

Tom let the words hang in the air between them for Jake to mull on. Then he rose up off his chair, stretched his arms and back and walked over to speak to his wife and another man nearby. He heard some laughter and saw Tom slapping the man on the back in a jovial manner. Jake already liked him. Then he looked around at the people who sat or stood in pockets of activity or conversation. Surviving. Simply surviving. No need for expensive cars, nor jewellery, no designer handbags or the latest must have accessory. No phones or Netflix to distract, no sports or activities like gardening or shopping to exercise the body or occupy the mind. Just breathing and surviving together individually and as a group, with one main objective – to not be mind controlled by a weapon as innocuous as a tiny pill.

By the time Tom returned, Jake had a couple more questions he felt the urge to ask.

"What happens when a drone catches you?"

"We don't really know, but safe to say that the person isn't ever seen again. Especially us rebels. When one of us gets caught, it's tough on all of us." Tom said with a sigh. His eyes lowered as he added, "We've all lost many people."

Jake looked around him. He guessed there were around fifty or so people in the room. The youngest was Tom's boy Will.

"Where are all the kids Tom? Apart from Will, there are only a handful and most are what, twelve and upwards?"

Tom's jaw clenched. He leaned forward and spoke through gritted teeth. "Don't say that too loud down here." he held Jake's eyes with his as a warning. Jake withered inside and his soul sank. "The Coming. At The Coming, they went into all the schools and...and...they took the kids."

"WHAT THE F...!" Jake's eyes widened. He looked over Tom's shoulder to his son.

"ANY KID off sick or not at school for any reason that day escaped. Will's older sister Hannah wasn't so lucky." Tom's face crumpled, yet he remained composed.

"I'M SO SORRY." Jake whispered. Tears threatened to form in his own eyes too as he thought of his girls; all three of them. He sat back in his chair and considered what he had been told. This was utter evil. All of it. And for what: money, power, control?

His thoughts were interrupted by a commotion to the front of the room near the trapdoor. Tom jumped up off his chair and looked for Bettina and Will. He gathered them to him and informed them to sit on the bed whilst he investigated. The voices at the front got louder. They were panicking and shouting. Jake felt the fear in his bowels as adrenalin electrified his blood. He looked back at Tom's wife and child and walked down towards the front. The men were gesturing, some were rubbing their faces with exasperation and a couple of women nearby started to sob. Something wasn't right. Danger had somehow made an entrance into this people hive and there was nowhere to escape to.

. . .

"How? How do you know they saw you? Are you sure?" the dour faced large trapdoor man screamed at a younger man whose face told the truth. He was sure. Jake watched the scene in slow motion. The look of panic on each of their faces, tears rolling down others, creating track lines as they passed through ingrained dirt. A man and woman huddled together, him soothing her and stroking her head as she stood sobbing against his chest.

He heard it before he saw it. The humming. So much humming. And then the explosion. There was no time to run, nor panic, nor say goodbyes. Simply time to fall or die. Jake fell. The blast knocked him backwards, but he was saved by Tom, who took the full impact of the blast. His body protected Jake, but it could not protect himself. He tried to shift Tom's dead weight off him so he could make an attempt to escape, but it was useless, he was pinned down.

And then he was face to face with a drone. He felt the scanner shift over Tom first then move to himself. Out of the corner of his eye to the right, he saw a drone blast a survivor. And Jake knew then what happened to the rebels caught by the drones. There were no survivors. He closed his eyes and waited for his end.

6

BACK TO REALITY

He awoke in his bed. Dressed in the pyjama bottoms and white tee, the same clothes he had on the last time he awoke. Once his eyes adjusted, he searched for his phone. 7.23am. Saturday. He jumped out of bed and ran into the bathroom and with anxious foreboding, glanced out of the sash window. There were no police, nobody protesting, no abandoned, graffiti coated cars or smashed up houses. Relieved, he sighed aloud. "Avorra!" he shouted as heading to the kitchen. A hot mug of tea awaited him on the small kitchen table and his blue angel stood beside the stove making an omelette this time.

"Oh thank goodness!" he ran up to her and was about to grab hold of her in elation, but stopped in his tracks. *She's an angel for goodness sake you idiot* he scolded himself retracting his arms back to his side. She turned to face him and smiled. He so missed that smile.

"I had the craziest dream, man, what a head f..." he managed to stop himself just in time. He hadn't realised how much he cursed until he had an angel for a best friend.

"Eat up!" was all she said as she hummed to herself. *I know that tune, what is it?* he wondered. He was so hungry at that point, that all thoughts dissipated to smoke.

"Mmm, this is soooo good Avorra. Oh my gosh, where did you learn to cook like this? Is there some kind of angel cook school or something? Do you get to take classes?" his eyes rolled in ecstasy and appreciation with each mouthful. "And I never knew I had so many eggs in that fridge!"

"Your neighbour leaves some in your fridge once a week. Along with some milk, cheese, butter and bread. Did you never notice?"

"What Gwyneth? Does she really? No, I guess I've been busy, you know, what with the project and Eloise and stuff." his voiced trailed off as he thought of his lovely elderly neighbour in the flat downstairs. He paid for her to come in and do his ironing every week, but wasn't aware that she actually left him groceries. "Wow!" he said astonished. "Why would she do that for me?"

"Because she sees your pain. And you helped her when her husband died, remember?" He did. Such a sad time for the old lady. To be with someone for fifty-three years and then suddenly be without them. He saw how difficult it was for her. Grief brought them close over the past few months, but he hadn't noticed the little things she did for him. He felt guilty for not realising. "She prays for you every morning and every night before going to bed you know; you're the son she never had."

"Really?" Jake's voice croaked as he considered that revelation. "Does she really pray for me?"

"Yes. In fact, many people do."

"They do?" he asked in astonishment. Avorra nodded.

"You mean a lot to many people Jake. You are far more blessed than you realise."

"I guess. I...I...it's just easy to forget that when you are trapped in the darkness of grief." They were silent for a moment. Then he reanimated. "I had the weirdest dream Avorra. It was so horrible, unbelievable really and so...realistic." He couldn't shake off the impression of the dream and strangely, remembered every moment of it.

"It wasn't a dream Jake." Avorra said turning to look him directly in the eyes. She had such a serious expression on her face that Jake wondered if he were still somehow in the dream.

"I don't understand." he said stammering the words out. He got up and checked outside his window. The streets below indicated that it was just another normal day. Then he glanced up at the sky. No drones. "If it wasn't a dream, then what was it?"

"A simulation. Of what the future will look like if the chip gets into the hands of those who do not have humanity's best interests."

"A simulation! What? I was in a game?" he was so confused. And shocked. He felt a surge of perplexed emotions and his hand found the chair to steady himself. "It was so real. I can still feel it." he said feeling discombobulated. Then a thought struck him. 'How do I know that *this* is real? That this isn't a simulation?" he asked waving his arms around him.

"This is real Jake. Trust me."

"I want to, I really do, but how can I, knowing you are mucking with my head? It felt so bloody real. That young girl, that man, Tom, Bettina, Will, the drones. I saw people have their heads blown off. And...and I thought it was going to happen to me." he said quietly.

"Sit down." she commanded in a soft tone. He complied meekly. "I told you I would show you the future Jake. You say you want to end this, but until you truly see and more importantly, *feel* the dangers of the future ahead for the human race, you won't have a true conviction about what has to be done to prevent it. I guess you could call it cause and affect. Until you see the affect, you won't be able to impact the cause. You can't change the past Jake, but you can affect the present in order to influence and change the future. Our choices set causality into motion before it becomes a future affect. Cause and affect is a natural law Jake."

He chewed on her words. He understood the reasons for the simulation, but at the same time, he felt uneasy knowing they could place him into a mind game like that. It scared him and he wasn't sure any longer, of what was real and what wasn't.

"I'm real Jake." she responded reading his thoughts. "Your family and friends are real. This is real. Everything you know is real. And unless you do what is right, what you experienced and saw in that simulation, will become very real. The timescale is an estimation. Those men in that meeting room haven't yet received the documents that Edward will pass on. That pill does not yet exist. Mind control and mind transparency is still just a nefarious dream of a few evil men. They do not yet know how to inject it into a living person. The method for which the people of this world will accept this as a cure to a proposed danger to them, has not yet been devised. Drones are being created, but for surveillance and not yet for destruction." she paused to allow him to process her words.

"The point is Jake," she added meeting his eyes and holding his gaze, "it's a matter of time before they get a breakthrough. And until that time, the Council will keep interjecting and delaying their progress."

"This keeps happening?" he asked incredulously. She nodded slowly.

"There has always existed in your societies, an elite group of people who want to rule and control the world. For many centuries, civilisations have had to face many threats of annihilation, social destruction and the abolishment of human sovereign rights, including those of freewill and freedom of thought. For some unknown reason, mankind is never content. The Universe gives them everything they needs to survive and thrive: food to eat, water to drink, companionship, nature to heal and nourish, a way to heat and cook, tools, intelligence and a never ending commitment from a Creator who loves them. Yet, for most, this isn't enough. They start to crave more: more food, more knowledge, more money, more power, more control. This can devolve the human being, until he or she becomes emptier and emptier and the connection to soul dwindles down to a faint memory.

Often, the further an individual moves towards the desires of their ego, the farther they seem to travel from the purpose of their soul. This is not the case for everyone, but a great majority. This pursuit of the ego, will often neglect that which is beautiful and good and kind. They forget that they are conscious creators in their pursuit of worldly desires. This can also mean they lose connection to the Creator. Think of a child pulling away from a parent's hand for example. Perhaps that child has seen something pretty, shiny or playful, and their desire is to go to that place. They pull away from the security of their parent's hold and often, will not see the potential dangers ahead. Yet the parent sees; the parent knows and the parent will try to hold on to prevent the child letting go. The Creator is like that, but because freewill is gifted to the human being, ultimately, they have the choice to keep holding on, or to simply let go and pursue their own path.

"Wow!" Jake replied. The way she spoke...he could see it unfolding before him. The devolution of the human race. "And you guys up there watching, what do you make of this human phenomenon?"

"It is not our place to interfere in the affairs of the inhabitants of this, or any other planet."

"But that's not true in my case is it? I mean, you are here aren't you? Trying to get me to change this trajectory path of man's history."

"This is different." Avorra added with a look of surprise at the question.

"Why? Why is persuading me, showing me all this, telling me all this, why is it different? Surely by doing so you are interfering with the future?"

"Yes and no. Yes, you are right of course. I have been sent here to prevent you from handing over the chip and the relevant data. But," she added peering into his face, "never before in the history of the human race, has one man entirely held their future predicament in his hand. Mmm," thought Avorra, "except perhaps Noah."

Jake was floored. "I...I..." he started but no further words came out. Given what he had already been shown, he knew she was right. It was he who made the breakthrough with linking nanotechnology to a mainline computer and sending electro magnetic wave frequency instructions from the computer to the brain. It was him who discovered how to inject this technology into the brain without causing any damage. He who did the research with psychologists and scientists about controlling certain brain patterns. In the end, it was all because of him. If he hadn't have done all that, hadn't continued down the path of creating this monster, then this particular danger wouldn't exist.

"Can you take me back? You know, to the past? We could go back to a time in my life when I didn't have this knowledge or desire to discover this information?"

"No. It isn't possible." Avorra said curtly.

"But why? We could stop this in its tracks. It makes perfect sense to me." Jake implored.

"No. It won't work." she reiterated. He sensed an agitation around her.

"But why? You can do time travel. We've already established that. Just take me back."

"Jake, we can't." she said then looked away. "The only way to do that, would be to prevent your existence on earth. You would never have been born."

"Oh." was all he could say. He thought for a moment. "So let's do that then?" Avorra sighed and shook her head. She remained with her back to him and head slightly bowed. She seemed resigned to a pre-designated fate.

"We cannot destroy life. It is not in our nature. We are here to love and protect the human race, not to destroy it. But if we fail this time," she said turning look him squarely in the face, "the human race destroys itself and we start again with the seeds of the next civilisation. It has happened before. The difference this time, is that there may not be anything of the human race that survives."

"I don't understand." he asked looking perplexed.

"You will see, but for now I can tell you that if we don't achieve our goal, then it won't just be Earth that suffers. If humanity is annihilated then the impact on the Multiverse could be devastating."

For a long while, the two were silent in each other's presence. Avorra closed her eyes and sat in council. Jake sat with his thoughts, trying to concoct other plausible options, whilst all the while remembering the feeling of impending death when faced with the laser of the drone directed at his head.

"Tell me what I should do Avorra and I will do it." he finally said. He was mentally exhausted and it was not yet 9am.

"To know how to get to the end, we have to start at the beginning." Avorra finally announced. Jake regarded her with bewilderment. "Get dressed Jake, we are going on a journey."

"Where to now?" Jake asked grimacing. He hoped it wasn't another simulation. Facing death in the face was not an experience he wanted to repeat anytime soon.

"We're off to meet some people who might be able to help you answer questions circling inside you. Oh and one more thing, look smart and no cussing."

7

SCHOOL OF THOUGHT

They arrived in a town centre in the streets of Madrid. Jake immediately felt the midday sun warm his skin and breathed in deeply and appreciatively. He had always loved this bustling metropolitan city, with its vibrant colours, various attractions and Spanish cuisine culture.

Avorra guided him to a cafe. She indicated that he take a seat at an empty table outside, which faced out onto a typical busy street. Jake's curiosity was piqued. *Can I be seen?* He questioned her in his mind. Avorra slowly shook her head and smiled.

"I WANT YOU TO LISTEN, interject and join in where required, but other than the direct conversation, you will remain a silent observer." she said cryptically. Jake furrowed his brow but remained watchful, simply out of curiosity. He had no idea what to expect.

He regarded his environment. From the way people were dressed and their style of hair and accessories, he guessed they had travelled back a couple of decades, perhaps to the late 1980's or even 90's?

His attention was alerted to a couple to his left. They were standing at a fountain near the street where his cafe was situated. The fountain created a central focus point feeding in from four other streets. From their hand gestures and body language, he guessed the couple were engaged in a heated discussion. Their voices raised louder, but nobody flinched or glanced their way. Bemused and transfixed watching them, he noted that the man looked to be defending himself against an accusation from the woman. His hands were outstretched in an obvious attempt at an apology, but she did not relent. This continued for a few more moments, until SLAP! The man winced and held his hand to his slapped face. Jake noted that he did not retaliate or become enraged. Instead he allowed his partner's anger to subside, then pulled her in close to his chest and allowed her to quietly sob. Then the two pulled their heads away and met each other's eyes. She wore an apologetic sad face, causing him to break into a loving smile. Then he leant in to kiss her tenderly on the lips. She reciprocated and within moments, they were engaged in a full, passionate kissing exchange. A growing feeling of accidental voyeurism, caused Jake to avert his eyes and turn away.

"THE HUMAN PSYCHE is fascinating do you agree sir?"

JAKE LOOKED around left to right behind him. The question was directed at him, yet Avorra told him he wasn't visible to others. Then he saw that the man who had spoken, sat occupying a seat at the table next to him.

. . .

"Forgive me. I did not mean to startle you, but I realised we were both engrossed in watching that scene play out. My name is Jose." the older man said stretching out a hand in greeting to Jake. Jake took it mechanically, since he was still confused as to why he was visible. He looked around for Avorra but she was nowhere to be seen. "I think she left us alone." the man added.

"You saw her? I mean, you could see her?" Jake asked in astonishment. He was bewildered.

"The blue woman? Yes I saw her." the man said wryly as he picked up his cup and sipped the coffee in front of him. "Curious colour blue wouldn't you say? Not quite belonging anywhere on the spectrum; slightly purple, slightly white and also deeply and unmistakably blue." Then he looked directly into Jake's face and met his eyes with his own in a deep stare, as though he were trying to read his thoughts.

"What is this?" Jake asked furrowing his brow. "Is this another simulation?"

"It seems so. Since I am deceased in your time and unable to have this conversation in real time with you, I suspect I am a projected simulation of a conversation which may, or may not have happened, if I was alive to respond."

. . .

Blimey, Jake thought to himself, taking a hand through his hair and running it back and forth. *Nothing makes sense anymore!*

"It is my understanding young man, that due to the work you do, that you have questions regarding the work I did. Is that correct?" He spoke in English with a deep Spanish accent that was both considered, clear and balanced.

"Wait...are you Jose *Delgrado*?" The other man nodded in a nonchalant manner. "Wow. Yes. Er...yes. I have so many questions for you. Oh my gosh, I have studied your work, read your many peer reviewed papers, which were amazing by the way. Man, I've watched countless videos on your work. Suffice to say, you are one of my heroes." Jake blurted out like a star struck fan. Jose smiled with genuine appreciation.

"Thank you sir, I appreciate your kind words. However, time is of the essence, so please, ask me anything, but do please try to remain pertinent to your cause. There is obviously a reason we are both here in this time space continuum. And whilst I am no expert on quantum physics or Einstein's Theory of Relativity, which may or may not, at this time, relate to the specifics of time travel, I do know from the energy emitting from both our brainwaves, that I have been brought here to help you in some way."

. . .

JAKE MUSED ON HIS WORDS, then decided to tell him everything he knew. He disclosed about Avorra, his work, the chip, Edward, Henry and the plan to sell the information to an unknown but obviously nefarious buyer. The manipulation of the data and chip for malevolent purposes and basically, the destruction and manipulating of the human being as an existing species for the purpose of control and power.

Jose, as a renowned and acclaimed neuroscientist, listened with interest. He nodded and grimaced, mused and winced, yet remained respectfully observant until Jake had finished his explanation. "Interesting." he remarked stroking his chin in reflection. "And what would you like to know today?"

"WELL," Jake began, "your work is similar to mine, in that we both developed brain technology for the purpose of helping fight disease, mental afflictions and disorders by communicating with the brain. Whilst your work relied on the use of implanted electrodes to deliver an electrical charge to the brain to achieve the end result, mine is focused on directly inserting nanotechnology into the brain via the brain fluid, where this technology then awaits instructions from an AI main 'Mother' computer. This Mother computer, sends out an electromagnetic frequency message to the waiting nanotech in the brain. The instructions are focused on a particular part of the brain that relates to a neurological, or bodily function. We both had the same idea of course, namely, to instruct the brain to change mental functions."

. . .

"Yes that pretty much sums it up, give or take an idea or two." Jose said nodding in agreement and winking. "Giving instructions to the brain instead of completely lobotomising the individual as some psychiatrists were more inclined towards during my time, is a perspective we obviously share."

"Indeed." Jake replied. "I am much more a proponent of your work than say, someone like John Fulton, though some of his work is equally as brilliant. My question is this," Jake added, "with both your proven work and my proposed work, namely, the use of inserted brain chips to send these electromagnetic pulse messages directly into the brain, would you say that we have interfered with nature? That perhaps, we have inadvertently, or even with intent, interfered with the human brain functionalities and created, what I can only describe, as something of a monster for those who follow in our footsteps? And, if I may add, may not have the best intentions for the individual?"

He watched as Jose pondered on this question, chewing over it as he debated the point raised in his mind. Finally, the man sat back, folded his arms and replied.

"You know young man, I faced an inordinate amount of criticism for my work in my day. I was called a 'madman' you know. Mmm... But let's see," he continued, "in response to your question, I will point out, that unlike your quest for nanotechnology, I was more interested in neurotechnology. Slight difference. From my objective viewpoint, I am unsure that handing control of the human brain to an advanced and advancing, technology such as AI, is a positive enhancement for the human race. In fact, I have to ask the question, 'is it ethical?'"

"Mmm." pondered Jake digesting the answer, "Truthfully, I've never really considered the ethical aspect of my work. Is ethics relevant in this context if my, or even *our* intent, is for positive purposes and not to deliberately cause harm to an individual?"

"Well, if it's an ethics answer you want, we should ask Socrates himself. After all, he is known as being the founder of ethical philosophy." Jose declared and pulled out a chair that was tucked underneath the table.

"Socrates?" Jake exclaimed in shock and confusion.

"Greetings men." said a voice from behind Jake. He turned around to see a portly and surprisingly unattractive man dressed in dirty robes. He was barefooted and wore his hair long and straggly. He slumped down into the chair beside Jose and grunted a greeting at the two men. "Why is he staring at me like that? Is there something wrong with him?" he whispered to the neurophysiologist, who simply shrugged and patted the back of the robed man.

"We have an ethical question and thought you might be the person who could help us to answer it." Jose stated, sitting back into his chair and waiting on Socrates to respond.

. . .

"WHAT IS THE QUESTION GENTLEMEN. I will see if it can be answered." the Greek philosopher replied.

"OKAY, WELL," Jake began fighting feelings of intimidation from sitting with one of the greatest and most renowned fathers of ethical philosophy, "it's to do with the brain."

"OKAY, THEN ASK ME THE QUESTION." Socrates replied.

"So, both Jose and myself have developed technology that can send messages to the brain, in order to affect a change to the individual brain's activity." Jake declared, then added for clarity. "For beneficial purposes to the individual of course." Socrates grunted and shrugged. He folded his arms and sat back in his chair and nodded for Jake to continue. He found the philosopher to be both unnerving and intimidating and also detected a slight sense of fatigue that his presence was being requested after so many centuries.

"Well," Jake continued, "we wondered, if in the pursuit of technological advancement for medicinal purposes, we have also inadvertently created a tool that could be weaponised to manipulate and control the human mind."

"YES, it is highly possible and likely, that given mankind's propensity for destruction and chaos in the name of greed, whether to attain wealth, or power, or control, that certain individuals would see the opportunity for manipulating this work for more nefarious intentions than those originally intended by the creators of such work. Namely, I imagine, since you are in attendance, both of you gentlemen."

"SEE, I knew he would know what to say!" Jose said with glee and smacking the Greek philosopher on the back again. Socrates in turn furrowed his brow and scowled at the Spaniard.

"BUT," Socrates continued, "that is not an ethical answer. That is simply a pragmatical response. For one must seek knowledge and wisdom before the pursuit of private interests. Thus, these individuals, if pursuing a quest to manipulate an individual's brain activity for their own private interests, jeopardises the sovereign rights of the individual being manipulated and controlled, then it is indeed, a question of ethics. If a person's freewill choice to be happy and live a free and fulfilling life is taken from them either by force or manipulation, to advance another's desire to develop themselves at the cost of this person's freedom and disrespect of conscious decision, then indeed, that is a poor ethical choice. And not just for the disadvantaged and manipulated individual whose freewill has been tampered with, but also for the person to whom personal advancement and gain is achieved through the sacrifice of another's happiness."

THE TWO PHYSICISTS sat and chewed over his words. *Philosophy is a real head fuck* Jake thought to himself as he took his time piecing together the jigsaw of words spoken by the philosopher.

"So then, would you say that it was unethical to allow this work to be out there, if a more nefarious type of individual decided to manipulate an idea that, despite being originally intended for good, was thus to be changed and utilised for malevolent purposes?" Jake asked fishing for an answer that was plaguing him since Avorra let him witness the meeting between Edward and Henry.

"I would say that you yourself, have the answer to that young man. You see, virtue is something that can be known and therefore, you must learn to know yourself what is virtuous and what is not."

"But how can I know that, if my intention was for good and not the opposite? Isn't it true that it is not I who is not being virtuous, since my discovery of the technology, was only intended for good?" Jake argued.

"Then I have two questions for you which may help you understand this better. Firstly," Socrates said stroking his long, wavy beard, "did you research where this work of yours would eventually end up and whose hands it was ultimately being delivered to? And secondly, what will you gain in the process? If there is gain to be made by you, for producing and thus handing over this work and therefore taking the control of it out of your hands, is your gain virtuous and is it ethical?"

Before he had a chance to respond, another guest joined the table.

"Hello gentleman." proclaimed a Germanic voice. Jake looked up and into the very familiar face of Albert Einstein. "May I join you?" he asked as he politely pulled another chair to the table.

"Ahhh Einstein. Good to see you again. You know Socrates of course, but I don't think you know Jake here. He's a physicist, researcher and scientist. And he is soul searching to answer very important questions for the future of the human race." Jose said as he winked at Jake, who in turn felt both humbled and unworthy of his place at this illustrious table of historically esteemed men.

'Einstein,' he said stammering, "I'm...I'm completely star struck right now. I mean, you're Albert Einstein!" The three men burst out into laughter at the comment. Jake had completely forgotten that he was in a controlled simulation.

"We are discussing ethics." Jose explained as way of introduction into the conversation. "Jake here has a pretty big ethical decision to make."

. . .

"Ah, ethics. One of my favourite topics. And yours too Socrates right?" he said nudging the Greek. Socrates rolled his eyes and grunted, sat back into his seat and stared at Jake, who then offered up the question of his research to Einstein.

"I suppose I am trying to understand my intention in relation to the outcome of a particular situation I am in." Jake stated with a big sigh. He was still unsure if he unintentionally meant harm to others or not.

"Well if you can't explain it simply, you don't understand it well enough." Einstein responded.

"True." agreed Socrates nodding in affirmation. Jake didn't feel at all enlightened in his predicament by that comment, despite it coming from his all time hero.

"I see you are unsure, so let us take your personal predicament and have an open discussion about it." Einstein continued. "Jose here used neurotechnology to advance an existing understanding of how defects in the brain could be assisted by the use of electrodes, in order to deliver electronic messages to specific areas of the brain. Whilst you young man," he said addressing Jake, "worked with computer technology, namely AI, to deliver this message directly into the brain fluid. Correct?" Jake nodded.

. . .

"I GUESS I want to ensure that I completely understand my actions from an ethical and moral point of view, before I know exactly what to do to rectify the mistake I made. In fact, truthfully, to know if I did in fact, make a mistake." Jake stated to the small, white and wild haired man.

"THE MOST IMPORTANT HUMAN ENDEAVOUR, is the striving for morality in our actions. Our inner balance and even our very existence depends on it. Only morality in our actions can give beauty and dignity to our life." Einstein stated.

"Wow!" Jake replied absorbing his words. "That's truly something to consider. The point is, that I discovered my work is going to get taken and manipulated by some pretty evil guys and then used as a weapon to control the human race. It was a huge discovery to make as you can imagine. Especially given that I was simply trying to help humanity."

EINSTEIN THOUGHT FOR A MOMENT. He glanced at Jose who found something interesting to look at near his shoes. Socrates stroked his beard as he contemplated the ethical and philosophical implications of the words just spoken. Then Einstein turned his attention back to Jake and gave him this response.

"THE WAY I SEE IT, the real problem is in the hearts and minds of men. It is not a problem of physics but of ethics. It is easier to denature plutonium than to denature the evil from the spirit of man."

. . .

JAKE CHEWED on these words as Socrates engaged Einstein in a debate about ethics verses physics. Jose joined in and in moments, the three men were deeply involved in explanations, theories and counter arguments. Jake's mind began to wander. They didn't notice that he had stepped away from the discussion and away from the table and the men. He heard their voices mute to just distant mumblings as he became lost in his meanderings through the streets of Spain's capital city. He watched as children played and giggled together, while dogs, lay in languor next to their owners glancing up hopefully at passers by in their quest for morsels thrown their way, or perhaps even a simple pat on their head. The busy mull of shoppers flowing in and out of doorways, conversations, standing, walking, talking. Faces of happiness, concern, anxiety, anger, detachment, animation, all passed by him without glance, intrigue or attachment. He was an invisible irrelevance in the minutiae of their lives. Prescient yet invisible.

Words, sounds, noise, all melted into one cup of human meaninglessness, as he floated up and away from them. Above the streets, above the buildings and structures, the statues, the mountains and hills, until the land mass below edged with water and then blue met green and became blanketed by a film of fluffy grey and white, until he lay back and felt the weightlessness of simply existing. And then there was only the dark above and the stars around. Nothing mattered, not him, nor time, nor meaning. Simply the experience of being.

He closed his eyes and listened to his breath. The rise and depression of his chest, the taking in of breath and expelling out from his nostrils, as he gave in to the sense and sound of his own breathing. And when finally, he succumbed to opening his eyes, he was surrounded by blackness, and colourful swirls of light and form. Inexplicable shapes and mesmerising colours melted around him, until the blackness that had moments before enveloped him, dissipated and disappeared. He saw, spaces of life. Planets without real form, that were mere swirls of light and colour claiming their space within the Universe. He felt the energy of life as he passed each planet, transmuting the space around him. Despite feeling deeply connected to everything, he concurrently felt an alien detachment to his surroundings. The duality of the experience rendered him incapable of any other thought other than the awareness of his presence..

He was heading towards a bright light. It grew wider and higher the closer he travelled and then his approach slowed until he stood just before it. This light, which suffused the entire space around him, had no form or structure, but instead, pulsated an energy of such purity and strength, that he knew within his soul, that he was standing before a Being of great significance. He knelt down in front of this energy and all the repressed emotions that he carried from his existence on Earth, poured forth from him like a waterfall. He sobbed and released without shame nor fear, and when the emotion was spent, he remained in still silence, without thought, intent or agenda. In that moment, he knew that he was present before the one Universal Creator.

He then felt the firm touch of a hand lift him up and into a standing position. However, no hand existed, since no form was visible to the eye. A voice, like no other voice he had heard before, transmitted out and filled the space around him. It beckoned for him to come closer, and with each step forward, Jake felt an incredible sense of peace and lightness, transcending through and around him. He kept moving forward, unconsciously, towards the light, until he became completely absorbed and as one with it.

Then he felt it. He became this being, this energy, this light. He was no longer who he knew himself to be. Every tiny, autonomous cell in his body fractured into minute, absorbing particles to take on this light form. He felt his human DNA dance and merge with the energy transmitting from the Creator, and all that once mattered to him, dissipated into a calm nothingness. Yet there was no emptiness, no void nor black hole that he once so eagerly craved. Instead what he became, was the everything. All of humanity: it's history, its people, faces, bodies, achievements, emotions; all of it. He saw and felt it all at once and in that unique moment of revelation, he saw the importance of his human condition and the relevance of the human race.

Then he knew, that the Creator existed in him as he existed in the created world. Jake realised at that moment, that he was indeed, the creator of his own life and that everything he needed to know, already existed within him, because it was of him and that the only truth that was of significant relevance in that moment, was that everything existed because he did. Without his presence in the world, the world as he knew it, could not exist, since he would not be there to witness its existence. Given that understanding, he realised that he was the conscious creator of his own world and in that knowledge and understanding, he felt at one with himself and the whole of creation.

He also experienced the overwhelming essence of love; from the Creator, from the Universe and from himself. Everywhere there was love and it filled him to the lowest depth of his being and to every corner of his soul's existence.

. . .

"Welcome to my world Jake." Avorra said, interrupting his thoughts as she appeared in front of him. She held out her hand and he took hold of it without question or thought. They travelled away from the light and into the coloured swirls of the Universal space.

"It's beautiful," he commented, "so calm and free."

"Yes. Some may say it's the inner sanctuary of our soul; perhaps even our purest nature."

"You say 'our' as though you are human, or a being like those on other planets around us. I can feel them you know, I can feel their existence. But you, you are an angel; so therefore how can you have a nature?" Jake asked looking directly into her eyes.

"I was alive once Jake. Actually, many times before that once." she replied wistfully.

"Do you miss it? Being human?"

"Missing implies lack and I have no lack, so how could I possibly hold a sense of loss within that which I am?" Jake's mind was already exhausted by all the surreal conversations and existential experiences from the past couple of hours, so he allowed himself the freedom of not musing or replying. "So tell me Jake, what did you really learn today?"

He took time to reflect on the answer. He thought about replaying to her, all the conversations with his three historical heroes, but that would be fruitless since Avorra had obviously arranged the simulation and probably witnessed all that was spoken. Instead, he reflected on his recent experience within the energy of the Universe and his experience meeting the Creator.

"The way I see it," he said, as they stood amongst the darkness and twinkling lights of the stars, "the French philosopher Descartes was right when he said 'I think therefore I am', for without thought, do we really exist as individuals? What determines our individuality, our personality or our character? For centuries, philosophers and scholars alike, have been asking if it is the consciousness or the soul that creates the individual? If we accept that the soul continues on forever, whether for good or for bad, in a cycle of up-levelling growth, or sold to the Devil, then we must question if destroying a person's mind equates to also destroying them as a human being? Is it the mind that makes the human being, or is it conscious awareness? Or perhaps is it something deeper that cannot be attained except through freewill? Could a person under hypnosis for example, consent to sign away his soul to the Devil and it stand as a forever contract, or since he or she, was perhaps, not making that choice through conscious awareness, could they be forgiven for signing under duress or through the malevolent intent of an external force such as another human being?

Thus, the question remains of whether a lobotomised, mind controlled, or mind compromised individual, still retains their sovereign, individual rights? And how does that affect the continuation of that person's soul if they are not consciously aware of the choices their hijacked mind and body are making at the hands of someone or, in the aspect of AI, some*thing* else?"

"I DO BELIEVE," Avorra said with joy, "that the student has indeed earned the right to proceed to the next step. Are you ready Jake?"

"READY?" he asked confused. "Ready for what?"

"THE FUTURE."

8

ONE STEP BEYOND

'The Future depends on what we do in the present' –
Mahatma Gandhi

THEY SAT IN HIS KITCHEN. Him eating another prepared meal by the blue cook and his blue companion in silent contemplation, her thoughts elsewhere. Since their return, she had remained in a non-verbal and reflective mood. Jake, having been over simulated with the depth of conversation, the brief exploration of the Universal space, the meeting with the Creator and his journey to philosophical wisdom, felt mentally exhausted. He welcomed the silence.

"Go rest for a while Jake. You have a tough road ahead." she finally stated, rising up from the chair she had occupied and clearing away the crockery. Despite her magical and non human appearance, she also did the physical job of washing up his plates.

"What's next? Another simulation or will you be with me this time?" He saw her shoulders lift and fall as she washed up with her back to him. *Did she just sigh?* He wondered, perplexed. She turned around to face him. Her face was serious and concerned.

"This next part will not be easy for you Jake." she stated. He noticed that a shadow of sadness clouded her eyes. She walked towards him and sat in her vacated chair. "This is the most difficult part of this journey together."

"Difficult?" he asked, his voice cracking with nervous anticipation. "For just me?"

"For both of us."

"Oh no. Do I die?" he asked, suddenly fearful. She shook her head in response, but still looked sad. "Then what? Why will it be so difficult?"

She took a breath, looked upwards for guidance, then explained what was going to happen. He would be put back into a simulation. A future time and a further development from where he was the last time. He would be placed into a simulation again, as a participant, living and experiencing it as though it were real life. Avorra would not be able to interfere at any stage until the simulation was over.

"So why are you sad? Is it because of what I will experience in this simulation?" he asked with growing concern.

"Yes. It will be very authentic and your emotions will be very real." she admitted.

Jake reflected on the experience of the first simulation with the drones and a trickle of ice cold fear coursed through his veins. "Will it be worse than what I experienced with Tom?" he asked. His heart had began to beat faster and louder within his chest.

"Much much worse."

He tried to nap, but thoughts of Tom, Bettina and Will kept poking him to stay awake. He felt back into the fear he experienced when pinned down by Tom's body and the drone's red laser beam directed squarely between his eyes. The anticipation and fear of facing death at that moment, unaware of being in a simulation, was authentically real, leaving an indelible mark on his memory. Would he carry the same fears if he knew that he was experiencing a simulation? He was aware, that every emotion, fear and danger he felt, would be truly authentic. And that Avorra would not be able to save him.

He got up, showered and dressed. Reflecting on the last simulation experience where he stood out because of his clothing, he searched through his drawers for something more suitable, and dug out some black jeans, white tee shirt and dark brown jumper. He considered taking a small, leather man bag, another gift from Mia. He could fill it with a mini survival kit, snacks and a notepad and pen perhaps? He was debating the bag to himself when Avorra entered the doorway to his room.

"It is time to go Jake." she said. Her tone was serious and authoritarian, but also empathetic. He held out the bag. "Take it, but no phone. Leave that here."

He took out the phone, sent a couple of messages to the family and placed it on the small bedside cabinet. After his earlier cleaning blitz, the only item that remained there, was a photo. He peered at it, realising it was one of the three of them together – him, Eloise and Amy. He hadn't consciously made that decision. *How strange,* he thought to himself as he smiled. Then he did something that surprised him. He sent a message to Amy.

Hi. Hope you are okay? Perhaps it's time we met to talk? J

He sent it without an X, but he battled internally with his conscience, so relented and sent another text with a simple 'X'. He placed the phone down and left the room.

Avorra was ready. She smiled at him and moved her mouth close to his ear.

"Remember Jake, even though I won't physically be with you, I will be there." she said indicating his heart. "And I will be watching you and watching over you, so if you need to talk to me, I am listening. I can't respond, but I will hear you." She smiled at him then and a memory of another time, a different place floored him. He couldn't place it, but he felt it. And for no reason whatsoever and one that made no sense, he knew that he loved her. She read his thoughts and smiled. "Oh and one more thing Jake, remember this...you cannot die." Then he saw her reach out and touch his arm.

He arrived in an underground tunnel running. He had no idea where to or who from, but his legs were automatically weaving him in and out of man made tunnels, water dripping onto his face and body, mud splashing up at his legs. His heart was filled with fear and his mind pounded out one main thought, *Where the fuck am I?*

He heard them before he saw them. Men up ahead calling for him to run faster. Instinct continued to charge his body and he ran as fast as he could towards them. Instinct also told him not to look back.

"Run man run. Hurry!" he saw a hand reach for his and he grabbed it mid stride and before he knew it, he was locked behind a steel door, panting and still. A hand was held against his mouth and Jake thought his chest would explode with the urge to expel breath. He had not run like that for more years than he could remember. He strained his ears to listen in the darkness, but the only sound he heard, came from his hard breathing.

"Okay, we're good to go. Follow us and don't say a word until we are in the clearing." the man's voice was croaky, rough and tinged with a strong London accent. He was relieved that they were still in the London area.

His eyes adjusted to the semi darkness. Dim orange lights peppered their path at intermittent points. He noticed that the man ahead of him was smaller than him and had dropped shoulders. Then he noticed that he himself was having to lower his head since the ceiling height was low, not more than his height of five foot eleven. He could not see who was ahead of that man, but he knew there was at least one other.

He couldn't help but notice that once again, he was being rescued and brought into an elaborate underground set up. This though, he became aware, was something much different. The man in front leading him, placed an arm behind him until it found Jake's chest. They both stopped. Jake's heart was racing with adrenalin. Why did they stop? Did this man notice danger ahead? Jake felt fear and panic rise. There was nowhere to escape to.

Then he heard a whirring sound coming from somewhere just ahead of them, or perhaps above them, he couldn't tell. The man turned his head to look back at Jake. His face was full of shock and fear. "Run!" he exclaimed and darted forward. Jake followed and kept running despite the sound of whirring getting closer and closer. The earth around them rattled and rumbled. Mud and water began to shake down around them. "Faster!" a voice ahead screamed.

Jake ran as fast as his legs could manage. He was astonished by how fast the men in front were. They darted and twisted, around curves and bends, all the while, following the dim orange lights. The sound from behind grew in crescendo, until it became a deafening crash. Whatever it was that was creating the noise, tore through the earth. Fear clenched Jake's heart in the tightest of grips and he felt sure that whoever, or whatever was behind, would at any moment, come up and seize him, or crush him to death. Then, in the swiftest of movements, he was pulled into a space away from the path. When his eyes adjusted, he realised they were in a metal box. It was small, enough for just a few bodies to stand. The doors closed and he felt it kick into motion and descend. Nobody spoke.

Jake fought against the rising fear of claustrophobia that had always haunted him. They were in near darkness in that tight space, which was some kind of lift heading downwards. His mind raced and in desperation, he prayed. *Avorra I need you. I know you can hear me and you are unable to get me out, but I want you to know that I'm bloody crapping myself right now.* He clamped his eyes tight shut as the lift slowly and roughly lowered itself down towards its destination. He felt every bump and jolt and after a short while, they could no longer hear the ground crunching sounds of the machine up above. He wondered where they were heading and if the men he was sharing this small space with were friendly. He worried that he was being led towards further danger and an unwelcoming environment? And then, despite his fears and questioning, her words sang in his ears like a lullaby. *You cannot die. You cannot die,* they repeated.

Did she mean that he wasn't allowed to die or that he wasn't able to? Thoughts on this distracted him enough for him not to notice that they had been travelling downwards for at least fifteen minutes. Then they came to a rough and sudden halt.

The doors opened, light flooded in and the two men walked out. They then turned around to regard their passenger. They didn't smile and their dirt smeared faces were full of suspicion. The first man pointed a pistol at him. "Out." he said indicating for Jake to exit the lift. Jake, unnerved but remaining calm, complied. He held up his hands like he had seen actors in films do when a gun was pointed at them. The two men looked at each other and laughed.

"We're not going to shoot you numb nuts!" said the one not holding the gun. He placed his hand on the other man's weapon and gently lowered it down. The gun man then returned it to the back of his trousers and the first man who rescued him introduced himself. "Beady. Well, my name's Jim, but everyone calls me Beady." he said holding out his hand.

"Hi. I'm Jake." he said shaking his hand in a firm grip.

"This 'ere is Mack. He don't say much, but thankfully he told us to run when he heard that Viper. Blimey that was a close one." Beardy said wiping his brow and face with a cloth. Jake noticed that the cloth was dirty even before the man had used it. "So, you new then by the look of you? Where'd you come from?"

"If I told you, you wouldn't believe me." Jake said with a laugh. Both men looked intensely at him and his clothes, which were a complete contrast to their own, which were not much better than rags. *Can't get the clothing thing right,* he thought scolding himself.

"Anyway, that was the first time the Viper got that close so we had better get a move on and see Hayden. I'm sure he'll be interested to hear your story." *My story?* Jake panicked. *I don't have a story.*

They walked along a white corridor, though the colour white was a loose description. The floors and walls were made from a type of marble Corian type stone. He was curious. *What type of place is this?* Their shoes echoed and bounced off high ceilings, with nothing to pad out the emptiness. They were the only ones in the tunnel. "Are there others?"

The two men looked at each others and chuckled. "This is the secure transport area. No one goes in or out without passing security. You're lucky we were up there at that particular time. Two minutes later and you'd have been mincemeat!"

"Oh! Jeez. What was that thing, that...what did you call it, a Viper?"

"Bloody horrible weapon. Kills anything and everything in its way." It was Mack who spoke up this time. 'We've lost many good soldiers to those monsters."

"Soldiers? Like in an army?"

The men laughed again and nodded back at him. "Hayden's going to love you." Jake winced. He had no idea what explanation he was going to give this Hayden bloke. But he had a feeling that whatever he came up with, had better be convincing.

Out of the blue, a quote came into his head from Ralph Waldo Emerson, *'Every mind must make its choice between truth and repose. It cannot have both.'* Thanks Avorra he thought, then added one of his own from Martin Luther King that he remembered, as he looked around him and wondered where these men where taking him: *'From every mountainside let freedom ring'*. He was sure he heard Avorra chuckle.

They came to a large metal door. It was similar to the one on the orange lit path above. He wondered if it was a coincidence or held some significance. He still had no idea at what stage of the future he was in, the year or what the state of the world was. All Avorra had told him it was that it was sometime past the drone period of the first simulation. How long past though, he dreaded to think.

The man punched in a code, peered into a security box on the wall beside the door, then proceeded to stick out his tongue and breathe hard. Jake watched the scene in bemusement. A loud beep went off and a red light lit up above the door. Then the security box spoke in a jovial female AI voice, 'Enter Mack. Have a good day.' Beady glanced back at Jake and smiled. "Hayden's humour."

"Stay close and follow us. Oh and ignore the looks; we don't get many visitors."

The doors opened into a white labyrinth of tunnels and activity. Beautiful, soothing colours swirled through the white, reminding him of a coloured sauce rippling into soft serve ice cream. Lilacs, blues, pinks and greens, flickered intermittently onto the white walls, floors and ceilings, which were made from the same material as the security tunnel they just emerged from. The energy the coloured lighting emitted, was so calming, that despite his situation, Jake immediately felt a sense of peace and warmth.

They walked past huddles of activity. People conversing, working, creating, sitting, standing, walking. Wherever, they were, the space was being utilised by a civilisation of humanity that seemed to have adapted to underground living. They had an air of peace about them, which reflected in the softness of their features. They did not look battle weary like Beady and Mack. And the clothes they wore were nothing like theirs either, which were far more suited to harsh outdoor conditions than the environment they were in. These people wore long light grey tunics, accessorised with rope or cloth belts and most of the women had accessorised with home made jewellery. Their shoes were like soft leather but of a different material he did not recognise. And mostly everyone wore their hair long, even the men.

He noticed their height too since at almost six feet, he

seemed to tower above most of them. They were predominantly short, no more than five and a half feet. This he found the strangest out of all the things he had so far witnessed.

Beady was right, his arrival into their underground world, created much curiosity. The buzz and hum of activity paused as they passed, then resumed to an excited whisper. He looked back at one point and saw that the people they passed were watching him with either curiosity, bemusement and in some faces, something else: fear.

They emerged from the tunnel and out into a vast opening. What he saw took his breath away. Beady and Mack continued their journey, but he stopped in his tracks and stood in awe and shock. They had walked out into a giant open cave-like space, which was unlike anything he had ever seen before. His mind searched for memories of similar scenes in a movie, but nothing, not even a sci-fi movie came as close to how breath-taking the view before him was. A vast city existence hummed around and below him. Cut into the whiteness of this vast open, white space, was a complex labyrinth of layers, with entrances to and from tunnels such as the one from which they had just emerged. Each layer had a glass type see-through safety wall cut into the white surface and interspaced along each path. He walked towards the glass wall that laced his own pathway, taking a closer look. It wasn't actually glass, but a Perspex type of material, more transparent than Perspex and approximately half a foot in thickness. He immediately felt safe, since the ceiling of the cave was hundreds of feet high from top to bottom.

"Come. Hayden's waiting to meet you." Beady instructed and Jake followed, his eyes darting everywhere in an attempt to absorb the fantastic views around him.

Everyone they passed gave the same reaction to the visitor. Mothers grabbed children closer, though he saw very few children. There were many more older people than younger, outweighing them three to one from what he was witnessing. He had so many questions to ask. Though first, he had to figure out what he was going to say. *The truth Jake. The truth.* Were those his thoughts or was Avorra actually communicating with him in some way he wondered? And then his attention was taken by an incredible sight. They had turned a corner and below them at the bottom of this city cave system, was a huge crystal. Jake ran towards the edge of the glass wall and looked down.

"Wow!"

Beady approached him and stood beside him. "It's beautiful isn't it? It feeds light and energy into this place." he said gesturing with opening arms at their environment. "It was here well before Hayden and the others discovered this place."

"What is it? *This place?*" Jake asked as he watched the crystal throw out colours like vibrant sunshine. Engrossed with the light show, he felt a sense of peace and calm he hadn't felt in a very long time. He saw too, that many congregated at the bottom and stood transfixed watching the colourful lights escape the huge white crystal rock.

"I'll let Hayden explain it. But let's just say, that it wasn't created by any human." Beady said as he beckoned for him to continue their journey. Now Jake had even more questions buzzing around his head.

They walked a few minutes more before entering another metal door and then into a lift. It was a lot smoother than the first lift he was in. In moments, they were emerging out onto the surface of the city. He couldn't see the crystal which he expected and the place they exited into was much darker.

"Through here." Mack commanded, indicating another door. It was a tunnel similar to the security one from above. He wearily followed the men, suddenly feeling exhausted. This tunnel went on longer than the previous and he noticed that it felt different. The energy here was not the same as the one in the city; this felt darker, more serious and altogether more humanly familiar. They went through yet another security door and this time they entered a corridor tunnel similar to corridors he expected to see in underground chambers. The lighting here created a more sombre and serious mood. The walls were decorated with arsenals of all types of armoury. Some were attached directly to the walls and others in and on cabinets and shelves. The closer they got to their destination, the more weapons were lined up along the walls like sentries. Then they stopped outside another metal door. Mack began to type codes into the security box. As he watched the entry process, adrenalin started to pump through Jake and his throat became dry. Given what he just witnessed and the change in the two environments, he had no idea what to expect.

The doors separated into two and they walked through another corridor, passing three different closed rooms with large windows. The one that piqued his curiosity most, resembled a military operations centre. It was unmanned and contained monitors, graphs, charts, sonar screens, chairs, desks. It looked as though it had been vacated mid project. He was led through a door and into a room that held only a large table and a few chairs, and instructed to take a seat. This room had no large windows like the other three, only two, dark internal windows. The room reminded him of those interrogation rooms in police stations he had seen in films. *I bet there are people watching me*, he thought as he sat down. He felt himself start to shake inside. He had no idea what to expect.

"Put this glove on." Mack said handing him a black glove. It looked metallic and felt like it should be weighted, but it wasn't. Instead, it had a silky feel. He slipped it onto his left hand.

"What is this?" he said indicating the glove.

"You'll find out.' Mack said with a smirk, then added. "Wait here, Hayden will come soon."

Jake watched the men walk out and then observed his environment. It was exactly like an interrogation room. He looked down at his hands. The ungloved hand shook and exposed his nervousness. He clasped the gloved hand over his bare one and closed his eyes. *Help me Avorra. Help me right now.* Then the words *The truth Jake, tell the truth* rang out in his ears once again. *But what if they don't want to hear the truth Avorra? What then?*

His thoughts were interrupted by the abrupt opening of the door. Jake opened his eyes with a start and looked up and to his left. In walked a tall man with broad, pulled back shoulders and a chest that seemed to fill up the room. He was dressed in army style combat gear, with a belt attached, that held a gun, a knife and what looked like grenades of some kind. The man looked to be much younger than him, possibly in his mid thirties and his hair was short, salt and pepper grey and his face deeply etched with the indelible marks of sorrow and battle. He had the air of someone in control, but also deeply exhausted with being resigned to the fate of his circumstances.

"Welcome to Heaven." he said and laughed at the connotation. It was obviously an in-house joke since the man's serious demeanour betrayed how he really felt. "Hayden." he said proffering his hand. Jake got up and took his hand in his left hand which was ungloved. The man had a firm grip that almost crushed his own.

"Jake." he replied.

"Okay Jake, take a seat. Before we begin, I have to inform you, that despite passing our security scanners for hidden weapons, explosives or the chip, you are a stranger to our colony and therefore, are to be viewed as a suspect. For this reason," he said gesturing around the room but keeping his eyes firmly on Jake's, "we have four lasers pointed at different parts of your body. So, if you so much as sneeze in a threatening manner, all I have to do is give the instruction and this room will be newly decorated with your insides. Do I make myself clear?" Jake nodded and gulped. He glanced around him and discerned that this was not just a room for interrogation, but perhaps even a torture room. He felt his tee- shirt dampen with perspiration, which leaked from his neck and trickled down onto his back.

"Right, let's get to it." Hayden announced leaning forward. At that moment, there was a knock on the door. "Enter!" he commanded. A man dressed in combat clothes came in carrying a tray. He placed in on the table and existed without saying a word. "Water?"

"Yes. Er...yes please."

"This is from the Internal Spring. It's part of the structure of the place. It's the purest form of water and nourishing too. In fact, most of the nutrients we need to survive down here comes from this." he said handing a glass to Jake. "Trust me, it's not like that shit they give them up in the Surface World. Drink!"

Jake welcomed the refreshment. He was suddenly so thirsty that his throat had constricted. Though that may have been the fear that coursed through his veins sitting opposite the most intimidating man he had ever encountered in his life. The knowledge that he could be blown to smithereens at any second, caused his heart to pound hard against his chest.

"So..." Hayden started as he sat back into his chair and folded his arms, "one minute you weren't in that tunnel and then there you were. And out of nowhere, came the Viper. Right out of the blue. Timing's a bit odd don't you think? And given that you don't look like anyone else in this city, nor like the New Humans, then we are wondering, rightly so we think, that maybe you are a new kind of spy?"

"A spy? Me?" Jake looked astonished. "No. No, I'm no spy."

Hayden glanced up and behind Jake's head. Jake glanced around him and faced a dark window. Whoever was in that room was watching and monitoring and feeding information back. They must have determined he was telling the truth since the questioning took a different route.

"Then why are you here Jake?"

Jake took a deep breath. "See Hayden, I have this dilemma. I want to tell you the truth, especially since I have lasers directed at my head, which is pretty unnerving to be honest, but then on the other hand, I'm concerned that if you don't like what I tell you, then you are going to zap me anyway. And if you do that, neither of us would learn anything about each other, right?" He watched as Hayden chewed on his words and observed him intently. Jake was obviously an enigma to him and to the rest of the people down there. He knew he didn't look like anyone else and he also wasn't *like* them. This wasn't his time zone; he wasn't meant to be there. Yet here he was, in a possible future that his work may have instigated. He had a feeling that everything depended on him convincing this man that he was worth keeping alive.

"Okay, shoot. Try me. And if I don't like what I hear, I'll decide then if you live or die. We have a deal." It wasn't a question.

Jake remembered Avorra's words, *You cannot die*. He still wasn't sure of the meaning behind it, but he hoped it was a positive outcome for him. He decided to tell Hayden and whomever else was in that room behind the glass wall, the truth. He mentioned Avorra and his state of mind before her arrival. He explained how the death of his daughter had imploded his family and sent him into a depressive and suicidal state. He saw Hayden wince and his action man features soften, his eyes clouding from a memory of something, perhaps from his past?

He then explained Avorra and everything he knew about her to that point. He risked sounding crazy, but it was the only way he could explain his presence in that room at that particular time in history. He also told him about the visit from Uncle Teddy and his being an unknown war hero. There was so much to say and it all sounded so ridiculous, apart from the sadness of Eloise and his suicidal quest.

"So this is some kind of simulation that you're in?"

"Yes."

"So are you not real, or are we not real?"

That stumped Jake. *What an interesting question to be asked* he thought. *What the hell is real?* He thought of Avorra then replied, "I'm in a simulation of your timeline, so I guess that makes this real. But then I am here in front of you, so that makes me real also." He shrugged his shoulders. He didn't know any better an explanation to give.

"Okay." Hayden replied leaning forward. Jake could see he was intrigued. "So, say this is all true, then why are you here?"

"Because...because," he began his mouth drying up, "because I created the brain chip."

Hayden jumped up from his chair and lunged for him. "You bastard!" he screamed through gritted teeth. "Do you know what you did? Do you?" Two men ran into the room to restrain him, yet there was no need, since he brushed them away. They left as quickly as they came in. Jake was literally eating his heart with fear. The prospect of being pummelled by a man of his strength filled him with terror. Yet at the same time, he sympathised with him. He was realising that his work was naive and open to manipulation, despite his good intentions in the creation of it.

"I'm going to destroy it I promise. This," Jake said indicating the room and everything around them, "whatever this is and whatever is up there, won't happen." He breathed a sigh of relief as Hayden relaxed back into his chair, though he saw that his jaw was still set and his eyes retained the embers of a murderous scorch of fire.

"This..." he said lifting out his arms, "this is our life. See the people out there in that city? They rely on us guys in here to keep them safe from the terrors above that want nothing more than their complete annihilation. And you know why?" Jake shook his head. "Because we are free. That's right, free. And *they* hate us for it."

"I...I don't understand."

"No. You wouldn't. Tell me, what year was it when you left to come here?"

'Er...2025. March 25th.'

"Wow. " Hayden said rising from his chair and running a hand through his short hair. "That explains your clothes. And your skin."

"My skin? What's wrong with my skin?"

"Nothing. It's perfect. That's the point. You have skin that lives under a sun."

"I don't understand. Don't you have a sun?" Jake asked perplexed. His mind was racing with so many questions and possibilities.

"Sure we have a sun. And a moon. They revolve around us 24/7 like with you in your time. But, we don't get to see them anymore. They," he said pointing upwards, "clouded the sun from us. They've been doing it for as long as I've been born, but recently, it's got worse. Nobody has seen the sun's rays or the bright light of the moon for a while now. We don't even know if they are still there. And if they aren't, then having read the many history books that sit in the library here, earth is soon going to be a dead planet."

"Oh my God, how? How did they do that?"

"Geo engineering and weather manipulation. I'm sure you had it back in the 20's? The books and articles showed that's when the population started to wake up to it. Though research shows that it had been going on for decades before then."

Jake thought back to articles and social media posts he had seen on chemtrails and weather manipulation, but truthfully, he had never taken any notice. He always avoided conspiracies and conspiracy theories. He had enough drama going on in his own life and work, without the desire to fall down dark rabbit holes.

"I heard a little, but truthfully, I wasn't aware such things were happening." he said before reflecting, "Surely, without the sun, life on the planet won't survive. Without sunshine, there would be no photosynthesis. Everything would stop growing; the animals would have nothing to eat and neither would we. Animals and humans alike, would starve. Not to mention that without the sun, the temperature on earth would be uninhabitable. Taking away the sun would be suicide. What kind of a person would make those type of decisions?"

"That's a very good question Jake. What kind of person indeed? Who's to say it's even a person?"

"What are you suggesting? Aliens?"

"We don't know. It could also be AI, or AI controlled by another species. It's all speculation of course, since nobody has actually seen the Controllers, or at least lived to tell the tale.'

"Controllers?" Jake asked perplexed. Hayden ignored the question. "It's hard to take in. Aliens, AI controlling people, weather manipulation? I just don't know. I guess I'm not ready to believe these kind of conspiracies."

"Conspiracies? Hah! Take a look around you man. Who do you think built this underground system? Humans?" Jake was flabbergasted. "This place has its own eco system that can sustain life for centuries. It has fresh mineral and nutrient rich water that is also somehow anti-ageing. The light emitted from the crystal changes colour to transfer the perfect amount of emotional balance and energy equilibrium, to live a perfectly harmonious and balanced life. It also sustains a permaculture that enables seeds to grow and be used to produce nutritious and life sustaining food. The technology in this place is so advanced, that you can literally think about a food you would like to eat, type it into a machine and that machine will then produce it for you."

"Wow, that's incredible!"Jake replied. Then looked at the angry man in front of him, adding. "I'm sorry for my ignorance. I hadn't realised that geo engineering was actually a real thing. You hear rumours you know, but trust what is told to you by the governments and such. It's easier to dismiss everything outside of that as a conspiracy."

Hayden grunted and shook his head. "That's about right. You scientists and medical people were so preoccupied with technological advancement and trusting your leaders, that you didn't give a rat's arse about what was going on around you. The destruction of nature, of natural foods, of the environment, of your own immune systems. Did you ever stop and wonder why there was so much growth in diseases like cancer, heart disease or the increase in auto immune issues? No, you were too engrossed with 'advancement' to notice anything of real importance; too busy having your head stuck up your own bloody asses!"

Jake shifted uncomfortably in his seat. Hayden was right. He could see that now and before all of this, he was exactly the person he described. Shame flooded him. "I'm sorry."

"I guess," Hayden relented sitting back into his seat and sighing, "you didn't know any better."

"Okay." Jake said taking in a deep breath. "You are going to have to fill me in. I have a lot of questions. That is," he paused and looked above and behind him, "if you decide not to laser my head off my shoulders." That broke the ice.

"Hey, you want something to eat?" Hayden asked in a more convivial tone.

"Gosh yes please. I'm actually starving!"

"Follow me. And you can take the glove off now."

"What's it for?" Jake asked removing it.

"It monitors if you are telling the truth. A lie detector as such, but a bit more sophisticated than the kind of thing you used in your day."

Jake followed Hayden out of the room. Two men stood guard on either side of the door. Hayden nodded to them and they followed behind them as they walked. They passed a couple more rooms until they came to a large door. From his end, Jake heard many voices.

"This is the mess. You're gonna raise a few brows but ignore them. They've seen some crazy shit in their lives so they don't take to strangers well."

The doors opened into a huge room filled with rows of metal tables and benches. Seated and standing around, were a few hundred men and women. All in a very dark grey type of combat uniform. He noticed that they all wore the same shoes as the long haired people in the grey tunics from the tunnels. And most of them had very short hair or shaved heads, including the women, and most had a square patch over the base of their skulls. When they entered, the noise of the room decreased down to silence, as though someone watching had just decided to turn down the volume.

"At ease soldiers. This is Jake. He's safe. Treat him with respect. He's about one hundred and forty years old!' Hayden turned to Jake and winked.

A hundred and forty? Thought Jake. *That means this must be less than a hundred years from my time? That's not that long!*

The noise volume raised again and Jake guessed that most of their conversation would have changed to centre around him and his presence there. He was shocked at the timeline, so he couldn't imagine how many questions the people around him were asking. Hayden led him through the mess hall towards a food area. This was like no canteen he had ever seen. They stopped in front of a large machine, similar to the vending machine he knew back home, but this was far more futuristic. Hayden looked Jake up and down, then pressed a few buttons. Two grey and silver packets dropped into a metal hole. Hayden took out the packets and slipped them into another machine. It took just two minutes before a steaming meal was handed on a metal plate to Jake.

"I guessed you'd be a meat guy." Hayden said handing

him what looked like a steak pie with mashed potato, peas and gravy.

"Oh man! This is amazing. I'm so bloody hungry!" Hayden regarded him then leaned in closer.

"Just a nudge Jake, cuss words were eliminated a long time ago. I'm cool with it and probably most of the guys in here, though we try not to use them ourselves whilst in the city. The people out there are, for want of a better word, more *unaware* than us." Another warning about his language. *Point taken Avorra* he thought with a wry smile. They sat at an empty table. "Eat. We've a lot to get through."

Jake was grateful for the food and the silence between them. This was his favourite meal at his mother's house and all the warming homely memories came flooding back to him. He felt comforted and found himself relaxing for the first time whilst in this strange simulation.

"This is delicious and exactly like how my mum used to make it back home. Where do you get the meat from? I didn't see any cows."

Hayden laughed. Then he called out to a couple of men standing nearby. "Hey lads, he just asked where we got the cows from?" They laughed and soon the word spread and raucous laughter filled the room. Jake looked around him in confusion then back at Hayden with a questioning look.

"Meat was eradicated from the human diet back in the mid 2030's. In fact, all dairy, poultry, fish and anything that lived, was eliminated from the human diet. Except for insects. For some reason, they didn't mind us eating them. In fact, they encouraged it, reasons for which we discovered much later down the line."

"But I don't understand." Jake proclaimed looking at his very empty and fork scraped plate. "That tasted exactly like beef and kidney."

"That's the point. It's meant to."

"So if it isn't meat, then what is it?" he asked feeling slightly queasy. "Bugs?"

"No, we stopped eating those around twenty or so years ago. We were devouring so many that the ecological process was not just disrupted by the lack of insect pollination, but also nearly destroyed. Insects are one of the most necessary things required for the sustainability of this planet and for indirectly feeding us as a species. They were wrong to make us consume them. You see, they can be pathogenic for humans, due to a substance called chitin. Seems this can't be digested or broken down in the body. Only birds have guts that can safely process insects. So, whilst we were told to eat bugs to save the planet, the very act of doing so was neither good for the planet, nor it seems, for us.

Unfortunately, we weren't presented with that information at the time, so as a result of humans consuming bugs on a mass scale, certain foods then disappeared completely, with no way of resurrecting them. Think about it, insects are not just crucial for food products such as coffee and chocolate, fruits etc., but also for breaking down leaves and bark from trees, eating decaying animals and their faeces, pollinating wild flowers and so on. Without insects, the world is colourless and grey. As well as ensuring a lack of varying nutrients for us to survive if they disappear. And boy, do I miss coffee!"

"And this happened? They actually did this?"

"Yup. Sadly, on top of all the other restrictions imposed on us, we were forced to eat bugs. As a result, many got sick and died. Whether this was deliberately intentional, or that the decision makers realised this a bit too late, we don't know, but suffice to say, it wasn't a good option for either the sustainability of humans, or for the good of the planet. And to top it off, these insects often have parasites and bacteria that are also detrimental for humans."

"Parasites?"

"Yeah. Ironic isn't it? This whole thing started with the fear of a parasite in our waters, then we are forced to ingest insects for food and getting sick from the parasites from the bugs. Honestly, you couldn't make it up!"

"So...do I want to know what I just ate then?" Jake grimaced as he regarded his plate.

"I typed in what I thought you would like. You enjoyed it right? Think about it, do you really want to know any more?" Hayden raised a brow and smirked. Jake shook his head slowly and remembered that this was after all, merely a simulation. *You cannot die.*

Hayden had to leave for a short while, so left him to hang around in the mess hall. Jake took the time to focus on his environment and collate his thoughts. The year was around 2120 to 2125 give or take a year. There was no living animal on the planet except for insects which had been eaten into near extinction. He thought of what the world above would look like. Did it resemble one of those apocalyptic dystopian films he loved watching, or perhaps something far more sinister?

He perused the other people in the room. He noticed that they all looked so similar, like action men and women figures. Muscular, trim, fit and chisel jawed. This intrigued him. He studied them further, then noticed a feature that he had failed to notice initially and he was shocked. They were all the same colour. Not white, not black, not Asian, nor mediterranean. Instead, they were a mixture of all of those races and became an undefinable colouring. It was as though someone had blended all the human race skin colours together, creating one colour. Why? Was the only word that came to him.

He tried to catch a glimpse of their eyes, but each time he looked, they seemed to be a different colour. And everyone he saw in that room had a patch at the back of the head. Just then, Hayden returned.

"Okay Jake, I have questions and I've no doubt you do too. Let's walk and talk." Jake got up and followed him out of the mess hall. He felt eyes watching his every move, questioning who and what he was, just as he was wondering the same of them.

"So are they all soldiers?" he asked Hayden as soon as they were inside another corridor and out of the mess room.

"Yes. We call them Protectors. And yes," he said as he stopped and turned to face him square on, "they are robots."

"Robots?"

"That's right. But renegade robots. Once connected to the Mother but then started to remember and question and, for want of a better word, became 'renegade' to the system. The other robots, who live in the city amongst the people are simply known as Renegades."

"Remember? Remember what? Do robots have memories?" Hayden carried on walking, ignoring the question. "Okay, okay, can we slow down a minute please? I...I don't understand what the hell is going on. I have no clue what the future, er...your present, is." Hayden stopped in front of a large metal door, sighed and turned to look at Jake with a mixture of exasperation, resignation and also, sadness.

"The future that faces you Jake, isn't pretty. Our present is in danger and not just for everyone in this city, but for the whole of humanity, even the Controllers of the Pyramid. We, as in myself, a few others like Mack and Beady, and the Protectors, are fighting a losing battle. We know it, but we can't let the people in the city know. They don't have the mental capacity shall we say, to survive knowing what's ahead. So whatever I tell you or show you, must be kept from them at all costs. Is that clear?"

"Yes. I understand." Jake agreed. "But I want to know everything, from start to finish."

"Oh boy. It's going to be a long day. We need coffee." Hayden said expelling a deep sigh.

"You have coffee?" Jake said excited. Suddenly, thoughts of a hot latte thrilled him.

"No numb nuts. Without insects there is no coffee. Just saying I could kill for a cup right now."

The door opened onto a white hive of human activity, along with the relaxing mixture of swirling, pastel colours bouncing around the walls and surfaces. He enquired about the crystal and the origins of the city. Hayden explained that it all existed before he was 'found' around the age of ten. He was brought into the city by an elder who was foraging for seeds. He was taught their ways but as he grew, he realised how different he was from them. They told him he was part of a manufactured human creation called the New Human.

"So if they are not like you and not like the Protectors or the Renegades, then who are they? Or, even *what* are they?"

"Humans. Well, the old style; the more authentic race." Hayden replied as he paused for Jake to take it all in. "I guess you could say that you are their predecessor."

Jake watched the people as they gathered before the crystal. Some were bowing, others kneeling and many were praying, but all were respectful and in awe of the huge white crystal structure. "What is that anyway?" he asked.

"Life. Literally. For everyone here, except of course the robots. They just go on and on, unless their plug is pulled, but I'll explain that later on. Come on, I'll introduce you to someone who will explain it better than me." Hayden led him through swathes of people, from those who gathered at the base of the crystal, to others engaged in activities or conversation. There were no vehicles, no phones or technology, no machines. Everything given or exchanged, was created by hand. The only equivalent way of life Jake could compare it to, was the Amish type communities in America he had read about. Except for one big difference – there was no land, nature or animals. Each new revelation within this simulation, brought him even further questions.

"Why are they so short?" he asked Hayden when they were out of earshot and heading towards another white tunnel.

"Lack of vital nutrients for growth. Plus no Vitamin D from the sun's rays. They receive life nutrients from the crystal, which by the way, is called The Queen." Hayden said as an aside. "Did you notice that there were very few children?"

"Yes. I saw that immediately. Where are they? Is there a school?"

Hayden shook his head then paused to look at him before responding. "There is no school. There is no requirement."

"No requirement?"

"Because there aren't enough kids or young people to fill a school." he left the words hanging and then stopped outside what could only be called a 'pod'. They had passed others just like it on their walk through the white tunnels. It had a glazed door in the same material as the safety glass that lined the layered pathways, though this one wasn't transparent. Instead, it had a frosted glass appearance. Hayden rapped on the door. They waited a moment, before the door slid open into two at the middle and disappeared into the walls either side. An elderly man with straggly long, white hair and an equally long white beard, greeted Hayden with a smile and a hug. The man was hunched over slightly and walked with a stick and a limp. He could easily have been well over a hundred years old.

"Papa, this is Jake. He's from the past and older even than you!"

Papa turned his eyes towards Jake and raised his brows suspiciously. "You don't look older than me." he commented and motioned for them both to enter. Jake gasped. It was the first time he had missed home since arriving in the city. The room they entered, was like a cave of all that was familiar to him in his own timeline. Two large, aged wooden bookshelves overflowing with books, adorned one side of the room. Against another wall, stood an old, battered chest of drawers, with varnish peeling or missing altogether in large patches. It held an array of bric a brac and treasure finds, reminding Jake of antique shops in London he used to visit with his daughters. Every ounce of space was covered with dusty and ageing items, from brass candelabras, to ashtrays, watches, bracelets and rings; a crystal vase, photo frames and even a pair of spectacles. There were also larger items, such as a brass Tiffany style lamp, a glass cafetière and a dusty, silver Dualit style toaster.

A blue, threadbare sofa sat in the centre of the room, along with barely there, worn down velvet cushions and to the right of the room, was a small table and two chairs. On top of the table, were more books and a Roberts style radio. Jake immediately felt comfortable in the old man's presence.

"I'd offer you tea or coffee, but that ran out about fifteen years ago. I do have something slightly more pernicious though." he winked at Hayden and ambled towards a small chest that sat underneath and to the back of the table. He pulled it out and lifted the lid. Inside were two bottles. Jake recognised one.

"Whisky? You have whisky?"

The other two men chuckled knowingly. Hayden went to a corner of the room and opened a cupboard. He pulled out two ancient crystal glasses and a glass cup. Then brought them over to where the old man was bent over extracting one of the bottles from the chest. It contained a quarter of dark liquid. Jake wondered if it was authentic alcohol or something made up like the meal he ate earlier. He still hadn't persuaded himself to ask them what he really ate.

"Here's to the end of the world as we know it." the old man said as he poured a small measure into each glass. "God save The Queen!" Then he laughed again. Jake was beginning to really like this old man.

"You mean the Crystal right?" Jake piped up.

"The only Queen there is young man."

The whisky hit the back of Jake's throat and he coughed. "Yup! That's good whisky right there!" he gasped. "Phew, I was worried a bit then."

"Rescued ten cases of these from an old warehouse about, oh, thirty years ago or something like that. What a find! Only one and a bit bottles left now. So I keep them for special occasions, you know?" Jake noticed he had an American twang, but also a little Asian and a twitch of London.

"I bet you have a few stories to tell?" Jake said as he savoured every drop that trickled like burning gold down the back of his throat.

Papa and Hayden raised their eyes at each other. Then the old man pulled out a chair from beside the small table and gestured towards the sofa at Jake. "Seems like we all do kid. But hey, since you are the newcomer here and far more intriguing than either of us, why don't you take a seat and tell us why you're here."

Jake sat in this little enclave pod in a white, non human constructed city and re-told the story about Avorra's visit and the chip project. He divulged about the private meeting between Edward and Henry and his proposed assassination. That raised eyebrows from the two men listening. He also informed them of the white pill plan and the nefarious intentions of a minority of evil men to create a mind control weapon against the human race.

He also confessed that this was not his first simulation and when recounting the story of the drones, Tom and the other people hiding in that basement, he felt sadness and fear rise in his chest and had to fight back the feelings of anger and loss he still carried. It may have been a simulation, but the indelible mark it left was like a dream he could never forget.

"So let me get this right," Hayden recounted, "you've come from the past to experience the future, which is our present, so that the future may not happen if you change the present; your present. Am I getting that right?"

"Pretty much yes. I guess Avorra and the Council want me to fully understand why the chip and all of my work pertaining to it, has to be destroyed."

"And tell me Jake, how do you feel about destroying this work?" Papa had been quietly listening to his story, nodding at places, reflecting in others. He watched as Hayden's face intensified when Jake recounted the story of the drones and the basement, noticing how his free hand clenched into a tight fist, whilst the other hand knocked back the strong liquor as it had done on so many previous occasions whilst sitting together in that room.

"I...I...It's the right thing to do of course." Jake blurted.

"That's not what I asked you."

Jake was dumbstruck. *How do I feel? Really.* He sighed, drained his glass, then looked at the floor. "I'm gutted truth be known."

"Gutted? Gutted? Do you not get it?" Hayden jumped up and loomed over Jake, who felt his blood draining from him at the sudden angry outburst. "Billions of peoples' lives were either abolished or destroyed because of something *you* created! And you are what? Gutted?" He looked to Papa. His face was enflamed with anger. "If I kill him now, will that stop all this from happening?"

"Kill me? No. I...I'm going to destroy it I promise. I was just answering the question that's all." *Avorra help* he pleaded in his head. *You cannot die* was the immediate response. *I still don't know if that means I can't, or I mustn't damn it!*

Papa placed his hand on Hayden's arm and met his eyes. So much love, respect and guidance passed through in that one look. The connection between the two was obvious. Hayden growled, slammed his fist against the sofa in rage, then headed off through to a small door at the back of the room.

"He'll calm down. Now, tell me more about this project. And about you." the old man said with such kindness and sincerity, that Jake's fear and guilt completely dissipated. He took a breath then explained how the chip was designed to be used for the good of humanity and how it could help eradicate diseases and ease mental health disorders by numbing or blocking receptors of the brain that enabled the growth of rogue, diseased cells and thoughts responsible for pursuing destructive paths. He told the old man that similar work had already been in process decades before his, mainly from other neuroscientists and neuropsychologists.

However, his breakthrough was finding a way to directly inject nanotechnology into the brain without causing injury, either immediate or long term. He then explained how this technology was developed to sit inside the brain fluid, awaiting instructions via EMF pulses that were fed into the brain by a main mother type computer.

When he finished explaining his work, Papa asked many more searching questions, including about his family and his private life. That's when he explained the death of Eloise, his plans to end his life and then the arrival of first Teddy and then finally, Avorra.

Throughout the entire explanation, the old man sat and intently absorbed each word, nodding and listening, without comment or interjecting, except to ask about his family life.

"Thank you for telling me everything Jake. You have experienced some tough times I can tell." Then he sighed, pulled the stopper out of the whisky bottle and re-filled all of their glasses, emptying the bottle.

"That's very generous of you sir, but don't you want to keep it for yourself? I mean, it's the last you'll ever see of this in your lifetime."

"Hah! My lifetime? I'm one hundred and fourteen years old Jake. I don't think there's much of a lifetime left in me to be honest. Besides," he said with an impish wink and a nod towards the small chest, "I've one more bottle left." Just then, before Jake had a chance to ask further questions, including how someone could live so long on the kind of diet and lack of core nutrients that they mentioned, Hayden walked back into the room. His upper torso was bare and he was about to place his shirt back on, but not before Jake saw a large blue tattoo on his right arm near his shoulder. It was simply one letter, the letter P. Hayden took a long, questioning look at Papa, sighed in resignation then returned to his position in the chair he vacated. He then turned reluctantly to face Jake.

"Okay, so let's look at this whole thing from another perspective." Papa said. "Say it's true that you came here to see what the future is, before you go back and decide your course of action in your present? Well then, it would help to know what the real future is don't you think? The one up there."

"Up there?"

"Yeah. The surface world is a whole different place to this city down here, trust me." Hayden said, glancing at Papa for affirmation.

"Why don't you tell him about you and why you got to be down here and not up above with the rest of them." Papa said addressing Hayden. "Then he might understand things a little better, especially about how the New Humans are created."

Hayden reflected, sighed and then began his story. "I went through the system the same as everyone else. Created in one of the birthing factories, stamped and passed into a teaching pod. The nanny robots are designated the role of bringing the babies from birthing pod to stamping and then to feeding. Round the clock, the developing fetus in these pods, are fed with a concoction of genetically modified nutrients that help grow the body and develop the functionality of each organ and limb movement, via a tube connected into the base of their skull. As the fetus develops, the tube acts as a technology feeding programme, passing instructions and information directly into the brain fluid before the child is born. Thus, at the end of gestation, when the child is fully developed and ready to be birthed, it is already initiated into the ways of the Pyramid."

"Sorry to interrupt, but you've mentioned it before; what is this Pyramid?"

"The Pyramid is the system constructed by the Controllers. It's a way of life that exists in the surface world. Anything outside of it is against the system and as such, they believe has to be destroyed." Hayden looked to Papa, posing a silent question with his eyes. Papa nodded. Hayden sighed. "To understand the Pyramid system, you have to understand why it is there in the first place.

You see," he continued with a heavy tone, "the only way the world they have created can sustain itself, is through ensuring that everything and everyone within it is contained and controlled. This means that individual thought, freewill, free speech or anything that contains any level of a person's individual sovereign rights, is disallowed.

At first they did this by the restrictions of rights and the reductions of freedoms. I guess it was around your time, the early to mid twenties they really initiated this. To begin with, it was a slow, incremental drip of subtle propaganda and elite psychological operations to produce mass formation psychosis, all propagated by a corrupt and paid for mainstream media. Basic rights were diminished by laws passed under the peoples' noses via the use of distractions..."

"Distractions? What kind of distractions?"

"Everything from wars, climate issues and virus mutation threats, to racial tensions, personal identity confusions and even the utilisation of celebrity status. Constant drama and crisis thrown out to distract from what was really happening around them – the restriction of basic freedoms and the increase of centralised control. The people were blind sided from every angle and all the while, their leaders were reassuring them that they knew best and the things they were putting in place was for their own wellbeing and safety. But it wasn't. No, in fact the complete opposite. Everything that was happening, was simply about control." Hayden finished his drink, stood up, walked around the room and continued.

"You see, keeping the people in a constant state of fear meant they were more malleable and therefore, easier to manipulate and manoeuvre into any direction they chose fit. A humanity experiencing cognitive dissonance, was ripe for ingesting higher levels of control than a free and critically thinking population. Any rebelliousness or dissonance, was portrayed as dangerous and against the wellbeing and safety of the general public. Thus it was easier to quell and squash protests from those who sought to wake people up to what was happening to them. It's pretty genius really, despite being downright evil."

"Bastards!" Jake exclaimed in anger. His mind searched for his own examples and came up with Edward and Henry. After the accident, they persuaded him to pour his grief into his work. Despite it being a hit and run, it was suspected that the driver of the other car involved, was allegedly under the influence of a banned substance. Thus his anger and grief was directed even more specifically towards finding a way to block off the receptor to a person's desire to exceed government guidelines for the consumption of alcohol or drugs. For him, the work was personal.

"Yes indeed. But you see Jake, it was so easy for them. We, in our time, keep asking the question, 'why didn't they see what was going on? Why didn't they stop it?" Perhaps, you could shed some light on this for us?"

"That's a really interesting question Hayden. Truthfully, I think it was as you said – the controlling measures are so subtle, that we weren't...aren't, aware of them. Until you just informed me, I didn't realise this was happening. I mean, the media? In on it too? I don't understand that; aren't they meant to be independent journalists investigating the truth?"

"Hah! Follow the money man. Look at who owns the media! Money buys anything and everything Jake. Though not in this lifetime. Currency of any type is a thing of the past. And there is nothing to purchase anyway. Not in the Pyramid system at least. No personal items are permitted and to be honest, unless you are survivors like us, or one of the Roamers, there is no reason to want for anything."

"Roamers?"

"The people who roam outside of the Controlled Cities. They are now few and far between, but we do come across a few. We tend to avoid them to be honest. They live like cockroaches, have a skewed moral compass and would sell you for a scrap of food in a second. Best avoid them if you can."

"What about food, or clothing, or items like vehicles, furniture, tools and stuff?" Jake asked. His mind was grasping for the necessities of his everyday life. "Don't the surface people need them?"

"Not in the Pyramid, no. The New Humans don't want for anything, they just are. They live in a carefully monitored environment, which we call Controlled Cities, with no transport to go anywhere even if they desired it, which they don't. They are alive only to feed the system one way or another. They get fed, watered, clothed and given a bed to sleep. They have no conscious awareness of individuality; no conscious choice and no desire. They wake, breathe, eat, drink, work, sleep. Repeating the same existence day after day after day. It's a sorry life and I would rather be dead than live like that."

Jake sat back against the threadbare, once canary yellow

velvet cushion and sighed out deeply. He shook his head attempting to absorb the imagery of the life of a human being in that world. "It's horrendous."

"Yup. And it's going to get a hell of a lot worse for the poor buggers. Indeed, for all of us, no matter where we are existing on this sorry planet."

"What does that mean?" Jake asked with concern.

"I'll tell you later. First I want you to get some rest. I'll find you a pod space and you can get some shut eye. You'll need to be alert and on the ball for where we are going next."

"Why? Where are we going?"

"To the Pyramid."

9

THE PYRAMID

His dream was vivid. He was in a crowd of people running; constantly running. Machines and drones were on every corner, in every building, alert and ready. Insect and animal robots, soldier and police robots, robot flying machines, gigantic walking machines and vehicle machines, like the Vipers, with gigantic corkscrew attachments that could bore holes into the surface within minutes, tearing up and ripping apart anything in its trajectory. There was nowhere to hide. And then he saw her: Eloise. She was standing, with a huge smile on her cherubic face, holding a bunch of handpicked wildflowers in one hand and holding her mother's hand in the other. She saw him and her face alighted. She pulled away from her mother's hand and excitedly waved to him.

A canine robot approached them. She stopped waving and paused to regard the animate metal object and, curious and full of childlike insouciance, reached out to touch it. Jake heard the annihilating bullets tear through the victims as he jolted awake, soaked in his perspiration. He didn't see it happen, but he could hear it and feel it.

He got up and used the bathroom, splashing his face with water to try to wash away the memory. Nothing was working. He saw her face, clear as day and heard the rat-a-tat-tat of the machine gun as it expelled bullet after bullet into petal soft skin. A sharp knock at the door caused him to jump into reality, but was a welcome distraction. "Come in." he called out.

Hayden touched the middle of the door and it disappeared into the walls. He stepped in, looked around him and regarded Jake with curiosity, watching as he emerged wiping his face and underarms with a towel. Jake replaced his tee shirt and jumper then sat down on the bed to put on his shoes. His head was still in his dream when a thought crossed his mind.

"Comfy bed. Where does the old guy sleep? I didn't see a bed in his room." he said.

"On the sofa. He hates beds but loves that sofa. Apparently it reminds him of his childhood." Hayden replied. "Time is short Jake and we only have a small window of opportunity before the sentries change shifts. We got to go."

"Sentries?"

"The guards. Robots. Solider ones, like the Protectors here, but with their plug intact."

"Plug?" Jake asked perplexed.

"Yeah, the connection to the Mother, which by the way, is the main AI computer that connects everyone and everything in the Pyramid, including the ones in the top three tiers." Jake's furrowed brow remained, so Hayden sighed and leaned against the table in the room.

"Tiers? Sorry, but I have so many questions still. So many!"

"Well you can ask me as we go along. I can't guarantee I will answer all of them and truthfully, I'm not one for talking much, but since you seem to be the reason we are in this mess and paradoxically, also can prevent this from happening, then I will accommodate as best I can. Fair?" Jake nodded.

"Okay, this is how it works. All New Humans and robots are connected to the Mother via electronic impulses sent to a receiver chip implanted into the brain, or in the case of robots, the back of the head area. I guess it's a further development on where you were going with your research. This connection from the Mother, happens during the gestation period and acts like a drip feeding tube into the New Humans. There is no memory or sub conscience as far as we know, but the DNA that they use to create them, stays in their central system and thus we believe, that if we can unplug as many as possible, then we have a hope of re-sparking the human DNA memories and help them to remember their human condition, or in the case of the robots, become more consciously aware and empathetic to the human cause. By becoming conscious again, they all have access to critical and free thought. At present, the humans are no better than robots; more like humanoids really."

"Wow. So how many have you saved and brought back to humanity this way?"

"No adults so far. Once they are in the Pyramid system then they are constantly monitored and receiving the EMF waves from Mother. We haven't found a way of unplugging a New Human adult yet."

"So they *are* just like robots then?" Hayden nodded and sighed. "And how does it work with the robots that escape the system? How can they escape and not the humans?"

"Now that's a great question!" Hayden answered animated. "We noticed that sometimes a humanoid type robot, as opposed to the drones, or machines like the Vipers, would pause as though affected by a memory. Then one day, during an altercation with a robot, the head was damaged. Something in the back of its head became what we call 'unplugged'. The robot stopped. We thought it was some kind of battery damage, but then the robot came back to life and asked us a question."

'What type of question?" Jake asked intrigued.

"It said, 'Where am I?'"

"So it expressed conscious thought?"

"Exactly!" Hayden replied. "From there we tried to unplug as many as possible. The Sentries we unplugged are our Protectors. It's in their programming to protect and to serve. The working robots became the Renegades who preferred to integrate within our community, yet they also feel safer being together, which is interesting. We believe the human DNA they used when designing these robots, gave them memories. Thus they feel both connected and also disconnected from the human race. It can be quite unnerving for them when they get unplugged. It's like all these human memories rush into them. I'm used to it now, but it can be strange when you first experience a robot talking about a memory from someone's past; someone long gone, like an ancestor of theirs. Yet they aren't flesh and blood. It's freaky when you think about it. On the plus side, they make great mates and they don't have the human emotions of love, fear, hate or anger. They do laugh though and their sense of humour is second to none!"

"Geez, that's fascinating." Jake proclaimed. His scientific mind whirred with possibilities. "What about the humans in this city here? Were they ever connected?"

"No. Did you notice, that all the human inhabitants of this city have long hair?"

"Yeah sure, I saw that"

"Well, that's something that happened with their evolution. Call it a natural defence trait or something. Whether it was conscious or unconscious, we don't know. But it protects the back of the skull from these electronic wave pulses that the Mother emits out into the pyramid. It never stops. It's like a radioactive wave of electromagnetic pulse energy that zaps anyone and everyone. And it works on one frequency. And before you ask, we have no idea what that frequency is."

"Are you, or were you connected too?" Jake asked trying to grab a glimpse of the back of his neck. He now understood why the Protectors he saw had a patch at the base of the skull. They had their plug to the Mother removed.

"No. I never had one. I was never connected to Mother."

Jake was shocked and intrigued. "But I thought everyone was. Weren't you also born in one of these factories?"

"I was. I also came from the Baby Nation. That's what they call these baby factories. But for some reason, whether it was by accident or by some kind of Divine intervention, I was and have never been connected.

"That's weird." Jake replied. "It was a lot to take in. "Well if you weren't plugged in and born into this crazy, controlled system, then how the hell did you survive?"

Hayden sighed as painful memories threatened to surface and hamper his focus as they had done so often in the past. The old man wasn't the only one who found crates of banned substances, but his crates did not last as long as the old man's. "It wasn't easy. I shouldn't have survived. They have a Reject bin for babies like me. But for some reason, I escaped it. I have no idea why. The first ten years surviving in The Pyramid was torture. There were many times I wanted to die; times I wished I had landed in that bin. I was close to death more times than I can remember and have countless scars to prove it. There was one particular time..." he started but then paused, glanced at Jake and regained his composure. "Let's just say that Papa found me in the nick of time. I was ten and we've been together ever since."

"Like a father figure?" Jake asked with tenderness.

"Hah! Kinda, but boy he isn't like any text book father I read about." he said chuckling to himself. "Anyway, the thing about the Pyramid that you have to remember is this: it's a dangerous system set up for everyone to lose. The only real winners are the Controllers. And if you are wondering who they are, then you are going to have to wait until we hit the surface, as we are running out of time. And if this is a simulation as you say, then I am guessing that time isn't on your side either."

"That's true, I never thought of that." Jake said as he got up and stretched, watching Hayden's back as he headed out of the room. Before leaving, Jake poured himself a glass of water, gulped it down and started to walk out, before swiftly turning back to look at the bed and the lingering nightmare he could not forget, "I'll fix it for them Eloise, I promise." he whispered, then walked out.

They headed through the tunnel and back out onto the main pathway. He watched the people going about their lives and wondering once again why there were so many older people in relation to people his age or younger. Papa wasn't the only centenarian in the city and like him, they seemed to be decades younger with regards to their physical state than in Jake's present time. They acted more like people aged in their sixties or seventies than forty or fifty years older. He enquired about this to Hayden, who said something about it being energy emitted from The Queen crystal. Decades of drinking water from a well that sat beneath the crystal, from which the humans managed to tap into, had given them life enduring qualities. However, in the past three decades, the crystal was losing its regenerating power. Less children were being born which explained the lack of youth. There were also significant changes up on the surface world and Hayden had evidence to suggest that the planet was dying.

"What's causing it?" Jake enquired.

"The over mining of all natural fossil fuel resources to create enough electricity to power all the Artificial Intelligence, robots, drones etc, plus the lost natural resources of vital minerals, forests, rivers and the destruction of the world's natural eco system. Deforestation, coupled with the obliteration of all animals on the planets and the over consumption of insects, including bees by the way, which became a particular delicacy of those in the higher Pyramid levels, then the planet has become nothing more than a mass of these constricted Controlled Cities pumping out pollution. They are literally sucking the life out of the planet and giving nothing back in return. It's unsustainable."

"Earth's going to die?" Jake stopped walking. His jaw dropped and adrenalin pumped through his system.

"I guess we all die eventually Jake, including this planet." He watched as Hayden tightened his jaw, straightened his back and walked on. 'I guess that's why we have to nip it in the bud before we get to this point. Come on."

They walked in silence, each chewing on their own thoughts. The knowledge that he had a major part in not just the destruction of the human race, but also the planet, was a lot to ingest. *I thought I was doing good for humanity?* He kept saying to himself over and over. *How could I have been so naive and short sighted?*

Hayden's thoughts were different. The arrival of a

human from the past, resurrected old memories of living in another time. This man reminded him of someone, yet he could not figure out who. He was also a reminder of familiarity; that somehow, he had been on earth in a different lifetime and also part of a loving family. He remembered experiences of sunshine, trees, a huge lake, cars, boats and planes. He scoured books that he had once discovered in an abandoned library whilst on a reconnaissance mission outside of the Pyramid city. He was searching for the answers to his soul, but found the books instead. He risked life and limb on return journeys to recover as many books as he could. He built the library himself from scratch, though very few people read. Only Papa and some of the other elders who had been taught to read or attended schools in their youth would spend time there. It was Papa who taught Hayden to read. Papa had taught him many things, not least of all on how to survive in an existence that was set up to destroy anything outside of its control.

They walked along pathways and through tunnels containing many pods. One pathway near the top of the city led them to a section that contained robots without the human skin. They were not like the Protectors. On first encountering them, Jake was reticent and on his guard. He knew they were not a danger since they lived within the city, but knowing that AI were the enemy, put him squarely on his back foot.

Hayden introduced him to one of the robots, whom Jake guessed was one of their elders. The robot approached him and placed a hand to his face and closed his eyes. It was reading him.

"Welcome Jake. You have come from afar to seek a very important answer to your destiny. In your quest, you will meet much challenge and quite possibly death. Though you will not die. But remember this...you already have the answers you seek. You are already home." Then it released its hand, stood back and added, "Have a good day men." before walking off and resuming the activity it was engaged in before the two men had arrived.

"That was Gregoria. He is the wisest of all whom you will encounter anywhere. It is said that he knows and sees everything. I have had many discussions with him. As you have seen, he gives pretty profound advice. Come, let's continue. We are close to the edge of the city and then we have to take a back way to the surface. We would have taken the lift, but Mack has reason to believe they are listening for activity underground. The upper lift is one of our making and not as sophisticated as the ones that already existed in the City. Whoever built this place, was way ahead of humans in their technological advancement."

Jake was still musing on Gregoria's words. 'You are already home'. What did he mean?

"Hey?" Hayden interrupted his thoughts. "What did Gregoria mean when he said you wouldn't die? Can you not die here? In this simulation?"

"Truthfully, I have no idea. I was about to be killed by a drone in the last simulation but ended up safe back in my flat. Whether that's the same this time, I have no idea. But suffice to say," he replied taking in a deep breath then exhaling, "I bloody hope it means that."

They carried on walking until they came to a large metal door. This one had the same security as the door on entering the city and on entering the area that Hayden and the Protectors occupied. Hayden typed into the metal pad and then stuck out his tongue and breathed into it, until the door opened. They entered another white tunnel, this time with no pods or pathways. Hayden indicated for him to follow. They walked for approximately ten more minutes, but in silence with just the questioning narrative inside their heads to break the monotony of the white environment. It was Hayden who finally spoke.

"This tunnel leads away from the underground city. It was uniquely designed to protect the original inhabitants from detection by the outside world. There are larger chambers than our city that lead off from this tunnel. We discovered them a few years ago but Mack, who is our main scout for detection of enemy penetration, thinks some of these chambers may have been compromised. We decided against risking the exposure of our city to find out if that really is the case."

"Were they, or are they inhabited?" Jake enquired.

"We don't know. I guess we will never know now. Come on, we're not far away from the stairs."

"Stairs?"

"Yes. A few hundred of them. How are your legs?" Hayden asked with a mock laugh.

"There's something I wanted to ask. Mack and Beady; are they Protectors too? It's just...they seem different."

"No, they are human. They are Rejects." Hayden said raising an eye.

"Rejects, like from the Reject Bin you mentioned?"

Hayden slowed down the pace and then stopped in front of a section of wall. He placed his hand over something invisible that Jake could not see. Electronic doors opened and slid into the wall, similar to the doors of the pod. Then he turned to face Jake. "There were hundreds of Reject New Humans like Mack and Beady living with us in the city, but unlike the Protectors, they don't survive long against the enemy out there. Now we take all Rejects to The Priest."

"The Priest? What, like an *actual* priest?"

"Without faith in this god forsaken world, what else is there?" Hayden remarked as he walked through the invisible doors that led out into another tunnel, although this one was made from rock and limestone. "Get ready to enter the Stairway to Hell."

They exited the tunnel and onto a staircase that was cut into the rock. It was narrow, with barely enough room for one man to stand comfortably. They could see neither ahead nor behind, since the stairway curved and twisted as it cut its way upwards. It was a steep climb. Hayden led the way. After a few minutes, Jake requested to stop and take a breather. Not only was it steep, but it was challenging on his legs, particularly his quads, glutes and calf muscles. He had so many questions still to ask, but Hayden told them to remain silent during the ascent. Jake was so breath challenged that he felt his lungs would explode if he even attempted to converse.

Finally, after at least twenty minutes of intense climbing, with a few stops to release the pain and tension accumulating in his legs, they made it to the top. Hayden allowed them to gather their breath and recover their bodies.

"My bloody ass is killing me!" Jake whispered through gasps of breath. It had been a while since he had exercised so intensely.

"We're close to the top. One more tunnel then we exit into the surface world. Stay close to me okay? There's danger everywhere. They have eyes all over the place. But just follow me and you'll be fine."

Jake nodded and prayed to God. And then to Avorra. *Stay with me Avorra. I've never been so scared as I am now. I have no idea what to expect.* The door opened out into semi darkness. It took a while for his eyes to adjust to the new environment, but the pungent smell made him gag immediately.

"Oh yes, I forgot to mention that the Underground tunnel system you once knew, is now their sewerage dump. Here, I brought you a face mask. It won't help much but it's the best I can do." Jake gladly took the thin black mask and slipped the loops over his ears. He pulled the cloth part over his mouth and nose and prayed the gag reflux would soon dissipate.

They walked along the track, avoiding strewn rubbish, discarded faeces and the intermittent squeals and squeaks of huge brown rats. Jake shivered inside; he hated vermin. Every so often Hayden would hold up a hand to indicate when to stop. Jake's heart beat a drum in his chest as his ears strained for noises that might alert them to danger. He went to speak, but was prevented from doing so with a finger placed to his lips. Hayden gave a sharp nod that they move to the left. Jake could sense it before he saw it. The sound of a Viper about 50 yards or so behind them. Hayden grabbed Jake's arm and yanked him up off the track and into a doorway. They pushed themselves as tight into the wall as they could and held their breath.

The corkscrew machine charged off in the opposite direction, corkscrew turned off but primed and ready for action. The two men remained slammed against the wall until the sound abated. Hayden expelled a large breath of relief. "Boy that was close."

"What would have happened if it came our way?"

"Mincemeat probably, though we may have stood a chance of not being seen. The problem is their infra red heat detectors. Let's just say, that it's best if we don't meet one of them face to face."

They continued to travel through the sludge, trying to

avoid as much of it as possible. Hayden explained as quietly as he could, that this was the overflow sewerage since the main one spilled out into the lakes outside of the cities. Another oversight of the greedy Controllers. They were so busy taking, he explained, that they hadn't considered the long term impact of their policies.

He then went on to explain that there were three ways out of the Underground and each one held danger. First, was the stairs that led up and out into the streets. This was the most exposed route since there was no guarantee that the cameras had been uninstalled as suspected. He was told by a source within the Pyramid, that the Controllers, in their attempt to prolong their existing resources, were cutting back on non essential monitoring. This would include the disused and long abandoned Underground. However, there was no verified proof that this had been actioned yet and to check out its validity, could very well end up as a suicide mission.

The second option was to take the lift. These weren't monitored, yet the noise of the aged lift mechanics, could alert a Viper to their presence. They couldn't take the risk. The last and least appealing option, was to climb through the pipe tunnels that expelled the sewerage and unwanted rubbish from the surface city. That was the option Hayden decided for them.

"We're going through there?" Jake exclaimed appalled by the internal state of the tunnels. The smell made him wretch.

"Look at it this way," Hayden said, "at least we don't have to crawl."

He was right. Although not high enough to stand up in, they could walk through by hunching their shoulders and head. It wasn't nearly as painful as walking up the stairs, but he soon felt the ache in his lower back and shoulders. After a while, he felt his neck start to ache also. "Much longer?" he whispered through clenched teeth. The stench was suffocating.

"Five minutes more." came the reply. Jake followed blithely, becoming unconsciously transfixed and absorbed in the motion of Hayden's boots squelching through the slop just ahead of him. Then Hayden slowed and held out a hand behind him to indicate that they had arrived. "Okay, we're here. Now stay close and follow me. And for God's sake Jake, do exactly as I say. Don't be a hero today okay? No matter what you see, remember that for me this is real life, but for you it isn't. There are times to die a hero, but today isn't it, got it?" Jake nodded, but he swore that his heart was going to leap out and betray his fear to whatever it was that may be awaiting them. This was the scariest and least brave feeling he had ever experienced in his life to date. He didn't feel like being a hero either. Was he ready? Not in the slightest. He was terrified.

Hayden slowly pushed the door until a crack of grey light slivered through. They had remained in semi darkness the entire time of being in the Underground tunnels, but his eyes had adjusted. To know that natural light existed beyond that door, filled him with excitement and relief, despite his nervous trepidation.

Slowly, more light escaped into the pipe until the door was a third open. Just enough for them to slip out one by one. Hayden held a finger to his mouth and Jake kept his own clamped shut. When they were fully out of the pipe and onto the street, Jake noticed that it was daytime. He hadn't anticipated that. He suddenly felt exposed. Hayden looked up and around him. He checked something on his wrist. It resembled a watch, but was more like the face of a dial. Jake watched him curiously. Hayden wiggled his index finger indicating the direction they were headed. He counted down with his fingers, three, two, one, then started running to the opposite side. Jake followed, heart in his mouth again.

Hayden held him still with his left hand firm across Jake's chest, he then glanced at him and nodded up to a tower. He held him back and counted under his breath then checked his 'watch' again. "Okay, go!" he whispered low and hard. Hayden ran low and close to the wall and Jake followed close behind. "Through here," he said as he opened a black door. They slipped in and then kept moving. They were in some sort of factory space. "Stay low and quiet. And don't leave my side."

In the distance Jake could hear whirring and mechanical sounds. Whatever was making that noise was beyond the large metal doors up ahead of them. He panicked and looked over to Hayden, wondering if a Viper could be nearby. However, the soldier man simply carried on determined, focused and unhampered by the noises. *What is this place?* he wondered.

"Whatever you see, don't say a word. Don't respond or do anything other than stay directly by my side, got it?" Jake nodded, too fearful to argue or question. They moved like stalking cats towards the large black metal doors. Hayden kept looking above and around him and then checking the accessory on his wrist. "We don't have much time."

They reached their destination and without warning, Hayden gingerly pushed the large door until it was just wide enough for them to enter separately, allowing the door to close behind them without much sound. Once in, they slid over to the left hand side and hid behind one of the big machines in the room. Hayden placed his finger to his lips and indicated that he observe. Jake took a moment to regard the surroundings. They were on a large factory type floor. To the left was a conveyor belt. On the far left end of the belt were a row of metal baskets with material inserts. From where he knelt, he could not see what was inside. The belt was stationery. He then noticed that there were three other similar conveyor belts, also motionless. Each one fed into one larger arm and at the end of that, was a machine. Beyond the machine, the conveyor belts separated out again into four lines, each culminating under a large sign with a letter – P, D, C, or F.

Jake looked at Hayden. He remembered seeing the P tattoo on his arm. He was about to ask a question, when Hayden pulled him down lower behind the machine they were situated at. He shot Jake a look that told him not to speak. Suddenly, the machine in the middle started up again and the conveyor belts sprung into action. The adrenalin pumped through Jake and his hands began to shake. Hayden noticed and placed his right hand over Jake's hands and nodded to him. This one movement of camaraderie reassured him. He knew that whatever happened, he was safe with Hayden.

Doors to the left hand side opened and in walked four robots. They were not humanoids like the Protectors, nor shiny grey metal like Gregoria in the city. These looked like scientists. They had faces of humanoids, but the rest of their body constructs were covered in a cream metal. The way they moved, the way they looked, gave them the image of being trustworthy and less intimidating than robots he imagined up on the surface. However, it was their faces that most unnerved him. They did not move. And then he realised, that the face was a mask, with painted on make up, just like a China doll. A shiver ran through his spine. He hated China dolls.

The robots automatically flicked on switches which sent the room into mechanical action. Then they walked towards the metal baskets and stood waiting. Wide black doors to the left fully opened into the walls. Four more of these robots entered, carrying something swaddled in each of their arms. Jake raised his head slightly to see what the white bundle was. He almost gasped aloud before Hayden jerked him down by his arm. They were carrying babies.

Jake watched the robotic production line in action. One robot handing a baby bundle to another who then placed it into one of the metal baskets, unwrapped the swaddling from the naked child and then placed the basket onto the conveyor belt. The basket made it's way towards the machine. Jake's heart threatened to tear out of his chest as he feared for the first child, unsure of what the machine was designed to do to the small human. When the baby was under the machine, the conveyor belt stopped. The baby looked up at the machine, just as a robotic arm came down and burned a letter onto the child's upper right arm. The baby did not make a sound. Jake shot a look at Hayden who was also watching. Anger and sadness filled the man's face, but also a glimmer of something else – hope?

After the stamping process, the child was then re-swaddled and retrieved by other, similar robot and taken to one of the four doors that led out of the room. Jake determined that it depended on which letter the child received as to which door it was then escorted from.

Suddenly, there was a noise like an alarm. Jake's heart leaped and he crouched lower in fear. Had they been seen? He glanced quickly at Hayden for reassurance, but he was alert like a crouching tiger about to pounce. He held Jake's gaze and indicated for him to move deeper down behind the machine in which they were taking cover. He then retrieved something from his jacket. It looked like a net of some kind. Just then, Jake heard one of the robots approaching. He closed his eyes in fear since he had nowhere to run to. Instead of being discovered, he heard the sound of metal lifting above him, then a thud, as though something had been dropped. The robot then walked away and back to its post to resume its work.

Jake opened his eyes and when he looked to the other man, he saw that his head, arms and upper torso, were half inside the machine. There was an opening at the back of the machine where they were situated and Hayden was half in there. Jake kept watching with both curious interest and raised anxiety. He had no clue what was happening at that moment.

Then another alarm sounded and the same thing happened. Jake watched the process repeat itself as though everything were in slow motion. All the while, Hayden remained in or close to the opening at the back of the machine. The conveyor belt system continued, until suddenly, a different noise shrilled out and then the mechanical noises around him terminated. He watched as the robots exited the large doors. He then moved closer to Hayden.

"Okay, got them." Hayden whispered as he retracted out of the machine.

Jake gasped. Hayden did not retract alone. He had in a net, two swaddled babies. Tiny things with huge eyes staring up. "What the...?"

"Right. Now this is the fun part. Grab a kid, put it in your jacket and remember that it's a living thing okay? And don't worry, most don't make a noise. Got it?" Jake nodded in shock as he took receipt of one of the babies. It was swaddled in a light pink and white blanket. Brown eyes and that same colour skin of the Protectors.

"Are these robots? Like the Protectors? Is this how they are created?"

"No idiot. The Protectors are robots; they were made like that. These," he said with sudden and unexpected tenderness as he gazed into the little boy's face, "are human, a New Human. Okay, we don't have much time. They birth them twice a day, so these Nursing Robots are done for the next six hours, but the sentries outside break in ten minutes, so we have to get out and past them by then. Ready?"

Jake looked down at the cherubic face looking back up at him and nodded. This was totally unexpected and he was lost for words. They exited the same way they came in. Stealth like as before, but this time, with a child swaddled inside their jackets, they moved differently. The warmth from the heat of another being's body next to his, brought memories of Eloise's birth flooding back. It was a difficult labour, with warnings of undergoing an emergency caesarean, but with the help of two midwives, stirrups and forceps, she was born at 5.17am on a Friday morning, weighing a healthy eight pounds and six ounces. Whilst Amy was being stitched up below, Jake held his gorgeous bundle skin on skin on his chest. It was one of his most precious, yet also most painful of memories.

As they crept along the wall, crouching low and staying silent, he couldn't help but glance down at the face inside his coat and recall those precious moments with his lost little girl. The moving motion and his own heartbeat had sent the child into a peaceful sleep. She looked so content. He had so many questions. Even more than he had before the rescue.

When they reached the doors that led out of the factory, Hayden motioned for him to wait. He checked his watch and sliced open the door, just enough to stick out his head to check around and above. It was clear. "We have to be real fast now. This is the tricky part, but you'll be okay if you stick with me. Ready?" Jake nodded. He was already neck deep in fear and had no other choice but to trust this man.

The next fifteen minutes happened as though he were in a dream sequence. They crept out of the factory doors then on a count of three, Hayden coarsely whispered "Run!" He ran and Jake followed. He saw but didn't stop to take in, that they had entered a crowded space of silent people, in what looked like a town square area. The people were walking and eating, standing and staring, but none were engaged in any conversation or activity. They ran past them and ignored the vacant yet observant eyes. The humans looked at them as they passed, but didn't actually see them. The two men dodged through buildings and doorways, only stopping when Hayden saw or sensed danger. And there was danger everywhere. Robot arm cameras constantly monitored the people as they walked zombie like around the streets. They reminded Jake of non player characters in a game; part of the scene, but insignificant and irrelevant players. And those vacant faces. *Are those eyes merely windows to nowhere, rather than reflections of their souls?* he pondered, unnerved by the emptiness he saw inside them.

They kept running like this, dodging people, running through and around buildings, stopping intermittently on Hayden's silent commands when he spotted a sentry or a drone, then running again. All the while, they each kept a hand underneath or on top of their jacket to protect their cargo. When they arrived at what looked like an outside wall, Hayden stopped. He was breathing hard, as was Jake.

When he managed to compose his breath, he pointed at a place beyond the wall.

"We have to get past this wall to an underground tunnel; a pipe similar to the one we emerged from earlier. But this leads outside of the wall not underground. The trouble is," he said catching at his breath, "we have to wait until the break is over or we *will* get caught. See those cameras up there?" he said indicating two surveillance robot camera arms that swivelled their lens from one end of the area in front of them, to the other. "If they see us, drones fly down and blast our sorry asses to smithereens."

Jake gulped at the way he emphasised the word *will*. "Break?" he enquired between catching breaths.

"The New Humans. They are on a work break. After a few years of the Pyramid, the Controllers realised that if they don't give these humans a break, they aren't as productive. As far as they are concerned, these humans are no better than robots. They just don't last as long."

"So what's the plan?" Jake was aware that he was no longer just responsible for his own wellbeing, but also for the baby's safety, which was still fast asleep inside his jacket.

"We wait. After the alarm calls, the humans will start to shuffle back to their work positions. This is when the drones are most active. They will be monitoring their behaviour and tracking them. Each New Human is born with a tracking device. This cannot be extracted like the tech tubes in the base of the skull. The tracking was implemented intravenously via the feeding tubes and inserted directly into the brain. And they can shut a person down immediately if they so choose."

"I have so many questions to ask right now. Forget that we both just stole a child from whatever that place was..."

"The Baby Nation. It's a factory. And we didn't steal

them, we rescued them." Hayden interrupted, gently patting the back of the sleeping boy baby he carried.

"Rescued? From what?"

"The Reject Bin. If we didn't they'd be dead meat. Trust me."

Then it all suddenly made sense to Jake. The story of Hayden's birth, how he managed to go through the system when he should have been rejected and the way the New Humans were like walking zombies, possibly because they had been lobotomised via manipulative programming into the brain during foetal development. Yet that still didn't explain why Hayden was unaffected. He asked him the question.

"I don't know the answer. Truthfully. I'm like this weird anomaly. From the system, but at the same time, not a part of it either. It's like I slipped through the net. I should have ended up in the Reject Bin like these little ones, but instead, I was passed through. I wasn't plugged in either, see...?" he said showing the back of his head. "No plug to pull out. I'm the only one I've ever met who was never connected."

"So what happened to you? How come they didn't detect that you were different?"

"Good question and one I have spent my entire life trying to work out. I was indoctrinated like all the other children in the School Nation and despite not speaking, just like the others, I still did not fit in. I saw through it all; I always saw it for what it was."

"And what is that?" Jake asked gently.

"Control. Total and utter control. That's what this is. The Pyramid, this triangle of social levels, is set up so that each level controls the one below it. At the top are the Privileged. These are the city leaders, the top politicians, the corporation owners and the heads of security. They are few, for only a select elite are privileged to enjoy that level of control. Below them on the second tier down, are the Directors. These are the factory owners, the security forces, the managing politicians and those who work in the Information and Propaganda section. Below that again, are the Managers. They manage and control the New Humans, plus the robots. They are told what to do from above and ensure the directives are carried out. And finally, are the New Humans and the robots. One leads the other, but both respond to commands and neither is capable of thinking for themselves."

"Wow. And who controls the drones and the Vipers?"

"Ultimately the commands come from the top, but Security in the Director level ensures that everyone and everything is kept in check. And they are given leeway to carry this out however they want. The Security Division are bastards. Make no mistake about it, they are heartless and devoid of any human compassion. I wouldn't be surprised if anyone involved with Security were AI and not flesh and blood."

"So let me get this straight." Jake asked taking a deep breath and trying to process all the information he had just received. "We are currently in an enclosed and controlled city, which houses a system of zombie humans, obeying robots and annihilating drones. There are levels of controlling humans, each controlled by another and all ultimately under the control of an unseen and powerful group called Controllers. Under our feet, exists a possibly alien constructed independent civilisation of people, called old humans, who are mostly oblivious to what it going on above their heads. And here we are, smack bang in the middle of these two diverse cities, trying to avoid being executed by watchdog drones. *And* with babies attached to our chest;

babies I may add, that have a tracking device inside them, that could give our position away at any moment. Did I miss anything?"

"Yeah you did. You forgot to mention that we are in this very position, because some selfish scientist decided to show the world how fucking clever he is!" Hayden glared at Jake. "Any further fucking questions?"

Jake shook his head in defeat, but he had grown in confidence since arriving and despite the soldier having a fair point, he was angry. At himself, at the system, at Edward and Henry and at Avorra for keeping him there. "Keep your fucking language down. Don't want to wake the babies now do we?" he spat out in defiance.

The two men glared at each other. A fight was brewing, but there wasn't time or opportunity to continue the argument. A shrill alarm rang out. It was time to move.

10

THE PRIEST

They made it to the door of the wastage system without being detected. As Hayden predicted, the cameras concentrated on the motions of the New Humans and not on the inside wall. There were however, surveillance cameras dotted along the top of the City wall facing outwards. The exit route they took must have been a weak, blind spot in the system, for Jake could tell it was a familiar route used by Hayden. Despite their differences, Jake knew he was a trustworthy companion and followed his every move.

Obscured by what looked like a blanket made of dirt and stones, was a trapdoor. In one swift and deft move, the soldier raised the covering, lifted the door and gestured for Jake to enter. There were steps leading down. Jake, more fearful of being caught than of what awaited for him below, obeyed without question. When Hayden was a few steps in, he looped the covering over the outer trapdoor and pulled it shut tight after him, thus concealing their escape route. They stood in darkness until Hayden flicked on a torchlight and moved in front of him to guide the way.

. . .

"Stay silent until I say any different." he instructed. "Vipers are all over this place."

They were in a disused tunnel. Water cascaded down onto them from small cracks at the top of the concrete above and their feet splashed through puddles created by the dripping water. Clusters of grass grew through some of the cracks on the lower edges of the tunnel. It was the first sight of natural green that he had witnessed since arriving.

As they walked, Jake thought about the sleeping bairn inside his jacket. He felt the warmth of her small body and then reflected on her creation and what she was formulated to become. He remembered the vacant, zombie like appearance of the New Humans in the streets above and shuddered. They were the new humanity. A human race deliberately degenerated by the design of a few controlling elite and their inhumane ideology, intent on controlling the human race with their hierarchical system of manipulating authorities and subservient lackeys.

He reflected also on his work and the quest in his time for further improvements to the human race. Despite his desire to do good and help eradicate disease, from his experiences in the simulations, he wondered if perhaps, humans should ultimately be left alone to develop on their own natural trajectory? What would be the point of technological and scientific advancement if it caused more harm, devastation and ultimately the devolution and perhaps even, the destruction of the human race?

They continued to walk in silence through the tunnel, which curved and meandered away from the city walls. He wondered where they were headed, since the underground city lay close to the Controlled City if not directly underneath. After walking for around fifteen minutes, he anticipated creating conversation, but given the tension between them before the alarm sounded for their escape journey, he thought better of it. He would wait for the nod from Hayden.

He looked down at the baby. His mind danced with questions that his tongue abated him to express. *What is going to become of you now?* He thought as he watched how peacefully content the child slept.

"Okay, we're nearly there." Hayden announced after they had walked for about forty five minutes. Jake was relieved. Suddenly, he was feeling weary and incredibly thirsty.

"I'm so thirsty. Can we get a drink at the place where we're heading?"

"The Priest will have refreshments."

"The Priest?"

"I'll let him explain." Hayden replied curtly dismissing the question. It was clear to Jake that he did not want to converse with the newcomer. The tension between the two had dissipated, but the breath of it still remained.

. . .

They turned another long bend and then came to a steep set of horizontal steps with metal holding bars either end. They led up to a metal covering above. It reminded Jake of the man hole covers in streets that he had seen in American movies.

Hayden went first. He shunted the round, metal lid with the palm of his hand. A popping thud resounded around them as it opened. He lifted it high over his head until it stood upright to attention. He then disappeared through the hole and out into the grey open air that awaited them. Jake followed and breathed a sigh of relief on emerging. Once he was clear, Hayden replaced the cover with care not to create unnecessary sound that could alert their presence. Jake noticed that the cover had a fold that allowed it to be lifted up. It looked like a street man hole cover, yet where they stood, there were no streets. They were in a wasteland.

"Where are we?"

"No Man's Land." the soldier replied glancing around him as he recovered from the exertion of gently lowering the metal cover without banging it closed. He breathed in deeply and looked up as though he were giving thanks. "Come on. We'd better get out of sight as quickly as we can. We're away from the city cameras, but the Vipers sentry the outer perimeter as well as inside the walls. Plus we need to ensure there aren't any Roamers around. Remember," he warned, "it's called No Man's Land for a reason."

. . .

JAKE FOLLOWED HIM WITHOUT SPEAKING. Despite his desire to ask further questions, his mouth was so dry that his tongue felt like a resting seal inside and he had no proclivity to move it. After another fifteen minutes of travelling through what was essentially a wasteland landscape attacked with a harsh, dry and abrasive wind, buildings appeared in the distance. He guessed that's where they were headed.

He surveyed the immediate area around him. It was mainly flat earth dotted with broken and decayed trees, aged and rusting abandoned vehicles and stone remnants of what was once upon a time, buildings. Nothing grew in this abandoned wasteland that felt post apocalyptic. They headed east and came across the derelict remainder of what was, just decades previous, a thriving town. Hayden told him that the area was subject to intermittent surveillance, but it had been weeks since anyone had seen a drone. They suspected this was possibly because of their requirement to reserve resources.

"JUST THROUGH HERE." he gestured and pointed to an almost intact and prominent building. Jake took a guess that it may have once been a library or town hall. Hayden checked around him and circumvented the perimeter of the building, before finding what he was looking for – a padlocked steel door. Jake, whose curiosity by now was fully piqued, followed close behind. He watched as Hayden extracted a chain from inside the green army tee shirt he wore. Attached to the chain, was a large key. He didn't take off the chain, but instead, navigated the lock with the key, whilst also trying to avoid disturbing the still sleeping baby he carried. Not for the first time since meeting him, did Jake realise how brave and resilient this man was. Despite how often he threatened to kill him, Jake realised that Hayden would be one of the few people he had ever met, who would be willing to give his life up for him.

"BEFORE WE GO IN, a word...you are going to meet The Priest. And he ain't like any other Priest you've met before. Keep an open mind and you'll be fine. Got it?"

JAKE NODDED. Then he took in a deep breath and followed the leader. *This simulation just gets better and better Avorra. Hope you're entertained!* The inside of the building displayed that it was neither a library nor a town hall. Instead, he deduced that from the way the rooms were set up, it was probably once an office building or school. Every window was smashed and what remained of light fittings, hung limply off walls and ceilings. They reminded him of amputated limbs left abandoned and decaying on a vacated battle field. There was no furniture in any of the rooms and nothing on the walls. Everything that could be removed had been. What remained was simply the exhausted and battered structure of something that once was probably, an important building. He spotted cameras dotted around every room they passed or entered, and he guessed that their every move was under surveillance.

"THROUGH HERE. MIND YOUR HEAD." Hayden took them through a door that led down a darkened corridor. He noticed the cameras again and felt the energy of many eyes trained on their movements. With the crushing thirst, the mental and physical exhaustion of the past few hours and the knowledge that all his moves were being tracked, he suddenly feint. He paused and held onto the wall to steady himself. But Hayden did not stop, so he gathered himself, breathed in deeply and continued moving. They came to another door. Hayden knocked, looked into the camera and stood back. The door opened and a bald man with a rifle met them. He greeted Hayden by name and nodded suspiciously at Jake, then softened his face as he saw the bundle he carried inside his jacket.

"The Priest is waiting to see you." the man said. They followed him through a short passageway then down some steep steps. Then another door.

"Remember what I said." Hayden whispered as the door opened.

The sight below him took his breath away. A huge room, busy with a mass of humans, Protectors and robots like Gregoria, all in various forms of activity. The room was constructed of plain concrete, had no windows and a fluorescent style lighting. There were monitors on the left hand side, in what looked like a security section. He spotted around eight. Some had images of the inside of the building, others of the derelict town and one that was entirely focused on the perimeter wall of the Controlled City. The main room had large black doors leading off. He counted four sets of doors. He couldn't see what existed beyond those doors so instead, focused on what he could see.

They descended the stairs and as he experienced when

he first entered the underground city, the uniformed Protectors stopped to study him. This in turn caused the robots to pause their activity followed closely by the humans. He noticed that most of the humans had shaven heads, but no patches at the base of their skulls like the Protectors. The robots without skin simply had a gaping hole. Jake assumed this was where they had all been unplugged. He didn't understand however, why the humans did not have the patch. *Are they still plugged in?* He wondered.

From the way he was welcomed and received by those in the room, Jake could tell that Hayden was a regular visitor. Two of the female humans approached the men and waited in front of them. Hayden unzipped his jacket and noticed that he had a mesh hammock holding the child in position. He unhooked the mesh and tucked it back into an internal pocket. Then he smiled at the woman and handed the child over. The female smiled broadly first at Hayden and then at the child who, despite all the commotion, remained contentedly asleep. Jake followed suit with another of the females waiting for him to hand over the little girl. When his package had been delivered, he suddenly felt lighter, but also incredibly weary.

Hayden spoke to one of the Protectors, who brought over a container of water and two mugs. The robot handed a mug to each of the men and filled their cups. Jake drank greedily. His mouth was desert parched and relief washed over him.

"That's so much better." he said wiping his mouth. "Thank you."

. . .

THE PROTECTOR HOLDING the container watched him with amused curiosity, then refilled Jake's mug. "You're welcome." he said before walking away. As Jake watched him depart, he pondered the question of soul. He thought of the Protectors, the New Humans and robots like Gregoria. Did they possess a soul? Gregoria, with his display of affection and conscious awareness, the Protectors, who readily fought for the security and protection of the humans, did they have a soul? And what of the New Humans, lobotomised and functioning, but without conscious thought or individuality; completely controlled and obeying directives. Where, if they possessed one, was their soul?

His thoughts were interrupted by Hayden, who, also refreshed and caught up on conversations, approached him with an open face. He seemed relaxed for the first time since he had left Papa's.

"IT'S TIME. The Priest is ready for us. Any questions you have, direct them to him. He knows more than anyone other than the Controllers themselves." He led Jake to one of the doors leading out of the room. They walked down a short passageway then stopped outside a door. "He wants to meet with you alone. I'll catch you later."

"THANKS HAYDEN. Slightly nervous to be honest." Jake added suddenly feeling quite sick. He had only eaten once since arriving and the anxiousness of the activities since entering and leaving the Controlled City, coupled with the thirst he experienced and the exhaustion, was taking its toll on him.

. . .

"Just be yourself. Be honest and tell him everything you told me. He's a good guy. Just...different." he said with a smirk, then he turned and walked away. Jake knocked on the door and held his breath.

"Come in." a gruff, heavily accented voice instructed him from the other side. Jake entered the room, expecting to see a religious man. Instead, he was face to face with a much older, grey bearded man with long white plaited hair, on top of which, sat a dusty and ageing, black Stetson hat. He wore brown trousers, a once white, greying shirt and a battered, brown leather pilot jacket. On his feet were black, army type combat boots like those worn by Hayden and the men, though his were far more beaten up and aged. In his mouth, was a fat cigar. Jake was taken aback. He resembled a rather battered, ageing Indiana Jones and was unlike any priest he had ever encountered.

"Not what you were expecting?" the man said with a chuckle. Jake slowly shook his head, aware that his mouth was slightly agape. "Hah! Take a seat."

Jake pulled out a chair from a large wooden desk and sat opposite the Priest. He took a second to glance around him. Well known famous paintings hung on the walls, a desk lamp on a filing cabinet in the left corner, books atop and a pot with pens. He couldn't figure out this man, the room or the underground bunker spaces. Neither The Priest not the place fitted into the world in which they currently inhabited.

. . .

"I can see you have many questions buzzing in that head of yours, but first, I think I need to know a little about you. I can see that you don't come from around here..."

"That's right. I'm actually a blast from the past and I'm pretty old apparently." Jake said raising his brows.

"That will explain the clothes and the sneakers. I haven't seen shoes like that for many a year. Okay, fill me in. But first, you hungry?" Jake nodded.

"Starving!"

The Priest chuckled and opened a drawer. He extracted a tin of fish with a pull top lid and handed it to Jake along with a small fork. "I found a whole crate of these in a deserted container near a port a couple of years back. Don't have many left now, but I'm happy to share with a guest. Especially a time travelling one." he added with a wink.

"You know?" Jake replied gratefully enjoying the tuna. He had never eaten it as bland and straight from the tin before, but was so hungry, that it tasted amazing.

. . .

"I guessed. You look too soft. Plus you've hair so you can't be a manufactured human. And you're too tall for the underground humans. And the way you walk tells me you're no robot that's for sure. So, who are you Jake?"

He explained to the older man where he came from and why he was there. He spoke of his emotional instability before Avorra entered onto the scene and about his work. He worried about being judged again when he divulged the information about the brain chip and insertion of nano technology in the brain fluid. However, the Priest didn't flinch, choosing instead to pick at his nails and chew his cigar around his mouth. Jake wasn't even sure the cigar was lit.

He also discussed Edward's plan to kill him in three days, which made the decision he had to make more palatable, especially given what he had witnessed since arriving in the simulation. The Priest sat and listened intently, nodding and shaking his head in response where appropriate. When Jake had finished, he sat back and awaited the questioning. But after five or so minutes of watching The Priest in deep thought, he realised that he would have to break the silence.

"What are your thoughts?"

The older man met his eyes, took the cigar out of his mouth and onto the desk, then sat back in a relaxed manner and asked, "What are your questions?"

. . .

"FIRSTLY, why do they call you The Priest? Are you a religious man?"

"YES AND NO. If you are asking if I am an ordained minister, then the answer is no. If however, you are asking me if I believe in one Almighty Being up and out there, watching and keeping an eye on us, then yes I most certainly do. In Hebrews Chapter 11, verse 6, the good bible says,

'AND WITHOUT FAITH, it is impossible to please God, because anyone who comes to him must believe that he exists and that he rewards those that earnestly seek him.'"

"SEE, that confuses me. I have always believed in God until he chose to take my little girl away. A loving God wouldn't do that, he just wouldn't. What did she do to deserve that?" Jake replied, his voice cracking with emotion.

"DO you believe God intended for her to die that way?"

JAKE HAD TO THINK. He didn't know. He didn't think so, but God also didn't prevent it. "I..I...I don't know. Truthfully, I don't know anything anymore. Think about it, I'm here but not here. A blue angel speaks to me. My bosses are plotting to kill me and I find out I'm partially responsible for killing the entire human race! What the fuck do I know?"

. . .

"Hah! Oh the language of cussing. I missed that. Nobody cusses anymore. You know why I think that is?" The Priest said leaning forward like a co-conspirator. Jake shrugged his shoulders, taken aback by the way the conversation was going. "Because nobody copulates anymore! It's true. They made the New Humans without sexual desire. They weren't designed to be fully human in that way. They gave them the external body parts for it, but that was probably some sick designer's way of making them walking, talking sex dolls for the Controllers and the elite bastards."

Jake wrinkled his nose in disgust. "Even Hayden? Mack, Beady?"

"Yeah, but they escaped the system early so they weren't abused in that way. The system is set up for the Controllers, not the controlled." He sat back in his chair and placed the cigar back into his mouth.

"That thing lit?"

"See any matches?" The Priest replied laughing. "I like the taste. It's almost as good as the real thing."

"Can I ask you why they call you The Priest?"

. . .

"My grandfather was one of the last remaining practising ministers in a Church in Southern Russia. The erosion of peoples' belief in a Divine Creator was a full on deliberate attack that had started a few decades previous. First they took away all reference to Mother. Take for example, Mother Mary. She became known as the 'One Who Birthed the Divine'. Next they destroyed the family unit by attacking conventional gender descriptions and affiliations to that gender. They pushed gender neutrality and blurred the known conventions and definitions, of what it was to be a man or a woman. This then led to accepted mutilation of children's genitalia, first from teenage years and then all the way from birth. This gave way to what we have today – no internal reproductive organs and no sexual desire in the New Human. Thus they have become non-gender by design. Except of course, that these designed new form of human beings are made with sexually shaped organs not for their own pleasure, but for those of the elites who pick them off as their preference chooses.

My grandfather was a very religious man and always quoting bible verses. He was electively deaf, dumb and blind to these forced changes, choosing instead, to remain true to what he knew in the bible and its written instructions. He chose to live a godly life and thus became a true role model as a man of faith, as well as a role model for all of us to follow. You could say that I'm ingrained with these scriptures. Hence my name. My real name given by my parents at birth, is now irrelevant. People refer to me as The Priest because they need someone to believe in; someone to provide them hope in a hopeless world and someone who reminds them that somewhere, up and out there, is a God figure who has their backs."

. . .

"I GUESS THAT MAKES SENSE." Jake interjected. The Priest nodded and continued.

"MY FATHER, though respectful of his father's faith, was a rebel. My parents realised what was happening early on and did not want to comply to all the bullshit. After the parasite attack of the water in the mid 2030's, life for us mere mortals changed. It was as though they were waiting for a reason to roll out the plan they had been working on for decades, centuries even."

"THEY?"

"THE CONTROLLERS WE CALL THEM. Those self appointed unknown elites who took control of the human race. We aren't sure when it began, or even what they actually are. We are not even sure if they are human like us. But they rolled out their control and like a huge, bulldozing machine, they destroyed, restricted and controlled our lives from that point onwards. Though truthfully, the system was always set up to control the populations."

"I THOUGHT that was all conspiracy theory. I mean, I heard the rumours and such, but I'm not the kind of guy who falls down rabbit holes."

"TELL ME, after being here and experiencing all this from a visitor's point of view, tell me one conspiracy theory you heard or read about that hasn't come true?" The Priest picked up the cigar and rolled it around his mouth a bit more, before replacing it carefully back onto the desk. Jake watched his actions, but his mind was searching through the archives of his memories for things he had heard, read and seen, but dismissed as made up theories. He was right. From a reflecting perspective, he was right.

"So what happened after they rolled out the pill; the wonder cure? Did it stop the parasite?"

"There was no parasite! That's the point. They created a story so they had an excuse to roll out their plan. The utilisation of mass media propaganda and manipulation ensured that the people watching were terrified. It was like feeding candy to a child. From there on, they brought in distraction after distraction, but it was all smoke and mirrors to disguise the laws and restrictions being put in place right under the peoples' noses. By the time the people realised, it was too late. There was no going back because they had their control mechanisms set up and in place.

Controlled towns and cities were set up under the guise of climate protection or something similar, I can't recall now. They used the threat of global catastrophe to ensure the people listened and obeyed. Once they saw how easy it was to get the people to comply, it was game over. The restrictions on peoples' movements and their rights was heightened. But it was always done subtly and incrementally, so it went pretty much undetected by the masses. The ones who saw it were labelled and publicly mocked as conspiracy theorists and the compliant were told these people were dangerous and did not deserve the same rights and freedoms as them. So they went underground and that's why there are underground resistance bases like this one, all over the globe."

'But I don't get why people allowed this to happen? I mean, did they not stop and think? Stop and ask why they were losing so much?" Jake asked his mind blown by what he was hearing.

"Hah! No. You'd think right? But how many times have you complied to something that was obviously causing restriction to you in some way, but you never stopped to ask why? You see Jake, they were dumbing us humans down for years before they rolled out their plan. Television, newspapers, smart phones, celebrity cult status, movies, programmes – all created by design to entertain and distract us."

"For what reason? Distract us from what?"

"From realising just how powerful we are as a species. If the average human knew what they were creatively designed to be able to achieve, they wouldn't believe it. The human being is far more powerful that you could ever imagine. That's why the connection to our Source, our Creator, to God, or whatever you choose to call him, is so important. And the very thing they have been attacking and destroying for decades."

. . .

"Wow! So how did you end up here all the way from Russia? Did you get out before the restrictions came into play?"

"Well, Russia back then was becoming like most countries around the world; our sovereign rights were being stolen from us incrementally, until it was becoming increasingly more difficult to live out normal lives. Neighbours were being told to dob on neighbours and even on their own families. As an awake and aware person, it had become not just difficult to live in this environment, but also dangerous.

Everything globally was being centralised. The push for one central bank, one central food supplier, one travel authority, one fuel supplier and one, dominating global government. Currency was eliminated and replaced by digital currency. First it was country run, then amalgamated into District provinces, such as Asia, Europe, North America and so on, until finally, it was centralised into one main global currency. And everything was monitored. From the food you bought and ate, to how many shits you took on the toilet. Everything. And suddenly the people saw that they were no longer free. Riots and rebellions rose up around the world. But they were ready. They had drones and AI situated everywhere. There was a centralised army in place, waiting and ready to go into combat with their citizens as soon as the protests erupted. They were supported in their cruel attack on the people, by armies of lawless illegal immigrants brought in with no loyalty to anyone except to themselves and their own religions. The fights were harsh and bloody and people simply gave up in the end.

The drones were becoming increasingly harsh too and much bolder in their terrorising and control. People were going missing all the time. They monitored everything we did and those who did not comply were publicly humiliated, beaten or killed. Terror ruled the streets and fear ruled the hearts of the people. It got to the point where my parents, for their non compliance and my grandfather for his faith, were put on some kind of 'list'. They knew that escaping Russia was their only chance. Rumours were that things were better in Africa, so we left as an entire family. My grandparents, my aunt and her family and us. I had an older brother called Aleksander. He was six. I was just three or four at the time and the only safe route, was what was known back then as 'the long walk'. Essentially, part of a six month journey from where we lived on the Georgia/Russian border town of Zazbegi, all the way down to Tanzania. We had close family there. It was the only way out. Citizens were being prevented from travelling internationally for anything other than essential travel. The ships were heavily monitored and impossible to get onto. Flying had been an impossibility for all but the very rich, for some years.

So, we packed up everything we had, took spare fuel we had been saving for months and drove an old van as far as we could. There was still gas back then, but it was expensive and like gold dust. However, my father was a successful businessman and had many connections back in those days. Our friends and neighbours were weak, fearful people and so we told no one. Essentially, we and anyone like us, were enemies of the state and thus the media portrayed us as enemies of the people. Propaganda was utilised to create mass formation psychosis. It was a very difficult time to be alive when you were awake and seeing what was happening around you. Very sad." The Priest paused and reflected internally on his thoughts, shaking his head and sighing deeply before continuing.

"So we drove through the back roads at night avoiding all checkpoints. It wasn't easy. By day we hid and by night we drove. We became like nocturnal animals. Despite the constant worry and fear of being caught, my parents and my grandfather were happy souls who sang songs and laughed and entertained us. My Aunt and Uncle had two children older than us, around ten and twelve. They were good people and entertained us younger two and ensured that we were kept busy in the long days of hiding. My grandfather recited bible verses and gave us hope. That was his gift to us all. He told us of a loving God and a faithful Son. Thanks to that hope, he inspired us to have joyful and grateful hearts in the first few weeks of our travels.

We crossed bridges and saw beautiful sights. In many ways, it was a dream journey for my family, who, other than my father, rarely travelled internationally. Most of his business was in Russia, so he had little need to travel elsewhere. And besides, with the rise of global inflation, high food and fuel prices, travel had become an unnecessary luxury."

"So you travelled all that way in a van? Wow! And you didn't get stopped at checkpoints or caught by drones? I've seen those things and they are uncompromising killers."

"Ah, you didn't let me finish. Your original question was why I was called The Priest, remember?"

"Yes. Sorry, please go on." Jake replied apologising and picking at the bits of fish stuck in the corners of the tin with his fork.

. . .

"I won't tell you the entire story. We don't have that much time, but suffice to say, that after the initial few weeks of feeling like we were on an adventure, it became a very difficult time for my family. By the time we eventually arrived in Tanzania, only my grandfather and I made it alive. He lived another five years and then he passed also. I was brought up by my cousin's family as their own, despite my strange accent. I managed to emigrate to Britain in my early twenties, but that is another story for another time.

My grandfather only spoke Russian, so he only communicated to me in Russian. My family spoke Russian at home, but we spoke English and a little Swahili in the community. That's why, despite living in Tanzania for most of my childhood, I still have a strong Russian accent. And why, thanks to relying so heavily on my grandfather, I adopted his penchant for reciting scripture. If I don't speak of a glorious and loving God, the people here would not know that salvation waited round the corner with loving and welcoming arms. My words give them hope, just as my grandfather's words inspired our family despite what was happening around us."

"May I ask what happened to your family sir?"

"It was their time to pass I guess. What else is there to say?" Then the older man got up, stretched and patted Jake on the shoulder. "When it is our time, it is our time. That's why we have to enjoy the moments we have whilst we still have them. Now," he said in a commanding tone, "shall we go see the children?"

"THE CHILDREN?" Jake followed him out of the room. His mind awash with images of the storyboard he was just given. He was saddened also, as he thought of the characters in the story and especially of those that did not make it. *So much unnecessary suffering because a self appointed and unelected select few decided to rule the world their way for their own benefit,* he thought to himself as he rose from his chair and followed the older man. "I get it now Avorra, I really do." he whispered to himself, resolving to burn every inch of his work before they could get their hands on it.

The place they were in, resembled an Aladdin's cave, but with underground rooms and chambers instead of treasure. They walked past a firing range, a combat and martial arts training room, a meeting room with a large TV monitor and large blackboard. The furniture was a hodgepodge of modern and old style, which were similar to what existed in his timeline. Since it was around a century since his timeline, he wondered where all the things came from. Except for those decaying in the car graveyards outside, there were no vehicles around and most of the buildings were either empty shells like the one above ground, or reduced to rubble. The more he saw on his walk with The Priest, the more questions he had. Finally, they arrived at their destination.

"WELCOME TO THE SCHOOL." the Priest announced as they entered a huge room separated into sections.

. . .

Jake gasped. There were children of all ages, from toddlers through to teenagers. All were bald and sporting the patches at the base of the skull. "Are they robots?" he asked in awe.

"Hah! No, these are real humans; flesh and blood. They get a basic level of education and most importantly, they learn to fight. They will all have to defend themselves soon. You are either in the system or you are an enemy to it and of it."

"So if they are not robots then why do they have patches at the back of their heads like the Protectors have? And why do the humans I saw when I came here, those in the large room, not have patches?"

"Because we have to unplug the humans too, otherwise they would remain plugged into the Pyramid and be of no use to anyone, including themselves. The hole heals, so the ones you saw were rescued as babies and the hole has healed over time. It takes approximately fifteen years before a patch is no longer required.

Unfortunately, we can't uninstall the tracker since we don't have the equipment to do so. It was deliberately planted into the brain fluid to remain undetected and unattainable. So instead, we shave their heads and spray them daily with a metal mist we developed. We aren't a hundred percent sure it works, but so far it seems to be doing the trick."

. . .

Jake winced. That was his idea, but manipulated for more malevolent results. He watched as the younger children silently laughed and played. The older children were separated into age groups and were being taught. However, they were being taught in sign language. When Jake queried this, he was told that most of the New Humans were born without voice boxes. Some bypassed this, but were thrown into the Reject Bin after screaming when the stamping machine burned their skins. Mack and Beady were like many of the rescued who could speak, but others were not so lucky.

"So Mack and Beady were rescued from the Bin when they were babies?"

The Priest nodded. "There have been many saved. But alas, not many make it to their ages."

"How old are they?"

"Age is difficult to accurately tell, but we think around mid-twenties. And before you ask, I'm a LOT older! Mid seventies at last count, give or take a year."

"And Hayden? How old is he?"

. . .

"Early to mid-thirties maybe. Hard to tell. He's had a tough life so far. And he's different from the others."

"Different?" Jake enquired as he watched the sign language classes with growing fascination. The children's open faces all shared the same innocent and insouciant respect for what they were learning and those who were teaching them. They reminded him of angels.

"He was never hooked up. As far as I know, he's the only one to come out of the system that way. Come, I want to show you something." he said heading towards the far right of the room. They opened a door and entered down a long passage. There were cameras on the wall. Then they stopped outside of a large metal door. It was a similar door to the one leading to Hayden's security chamber in the underground city. The Priest did the same security measures to enter through: the punching in of a code and the tongue and breath. "It can read our breath. It's tech we developed based on the back of their own security. Pretty fool proof as far as we can tell."

The door opened into a security chamber. It was manned by a combination of Protectors and humans. Some of the humans sported hair like Mack and Beady and others were bald. All were engrossed in activities in front of monitors and screens.

"What is this place?" Jake enquired in awe. It was high tech and compared to the apocalyptic conditions outside of the Controlled City, this was way ahead of anything he had seen in his labs.

'WE CALL IT THE HUB. It's actually our control centre. The Controllers watch everyone in the Pyramid, the Directors and Managers watch the New Humans and Robots and we watch them. We haven't managed to track down the Controllers yet, but it's just a matter of time. They'll expose themselves soon; psychopaths like them always do."

"WHO ARE *THEY*? THESE CONTROLLERS?" Jake asked in awe of the scenes he was witnessing. He saw Hayden in front of a monitor along with Mack and Beady. He wasn't sure if they were aware of his presence as yet.

'TRUTHFULLY, nobody knows. They've never been seen. But we've all heard the rumours."

"RUMOURS?"

"YES. Some say they are a corrupt world elite of old time humans. Whilst others are convinced they are something else..." he glanced at Jake and raised his brows.

"SOMETHING ELSE? SUCH AS WHAT?"

. . .

"Aliens. Another species. Possibly here for millions, if not billions of years. You saw the underground city right?" Jake nodded at the question. "Well, they weren't built by any normal humans. And there are hundreds of these cities across the world. How many, we don't know. They destroyed our surface communication, but we have a subterfuge network recently set up linking other cities across the country and are just connecting to other parts of the world. It's still in progress, but we believe it could be up and running globally in the next few months. That's why we are building an army."

"An army? What kind of army? Against who?"

"Against the system. Every child and robot we save and unplug from their system, we explain what the system is and what it's designed for. Everyone is prepared to fight." He saw Jake's shocked face as he glanced over at the children. "Make no mistake about it, what has been happening to humanity well before your time, has been a war against the people. Whoever the instigators or the Controllers are, we are getting ready to fight back. We have our own plans in place. It is time for us to take back this planet and claim what is rightfully ours."

"Wow!" was all Jake could say. His mind was racing with images and possibilities. The thought of there being cities like both the Controlled City and the underground city all over the world fascinated him. And in between, were vast patches of wasteland acting like graveyards for lost civilisations. The realisation that one day his descendants would exist in a controlled, dystopian world like this and that they would have to learn to fight against the machine that is the system, sent a cold shiver running through him.

"You got the full tour?" Hayden asked him as he approached. Jake nodded. "Did he show you the Training Room?"

"No. What's that for?" Before anyone could respond Jake's stomach rumbled loudly, causing the men to chuckle.

"I think we'd best feed you. Can't have you falling down on the job!" Hayden slapped him on the back and said something quietly to Beady, who then headed out of the room. "Beady will sort you out something to eat."

"Should I ask what it is, or do I not want to know?" Jake winced.

"Relax. We grow our own food here. Permaculture at it's finest. It'll be a veg meal, since there isn't any meat. Unless you like rat that is?" The Priest added with a knowing wink at the men.

"When did that happen? You know, the animals dying? How long have you been without meat? I'm surprised the

Controllers and higher Pyramid levels allowed it to happen, or do they keep a supply of all the best stuff hidden for themselves?" Jake enquired since nothing about the Controllers surprised him anymore.

THE MEN all looked at each other conspiratorially. Mack raised his brows then shrugged.

"HAVE I MISSED SOMETHING?" Jake asked.

"THEY DO EAT MEAT. But it isn't the kind of meat we would ever eat." Hayden added looking sad. Jake raised a querying eye and shook his head indicating he didn't understand.

"THEY ARE REFERRING to what happens to the babies who end up in the Reject Bin. And all the other New Humans who don't make the grade or fall out of step with the system." The Priest commented. He looked at Jake who was still confused. "Humans make great patties by all accounts."

"WHAT? They...they eat humans? Are you kidding me?" They shook their heads or looked away.

"IT'S why we risk our lives everyday to rescue the kids. Then we bring them here." Hayden added.

. . .

"That's, that's disgusting. Ugh." Jake felt queasy thinking about it. "I don't even want to know how they do it."

"Mincing machine." Beady chipped in. "They have machines for everything. One day, those machines are going to take over the world."

"Now now with your conspiracy stories Beady. You know they always come true." The Priest added mockingly. "Actually, with the amount of control they are giving Artificial Intelligence, it wouldn't surprise me."

Suddenly, they were interrupted by a commotion outside of the room. Voices were raised in panic. The men looked at each other then ran to the door. After speaking to one of the men outside of the room, Hayden came running back.

"Sound the alarm. Grab weapons. They've found us!"

"Found us? Who has found us?" Jake asked panicking. Everyone seemed to know what to do except him. He felt helpless and unprepared.

"The drones. They'll be sending Vipers in and then it'll be over. They won't stop until everyone is dead." Hayden's jaw was set, his eyes like black coals flickering with fire. "We've been training for this but it doesn't make it easier when it happens."

"What can I do?" Jake screamed. His stomach twisted in knots and his blood chilled to ice as he recalled the memory of facing annihilation by drone.

"Grab a weapon and go with the children and young people to the other bunker. We have to keep as many of them alive as possible." said Hayden.

"Why, tell me. What's so important about the children?"

"They are the future of humanity."

Jake started to move, but before he got the chance, there was an almighty tearing noise and the roof and walls collapsed in on them. Just before the metal was about to rip him apart, he saw his new friend Hayden being pushed away and saved by The Priest, who took the full brunt of the twisting corkscrew. His words 'When it is our time, it is our time.' was the last memory Jake had before the blackness came.

11

THE PAST LEAVES CLUES

He awoke with a jolt, feeling as though he had emerged from a dark tunnel. He felt sick and hot. Perspiration poured from his neck, dampening his pillow. His mouth felt dry and gritty like the morning after the night before. 'Ugh.' he groaned.

He looked up at the ceiling above him to the familiar sight of the rose decoration circling the cheap lampshade which he had inherited from the previous owner and always intended to replace. Sunlight poured through the open curtains and warmed his face. He turned his face towards it and gladly welcomed the sun.

He knew he had to rise up, but his body refused to move. He felt the dead weight of it, creating a Jake shaped mould on the memory foam mattress. His mind was calm, though his thoughts spent. He simply just was. *I'm alive* was the only thought in his mind as he closed his eyes and allowed the yellow-orange sun fire colours to permeate through the thin layer of skin on his eyelids. A sound from somewhere outside of the room caught his attention and sent the colours scurrying away. *Avorra!*

He eased himself off the bed and changed his tee shirt and pants. He wanted to shower, but curiosity pulled him towards the kitchen. He knew she would be there and he had to see her. He noticed how warm his flat was compared to the harsh coldness of the other world; Hayden's world; The Priest's world. He sighed as he remembered them and sighed even more deeply when he considered their fate. 'You cannot die.' he also now understood that instruction.

"Hello Jake." she said warmly as she handed him a hot mug of tea. He sipped it gratefully. It was always just so perfectly right.

"I would love coffee if I have any?" was all he could think of to say. He rarely drank coffee; his constitution repelled against it. Yet this morning, in memory of Hayden, he craved coffee.

Avorra smiled in acknowledgement, but did not respond to the request. "I made you frittata again. There was bacon in the fridge. And mushrooms. You must be doing something right.' she said referring to the angel that was his neighbour.

"That sounds so perfect. I'm famished." he replied taking a seat and then rubbing his hands through his hair and then across his face. "I missed you." His blue angel gave him a coy look and smiled. Once again, he was reminded that there was something similar about her; something comforting and beautiful. She felt like home. She took a seat opposite him.

"Do you see now?" she said gently. Jake nodded slowly and closed his eyes. For the first time in years, he gave thanks for the meal he was about to eat. He ate in silence and when he was finished, he downed the glass of milk beside the plate and wiped away all remnants from his mouth with the back of his hand. He turned his face towards the bright sun and allowed his face once again to absorb the warmth. Then he turned to face Avorra.

"I'm ready. What do you want me to do?"

"That's great Jake. I knew you would be. But first, we have to take a visit to the past. It's going to be difficult for you, but also necessary."

"The past? Difficult? What kind of difficult? I already feel as though I have had my insides literally torn apart twice by killing machines from the future. I've witnessed my family falling apart, my bosses plot to kill me, my entire life's work destined for the destruction of the human race and I have no idea what time, what day, or even what decade it is! How much more difficult could my life possibly get right now?"

Avorra simply smiled. "Everyone has their purpose Jake. Some get to live long arduous lives with no respite from struggle or trauma, whilst others blaze their short lives by bringing love, joy and blessings to themselves and to others. Both may have started on the same journey, with the same opportunity, but they may have different purposes to fulfil. That in turn depicts the type of life they may go on to live."

"I don't understand this. Did Hayden have to suffer without love or a family and always having to fight just to survive? Did The Priest have to lose most of his family only to die at the metal end of a machine he was gearing up to fight? Did Eloise have to die so young without experiencing any of the beauty that life could have given her? Did she? Well, DID SHE?" Anger arose from nowhere. And it exploded like a sudden volcanic eruption from a fiery place deep down within the guts of him. He could not stop the angry tears. They poured forth from him, his grief buckling his legs until he was sobbing on the floor.

Avorra knelt beside him and placed his head in her lap,

cradling and soothing the back of his head with the most tender of touches. It was only when his tears abated and he realised his position, did he raise his head and sit up to kneel opposite her. "I'm sorry for being so weak." he said, wiping his nose with the back of his hand and raising his face to meet hers. And then he saw her eyes. There were tears in both corners. "You're crying?"

"I feel your pain and the pain of all humanity." she said as she allowed the droplets to zigzag down her cheeks. "It is human to cry. I feel your humanity and that is all I ask of you; all *we* ask of you, to feel your humanity and to understand the importance of being human."

"It kinda sucks being human."

"Sometimes perhaps, but it is also the most amazing of gifts. To live on this most beautiful of planets, where everything you require to survive and sustain you is a gift. The plants that both nourish and heal you, the animals that give you both unconditional love and themselves as food, the sun that warms you and gives you daylight; the moon that both guides the tides and is the light in the darkness. The people we interact with that are both a source of friendship and support, but also have the ability to destroy and isolate us. And at the centre of all that is good and all that is sent to support you, is a connection to the Creator who made all of it possible. Everything a human requires to survive and thrive on this planet, is either around them, beside them, or of them."

"I have never looked at it that way before." he remarked before adding, "So why are we so willing to destroy what we have or allow others to? I mean, surely there are far more of us than them? We could stop them right?"

"Of course. You have freewill. You have sovereign rights

just like any other creature on this planet, but like the many sheep in the field controlled by the lone sheepdog, on the commands of one man, for some reason, humans feel the need to obey commands and orders, even if they are detrimental to their very survival. You want to be led; you like having your boundaries imposed on you."

"It's madness! Why don't we just say no? Why are we so compliant?" Jake reflected on himself and realised that he was no different. He had never been a rebel, nor really an individual thinker; he had always been a compliant box ticker.

"The system you live in is designed to keep you penned in. From the moment you are born, you are assigned a birth certificate that indicates you belong to someone. You enter the discipline systems of learning – kindergarten, school, college. Then you go through the work system. All the while you wear uniforms or suits, you belong to someone or something: a building, an organisation. Think of the word 'belong'. What does that symbolise for you?"

Jake reflected, "I guess it gives me meaning, a sense of being, of belonging to something. It means I am not alone in this world."

"And how do you feel right now? Do you feel you belong anywhere Jake?"

"After what I have witnessed this weekend, truthfully, I don't feel I belong anywhere. But I feel safe in this flat; with you." he said earnestly.

"So being alone and isolated in your living space with just a blue angel for company, that makes you feels safe?"

"I...I...don't know." he said getting up awkwardly off his knees and sitting wearily in his chair. "I don't know anything anymore. It's all too much to take in. It's not everyday you discover you're the creator of the future destruction of the human race!"

"Okay, let's look at this from another place." she said rising and standing in front of the kitchen window. "What does it mean to you to be human?"

He thought for a few moments. He thought of Hayden risking his life to rescue the babies, of the communities outside of the Pyramid system that were trying to survive on very little resources. Of The Priest and his family's enduring journey to escape tyranny and find a better life elsewhere and how his grief was directed towards helping and leading others.

He thought of his mother and the way she read his messages but didn't let on; of the way his daughters worried for him; of the struggle of his sisters and how much him not being there had affected them; of Amy and how much they needed each other and how he had allowed pain and grief to create the barbwire fence between them that tore apart their wounds even more. Of Eloise and her infectious laugh and those beautiful, twinkling and knowing eyes, like she had lived lifetimes before and chose to be there as a gift.

He thought of his neglected friendships and how he missed having men around; men who had known him since he himself was a child. He missed being known and seen and loved for who they knew he was; they all allowed him to be himself freely and without condition.

Then he reflected on the darker side of being human. The long hours at work, the pressure to achieve and perform that kept him there rather than with those he wanted to be with. The pressure to conform to having the right type of house in the right type of street, driving the right type of car, just so he could be ignored by the wrong type of people. When he was married, he hated living the life they had because it wasn't him. Private education for the girls, dinner parties, charity functions, playing golf with work colleagues or dads from the kids' schools, yet no time to play golf with his own friends. He could see now that by throwing himself into his work and not being home often, was actually a way to enable him to escape from the life he had created. He had given himself over to fitting into an expected ideal, but it wasn't his ideal way to live.

"It's about choice. About being free to make choices about how you want to live your life." he said finally. "And yet," he added looking directly at Avorra, "we deny ourselves this right daily. And it will come to a point where we no longer have that freewill to choose, because we never fought to keep it."

Avorra nodded then smiled and declared, "It's a gift from the Creator. It is free and it is beautiful."

"And we are going to lose it. Soon, unless we stop them taking it. But how can we do that?"

"I will show you. But first, I wanted you to see the importance of being able to think freely, to have free thought and to know that it's a necessary part of being human."

Jake nodded, digesting her words and feeling more content after the release of emotions he had been hiding for far too long. "Hey Avorra," he said, "do you think I could have that coffee now?"

The coffee was just as he hoped it would be: perfect. He toasted Tom, Hayden, Mack, Beady, Papa and The Priest and vowed to not let them endure that type of future. On Avorra's instructions, he showered, shaved and dressed. When he was ready, he glanced out of the window. It was a beautiful Spring Sunday with the sound of birds and the gentle hustle of life in the streets around him. He opened the window and stuck his head out, breathing in deeply. *It's good to be alive* he thought as memories of the future washed over and through him. He tried not to remember the corkscrew machine impaling and ripping through The Priest, but it was framed and placed centre stage on the wall of his memories. He shivered, withdrew his head, closed the window, then headed back into his bedroom.

He caught his image in the mirror as he passed, then reflected. He looked different. The slump in his shoulders had disappeared; the defeat in his eyes gone. The man staring back, reminded him of the teenager who scaled abandoned buildings with his friends on the nearby council estate and who rode out on his bike until way too late on a school night; the kid who broke his arm twice from swinging from ropes on trees across rivers and occasionally bunked school to hang out by the disused factory and smoke a fag that always made him cough. The young man who helped his mother cut the vegetables for Sunday roasts, the boy who made daisy chains for his little sister. *I'm back!* He announced in his head. He smiled, then walked towards the kitchen.

"You look good Jake." she said noticing the new spring in his step.

"I feel better to tell you the truth. Which is kind of weird given the situation and all I have just experienced."

Avorra did not respond. Instead she turned her back and looked upwards. Jake guessed she was communicating to the Council. But he felt her energy had changed. There was a definite aura of sadness around her. Then she finally turned around and met his eyes. She sighed. "This is going to be the hardest part of everything you will experience. I'm sorry Jake, but it is necessary. In order for you to make the right choice out of freewill rather than doing the right thing for others, you have to go through this experience."

"What type of experience?" suddenly he wasn't feeling so brave. His stomach contracted and he could feel perspiration rise up and onto his neck.

She reached for his hand. "I will be there with you every moment, remember that. I will not abandon you."

There was no time to respond. The next moment he was standing not in his kitchen, but in the house he shared with Amy before he left to rent his flat. It was raining outside; torrential rain. He heard it bouncing off the conservatory roof. He watched Amy as she finished making a sandwich, then place it into an open bag on the countertop, alongside an apple, a banana and a cereal bar. She brought the lid of the bag down and zipped it, then placed it next to a school bag that sat on the bar stool next to the island unit. He recognised the bag, he recognised the lunch bag; they were Eloise's. He looked closely at Amy, at what she was wearing, listened to the crashing sound of the rain against the glass, then horror filled his soul.

He urgently searched for Avorra. *Where are you?* he cried out as fear held a crushing hand on his heart.

"I am here."

He turned around to look at her, horror and disbelief on his face. *Why would you do this?*

"You can talk. You are merely a silent observer." she added as she held his eyes.

"Why are we here?" he screamed out.

"It is necessary."

He turned around abruptly on hearing a voice he instantly recognised. It was his own voice. Yet the man who walked into the room and spoke, was the past version himself on the morning of *that* awful day. He watched everything in slow motion, like the re-run of a familiar yet forgotten movie. He noticed how happy he looked. He was slim and fit and looked relaxed. He remembered the moment well. It was the day he was going to hand in his notice at his company. He had plans to set up his own research consultancy. He wasn't happy with the way the company was progressing their plans to interfere with the human brain.

The day before he had expressed his concerns to Edward. Harry was on vacation and so he reported directly to the CEO at the monthly team presentation. Edward suggested creating a shared database of Jake's progress and research. But Jake was unhappy about who could access the sensitive data. He was close to a breakthrough, but he held concerns about the ethical aspect of invasive technological advancement on the freewill of a human being. Edward wasn't happy and threatened to close him down. But Jake held the patents on the data and research so they couldn't take it from him by force or coercion.

He and Amy had discussed the situation and his choices the night before. He glanced over to the almost empty bottle of red that sat next to the kettle and the two wine glasses drying on the draining board. A Penfold's Ruby Cabernet: Amy's favourite wine. There was just one bottle remaining in the wine rack in the garage. He planned to surprise her that week with another two cases being delivered, along with a case of pink champagne. Amy loved pink fizz.

Amy. He watched how content she was preparing her little girl's bag for school and handing over a mug of coffee to the man she was due to marry shortly. Watching her, the ice castle he had erected to keep her out, started to melt. He wanted to place his arms around her waist and snuggle his head down into the base of her neck as he did so many times before. Then this past version of him spoke.

'You take my car honey. It's torrential out. I'll get a cab to the station today. I'm meeting Dave tonight for a beer after work anyway."

"Are you sure? My car will be out of the garage later today. They said it was just the points. The brakes are fine. Do you want me to pick you up from the station tonight, or will you be back late?"

"I'll get a cab. Don't worry about me, you just chill. Where is the monkey anyway?"

"Watching her favourite film of course! You know how much she loves it. I swear I know that film off by heart. She's obsessive." Amy rolled her eyes but also smiled.

"Okay well I'll go say goodbye to her and see you later. I'll call her before she goes to bed okay?"

Jake watched as his past self drained the coffee, place his phone and keys down on the kitchen unit and walk out of the room. Jake wanted to follow, to see his girl again, but Avorra held him back.

"Watch. Observe." she reminded him, then indicated towards the phone on the unit. Jake walked over and looked at it. A message pinged. 'Hey, are you bringing in the chip to the Centre today? I want to talk something through with you.' Jake looked at Avorra in confusion. He had forgotten about that text. It was from the chief research scientist at the Centre for Neurology he was due to meet with later that morning. He rarely took the chip with him unless he was working on specifics. It was unusual to be asked to bring it in. He remembered thinking that at the time, but he didn't query and took it anyway.

They watched as the past Jake re-emerged into the room,

pick up his phone to call a taxi and then read the text. His brow furrowed, but then a voice called for him in the next room. Jake's heart leapt when he heard *her* voice. He asked Amy to call the taxi whilst he went to Eloise. It was during that time he also grabbed the chip from the hidden safe in his bedroom. Amy went to tell him the taxi was just minutes away and the two of them re-entered the kitchen. They kissed and he told her he loved her and couldn't wait for her to be his wife. Jake watched the way her face lit up and the way his own filled with adoration. The love between them was palpable.

There was a beep outside and then the old Jake left. They watched as Amy exited the room and re-entered with Eloise wearing a coat and looking content and happy.

"We have Daddy's posh car today pickle." she announced happily.

"Yes. I love the music in Daddy's car." the little girl replied with glee.

Jake watched them with a heart both tearing apart and also overflowing with deep, indescribable love. Then Avorra touched his arm and suddenly they were in the back of the car. Amy and Eloise were singing to Driving In My Car by Madness. It was the song he always played when they went on day trips together. It was their happy family song and Eloise loved it.

Jake felt Avorra's eyes on him. Then he realised what was coming. They were going to be in the car the very moment the other driver was about to lose control and the moment he would lose his family. Then he saw something in Amy's eyes in the rear view mirror that caught his attention. She had spotted something behind her. Her brow furrowed and she stopped singing.

"Sing Mummy!" Eloise cried out still happy. Amy

murmured some of the lyrics but was too distracted to continue. Her concern turned to fear and her speed picked up. "Ooh we are fast!" the little girl yelled with glee. Amy didn't take the turning towards the school and instead headed onto a main road.

"This isn't the way to school Mummy."

Jake looked behind him to see what was causing Amy distress. There was a black SUV close behind. It kept flashing its headlights at her. Jake knew that Amy would have given way or slowed down usually, so something didn't feel right for her to choose to speed up and take a different direction. He could see she was trying to escape or even to shake them off. Suddenly there was a shunt from behind and they all jerked forward. Eloise screamed and Amy tried to calm her down. The car behind shunted them again.

"Eloise call Daddy on Mummy's phone. Quickly!" Jake watched as his little girl who was now sobbing, picked up her mother's phone and tried to call him.

"It's not working. It's not ringing." she said in anguish.

"He must be on the Underground. Damn!" the car was shunted once again and Amy panicking, pulled off the street they were on and headed fast along many unknown roads until she entered a side road near some abandoned buildings. Jake screamed out "No don't go down here Amy. It's a dead end!" But it was too late. The car behind shunted them so hard, they went into a spin and the car rolled over twice. Jake was outside of the car and witnessing the next few moments in slow motion. The screams, the crunching, the sound of glass breaking. The song playing in the background. Then the car finally came to a halt upside down on its roof, wheels facing the sky.

Two men exited the SUV. One of the men looked

around, then walked to the driver's side. The other one checked the passenger window.

"Where is he?" the man checking the driver's window asked. He sounded surprised.

"Oh shit!" the other man said as he checked the pulse of the child in the passenger seat. "This one's dead." Then in shock he looked up and said, "We just killed a kid."

"Fuck! This one is unconscious. We'd better call in and let Edward know he wasn't in the car. He must have taken a different route in. That means he still has the chip. Shit. What a mess! Call in the guys. They will know what to do. Thankfully," he said looking around him, "we don't have any witnesses." Then the two men got in their car, did a U turn and sped off.

Jake went to run to the car and to his family, but Avorra touched his arm before he could run to them. In a moment, they were back in his kitchen, where a mug of hot tea was waiting for him on the kitchen table.

"What the hell just happened? That's not what was reported? They said a guy high on drugs hit them. I...I don't understand." he said running hands through his hair. "Who were those guys and why did they do that to them?"

"Your family weren't their target Jake. You were."

"Me?" and then the penny dropped. "The chip! They wanted the chip. So, they were going to kill me to get it? I'd be out of the way and they could proceed with their plans without me. But...I let the girls take the car instead. Oh my god!" he looked at Avorra in shock, the colour draining from his face. "It wasn't Amy's fault at all. It was mine for letting her take the car. It should have been me." he said slumping down heavily into the chair. "It should have been me."

"And you have always blamed yourself for that. For

loaning your car that morning and taking the taxi instead of driving."

"Yes." he replied defeated.

"But ultimately, neither of you were to blame were you Jake? And you didn't intend this harm to come to your girl. You both loved her. And you love each other."

Jake looked up at Avorra. What she said made perfect sense. All this time guilt had created chasms within him and barricaded his heart from everyone, including the one person who could make it better...Amy. He didn't understand why she never spoke about what happened.

"Because she has blocked it out. She can't remember. She has placed it in a dark and painful place deep inside her, but her subconscious knows and has access to it. With time she can acknowledge what happened, feel the emotions that are also trapped inside and then heal. Until she does that, she has confined herself to a cell within, where she is both the judge and the jailor."

Jake reflected on her words. "There's so much to take in." he said placing his head in his hands. "They killed her. Whether she was the intended victim or not, they killed her. Edward killed her." he said raising his head and setting his jaw. Anger swept through him and his hands balled into fists. "I'm going to kill him! A life for a life!"

"It doesn't work that way Jake. Revenge really is a bitter pill. It won't help."

"So what can I do then? They killed her thinking it was me. And destroyed Amy. I...I was ready to kill myself because of them."

"Yes, but you are now past that moment. And you will let this moment pass also. It is time for both of you to heal Jake. You and Amy. You can still create a life together."

"But without her? Without Eloise at the centre? She was the reason we decided to stay together."

"Trust me, you were destined to be together, with or without Eloise in your life."

"How do you know? Oh yes, because you see everything right?" he was slightly sarcastic in his reply. Avorra laughed it off and smiled.

"Eloise was a gift to you both. Perhaps she was there to bring you together? Perhaps," she added with a knowingness that made him regard her questioningly, 'perhaps that was the main purpose of her short, but beautiful life."

He couldn't think about that for the moment. It was so much to take in, but a feeling stained his conscience regardless. *What if she's right?* The feeling whispered to him. *What if she is right?* "So what's the plan? What's the next step in this surreal adventure? Am I about to find out my mother is actually Marilyn Monroe, or that I am Jesus or something as equally crazy?"

Avorra laughed. And once she started, she couldn't stop. It reminded him of Amy. He tried to get her to stop but she couldn't. He was never able to stop Amy either; he had to wait it out until she could recompose herself. He noticed that Eloise, before she passed, was becoming just like her mother in many ways, including her infectious laughter.

He couldn't help himself. He started to chuckle. And the more he chuckled, the more Avorra laughed, until it wasn't long before tears were running down both of their cheeks. Despite himself, it felt amazing to be so free with emotions. "Thank you. I needed that." he said wiping his eyes with the back of his sleeve.

"Now we destroy the chip. And all the documentation and data relating to it." she said suddenly in serious mode.

"Okay, but how? You told me the office and the research

centre and labs were now heavily guarded with added security. How are we going to get in?"

"Henry. He's going to let you in."

"Henry? But he's in with it! Why would he help us?"

"Trust me, he will do anything you ask of him." she added with a wink.

"Why, what have you got on him?" Then he felt her hand on his arm and they were off to find out.

12

AN ANGEL CALLS

They arrived back in Edward's office. He was on a phone call coming through on the speaker. The man on the other end of the line was American, with a curt, gruff voice. He was instructing the CEO on the next course of action. They had to be in possession of the chip after the contract signing at 2pm Monday. Jake would be terminated as planned by early hours Tuesday. A gas explosion in his flat was suggested. He was instructed that this time there were to be no mistakes.

Then they mentioned Henry. He was being sent on an urgent business trip. He was to be scheduled to take a private jet to Dubai to meet a new business associate. He wasn't going to be returning. Edward asked why Henry had to be disposed of and the answer he heard, chilled Jake's spine.

"THE GUYS in charge want no loose ends." Edward then sat back, reflected and took a large gulp of his drink.

. . .

"And what of me? Am I disposable too?"

"We are all disposable except for those at the top. You know that Edward. But you have time to get your house in order. For now, it's those two who are the immediate threat. You know what to do."

Just before they left, Jake took a long look at the older man in his executive leather chair, drinking expensive bourbon and surrounded by the best of everything. He had sold his soul to get to where he was and now he was faced with the reality that the devil always claims his prize. He left the shell shocked man to wallow in his self pity.

They were still in the office building. Avorra had not transported them anywhere else. *What now?* he thought as she walked ahead and he followed. Once again, he wondered if she glided or walked. He was transfixed watching her ahead of him and he thought back to watching Hayden's footsteps in the tunnel with the baby inside his jacket. He thought of Eloise, of Amy, of his girls, his sisters, his mother and everyone he loved and knew. Perhaps this was his destiny, his purpose? To be the person who develops this invasive brain controlling nanotechnology, just so that he could destroy it before anyone else could get there first. Was it possible that he could ensure that the future of humanity did not happen the way he was shown? Could he actually stop it?

Avorra stopped outside Henry's office. Then she touched his arm and they were inside.

. . .

"Why are we here? It's Sunday evening. He will be at church with his wife and her family. It's what they do every Sunday." Jake said raising his arms in confusion. Ironic he thought to himself. *Plotting my assassination whilst giving thanks to God. Tosser!* Avorra scowled at him. "Sorry."

"Henry doesn't know how Eloise died. He wasn't involved. Edward told him that focusing your grief into your work would help you and that distraction was a good thing for you. Henry didn't know half of what Edward was up to. But he found out."

"Found out? What did he find out?"

"After Edward told him that you were to be killed off, Henry panicked. He knew that if they could come for you, then most likely, they would come for him. Of course he was right. So," she said reaching into the locked safe behind the painting on the wall at the back of Henry's chair, "he made himself a safety net." She extracted a document and handed it to him. The safe remained unopened and intact.

"This was going to be handed over to someone he is connected to in the House of Lords." she said ignoring the querying of his thoughts.

Jake scanned the document. It was an unredacted file of transcripts between Edward, the military, secret services and diplomats in a formidable Asian country. Conversations, messages, emails and bank transfers were all recorded. The file had been collated over months.

"He must have known he couldn't trust Edward. This is huge. If this got out, Edward would either be killed off himself, or face a very long time in jail."

"Knowing the type of people he was involved with, I would say the former." Avorra replied.

"So, what next? Seems like everyone is on a list to get killed, nobody can be trusted and the real criminals are going to get away with the chip, murder, espionage and countless other international offences. Damn this stuff is unreal!"

"Now we go ahead and destroy the chip as planned."

"But how? You saw this place, it's now like Fort bloody Knox! How the hell are we going to get it out of here? You know where I keep it right?" Jake said pacing the room.

"In the base of the Peace Lily plant on your desk. That's why you have a double pot. The outer pot is a ceramic one made by Amy and Eloise for your birthday. The plant was a gift from your daughter Mia. No one would dare touch such a sentimental possession. The inner pot is the real one that houses the plant. At the internal base of that, is the chip. Genius."

"Thanks. Boy, you really do know everything don't you?"

"Not everything. I still don't know the end. You have free will remember?" she added with a wink.
"We don't have much time though. Henry plans to leave the country at 8am, via a flight to Mexico and then on to Chile. He's planned some plastic surgery in Mexico; a little face re-arranging."

"Wow. And what about his family?"

"Henry doesn't look out for anyone else. You should know that. When he found out they planned to kill you, he guessed he'd be next. So he opted to save his own skin. He's arranged a fishing trip accident in Mexico. That way his family gets the life insurance and he gets the nest egg he siphoned off from the company in a private equity fund with offshore dealings. What that man doesn't know about dodgy dealings, he knows people who do."

"The bastard!" Jake sat in his chair and frowned. He suddenly felt exhausted. He reached for the whisky bottle that always sat in the cupboard of Henry's desk and poured himself a large glass. The brown liquid burned down into his stomach like a flow of lava. "Hah! That's better." Avorra stayed silent and watched him. "Okay. Let's do whatever we've got to do and get this over with." He re-filled his glass and said a cheers to the painting of a Phoenix that sat opposite the desk. It was an original from a renowned worldwide artist and one that Henry loved.

"To the rise of the Phoenix!" he toasted and knocked back the liquid. He rose up out of the chair with a stiffened resolve. "Let's go kick some ass!"

"I like this new Jake." Avorra proclaimed with a smile. "Let's see if Henry likes him too."

"Whaa..." there wasn't time to complete his question. She touched his arm and they were outside the Midnight blue Victorian door of a huge white house: Henry's house. Jake shot a glance at her before she rapped on the door. He wanted to hide like the younger kid version of himself who played 'Knock Down Ginger' before he got caught and slapped across the ear by a retired policeman he happened to knock the door of.

"What am I supposed to say to him?" he panicked as he heard footsteps heading towards them from inside.

. . .

"Trust your instincts. I will help you." said Avorra before disappearing.

"Jake?" the older man quizzed when he saw him.

"Hey Henry. How's things?" The two men regarded each other. Henry stood in shock and disbelief and Jake felt awkward and unsure of his next move.

"What the hell are you doing here?" Henry asked looking around him and closing the door a little behind him. "Is everything alright?"

"Actually Henry, no. Everything is not alright. Can we walk and talk? I assume you have your family at home there?" Henry nodded slowly, the colour draining from his face. He went inside and returned a few moments later wearing a coat. The sun had already set and evening was welcoming in the darkness. The men walked in silence towards a nearby clearing. Jake could feel the fear and nervous energy exude from the other man. It gave him confidence to speak.

"I know that you and Edward are planning to have me killed." he announced.

. . .

"Wha...? Don't be ridiculous man. How? How could you say something like that? Are you suffering with a mental setback, is that it?"

"Shut up Henry. I know far more than you think I know. Like your little 'vacation' to Mexico for some face adjustments shall we say?" Henry stopped walking and turned to face him. "I know *everything.*" Jake added.

"I...I..." Henry was trying to think quickly. Dumbfounded, he scanned their surroundings to see if anyone else was with him, or more importantly, to see if Jake had brought an assailant with him.

"Don't worry, I'm not going to harm you or take my revenge. I'm not like you or Edward."

"So what do you want then? If you really do know what you think you know, that is?" Henry recovered from his initial shock and attempted to regain the upper hand.

"Well I know that Edward got the directive to assassinate me after I sign the contract and hand over the chip tomorrow. I know that around nine months ago Edward tried to kill me to get the chip, but ended up killing my innocent child and putting my fiancee in a coma for a few weeks. And,' he added moving his face closer and almost spitting the words out into his face, "I know that plans are in place to get you removed too."

HENRY'S SHOULDERS slumped in resignation and his face paled. He walked towards a bench situated on the entrance to a park next to the field they had just walked on the edge of. "I didn't know about your daughter until recently. I wasn't told; I found that out myself. You are not the only person to go digging for dirt." He sat down heavily. At fifty six, he was eleven years older than Jake. "I'm so sorry. She was such a lovely and sweet little girl."

JAKE SIGHED and sat beside him. "So how much do you know?"

"MOST OF IT I THINK. The chip and the data are not headed to the government for the purposes you think they are."

"I REALISED. Do you know who is getting the data?" Jake asked.

"NOT REALLY NO. I do know that you don't mess with these guys. After you, they are coming for me probably and then possibly for Edward. I've seen that guy drink more in the past few weeks than in the entire fifteen years I have known him in that company. I think the old guy has cancer, but whether it's that that gets him or a bullet, I couldn't say."

. . .

"And your answer is to run away right? From this, and from your family. What happened to doing the right thing Henry? We used to be friends. For goodness sake, you were going to be an usher at mine and Amy's wedding! What happened to you?"

"Money." Henry replied without thought. "Simple as that. A shit load of money."

"Is being rich worth all of this? The death of my girl, destroying the life of my family, my murder, your scheduled death; leaving your family? Damn Henry, what happened to the decent man I used to admire?" Jake shook his head as he thought about it. *All this for money?*

"You wouldn't understand Jake. You're not like me. You don't know what it's like at the corporate level I'm at. The pressure to stay on top with all the younger guys creeping up below and tugging at your trouser legs. And then at the summit, at the top of the mountain you've worked so hard to climb to, when you get up there, you realise it's scummier up there than at the bottom. The guys up there are unscrupulous, self serving and ready to stab you in the back without a second thought. It's tough."

"Tough? Tough? Earning hundreds of thousands a year, living in a huge luxurious house, fine wining and fine dining, with a wife and kids and a mistress or two tucked away in some fancy penthouse somewhere, just so you can play chess with peoples' lives? If you think that's tough, try living with the death of your four year old girl and finding out your bosses killed her instead of you! Tell me that's not more fucking tough you arrogant arsehole!" he stood up and started walking around. Anger raged inside. The temptation to kick the legs of the man who sat in front of him was overwhelming.

He heard Avorra's voice inside his head that calmed him down. *Breathe Jake, breathe.* He sighed. Looked upwards with his eyes closed for a moment, then opened them and returned to the seat beside Henry. For a few moments, they sat in silence.

"So, what now?" Henry finally asked.

"Now we fight back."

Henry heard Jake's proposal. Jake would retrieve the chip from the plant pot and Henry would recover the documents from his office safe. This would be both his protection and ammunition. Jake would then remove all the files relating to the chip since he also retained all security codes that he had created to protect the information from being stolen or copied. When all information had been transferred onto a USB stick that Jake would keep possession of, a fire 'accident' would occur in the lab at the basement of the office centre where all the other data was kept.

Once all information had been extracted then Henry could catch his flight and Jake would go his own way. Thus neither of them would be able to attend the Monday meeting and no data would be exchanged or passed on to the relevant parties.

"It will never work. They stepped up security on Friday in preparation for the meeting. They've thought of everything and nothing is going to get in their way." Henry commented. By now, they were in the office of his house drinking thirty year old aged whisky, which ironically, was a Christmas gift from Edward.

"We have a way in. You are going to have to trust us. All you have to do is retrieve your documents from the safe."

"How do you know about the document and where my safe is?"

"Let's just say that I have heavenly help." Jake replied with a wink and a nod to Avorra and the Council. "Oh. And nice painting by the way. My sister Suzannah collects the artist's paintings. She'd loved that one." he added with a wink.

Henry sighed deeply and rolled his eyes. "Okay. You do your part and I'll uphold my end. But one thing...if and when we get out of this alive, we're done okay? I'm starting a new life and I'm completely walking away from the old one. Got it?"

. . .

Jake nodded. Then reflected and asked, "How can you do it? You know, leave your wife and kids like that? Faking your death and just walking away?"

The older man got up from his chair, took the glass out of Jake's hands and looked at him squarely face on. "Because if I don't disappear, they'll probably torture or kill them. It's the least I can do."

He left Henry's house shaking. He couldn't believe the gumption he just expressed to his boss. *Who have I become Avorra? Look at me!* He looked up and sighed and let out a deep breath. He really had no idea how they were going to get away with what they had just arranged. Avorra had presented a plan to him before they visited Henry's house. A crazy, wild and outrageous plan that belonged more to a Hollywood blockbuster espionage film script than to his once normal life.

What's happened to me? He asked himself as he walked away from the house, still physically shaking from what he just accomplished. *One minute I'm an eminent research scientist discovering a way to help humanity and next I discover that everything around me is a lie, that my girl was murdered instead of me and that my immediate bosses and myself, are due to be assassinated by an unknown group of people linked to an elite who want to dominate and manipulate the world into near extinction. Fuck! Fuck, fuck, fucketty fuck!*

"Hey Jake. I leave you alone for five minutes and I have to wash your mouth out?"

. . .

"Avorra! You scared me! Please don't jump up on me like that again. My heart can only take so much. It's been a tough few days, don't you reckon?" he said holding his chest and breathing deeply with relief. He was still unnerved after confronting Henry. Avorra smiled as way of apology. "Okay, Henry is on board. Hopefully. Now where to? What great adventures have you got up that blue sleeve for me now?"

"Now we are off to take a visit to Edward."

"Edward? What the f…?"

"Now now Jake. Language." she mocked with a raised brow.

They arrived at midnight inside Edward's house. It was dark except for the shimmering, white blue light that radiated out from Avorra. In just over four hours time they would be carrying out their plan. Edward was asleep in the spare room. He was snoring so loudly that Jake guessed it was the reason he wasn't in the master bed. Avorra instructed Jake to remain in the background as an observer. He would not be visible to Edward, but at no stage was he to speak.

. . .

"Edward wake up." she instructed in a stern voice. He grumbled but remained asleep. She repeated the instruction in a louder voice. "Wake up Edward!"

"What? Wha...?" The older man sat up and looked around him. Peering over him and then walking backwards, was a tall, shimmering, light blue female figure calling his name. "Edward, wake up!"

"What the hell? Am I dreaming? Is this a dream?"

"No. It's really happening." she replied. Jake noticed how serious and stern her voice was compared to how she spoke to him. Given how petrified the older guy looked at that moment, he much preferred the way she spoke to him. "My name is Avorra from the Council of Angels and I come to you because you have a chance to save your soul from eternal condemnation. But only if you do exactly as I say. Do you accept this request?"

Edward sat up and pulled his duvet closer up his body and clutched it under his chin. "I don't understand what is happening." he cried. Jake saw how childlike this old man looked as he withered before her, gripped in fear. He didn't know whether to have pity for him, or to despise him for his weakness.

. . .

"You have done terrible things for your own gain and now it is coming to pass. Soon those whom you compromised so much for, will be calling for your demise. You have been wretched in your choices, responsible for the suffering and death of others and now there is little time left for you on this planet."

"I know. I know. I'm sorry. I didn't mean for so much harm to be brought on those people. But my hands were tied. If I didn't do it, they would come for me, or even my family." he snivelled.

"The instruction may have come from someone else, but you made the final decision Edward. And the pain and suffering endured by others, will have to be repaid with your soul. You must know that they are going to take that soul soon? Your time here is scarce." she added in a deep and condemning voice. Jake had never seen this side of Avorra and he feared for Edward. He watched the old guy's response with fascination.

"They are going to kill me soon. I know. I don't know how or when, but they will. They don't like 'loose ends' apparently." he stated mockingly. "What, what do you want of me? Why are you here?"

"To offer you a chance to redeem some of the awful things you have done. They have demonstrated no loyalty to you, except for these material things. But what use are they when you are not around to enjoy them? That bed imported from a hotel in Dubai you once stayed in, the luxurious silk sheets from the finest silk designer on the planet. Your wife's expensive body enhancements. All for what? So you can end up sleeping in the spare room and not enjoying your wife's company and her body? Because despite everything you have done to create the perfect sleep environment, you cannot stop yourself from snoring. Ask yourself Edward, was it worth it? Everything you did in the name of power and greed and money...was it worth it in the end?"

EDWARD WAS silent for a few moments as he reflected. She was right. His wife despised him and his snoring was an excuse for her to not sleep with him. His mistress tolerated him because he paid for her company and to be his whore for one night a week. Maintaining that one copulation where he was lucky to last ten minutes, cost him at least a hundred thousand a year in rent, fine dining and expensive gifts. He asked himself was it worth it.

"NO. IN THE END, NO."

A PART of Jake wanted so much to feel empathy for this man, as he sat up in his bed looking wretched and defeated, but thinking of his daughter upside down in the car, her life ebbing away because of a call this man made to kill him, stopped that emotion abruptly at the door.

. . .

"So is this some Angel of Death thing? Am I about to die?" Edward asked forlornly.

"No you are going to do some retribution for all the bad things you have done in your life Edward. After that, it's up to you." Avorra said sternly.

Edward sighed. He already knew they would be coming for him soon. He guessed he had no real choice. "What do I have to do?"

13

THE PHOENIX RISES

It was set in motion. Edward and Henry had their parts to play and neither was aware of the other. The last part of the plan, was a visit to his sister Helen.

It was close to 1am when he arrived at the door. It took a while for her to awake, but she slept lightly and so was able to answer the door before anyone stirred. She was shocked to see him for many reasons, but given the family's concern over his mental wellbeing, she welcomed him in. She made them both coffee and then sat with him in the living room.

"Okay, tell me again. I think I'm either still dreaming or the coffee hasn't kicked in yet. You want me to do what?" she asked, with a look of shocked disbelief on her face.

"Since you work as a cleaner at my office building, I need you to let us in legitimately, through the front door so to speak. It's the only way." he explained. He hadn't realised it at the time, but the building he witnessed her cleaning in on the visit with Avorra, was his workplace. They were simply in another part of the building on a different floor.

"But you are not coming in the front door? I have to open a back door and let you in right?"

"Yes. Myself and my boss Henry."

"Your boss? But why is he going to be with you? You're not in trouble are you Jake?" she queried, adopting a worried expression that reminded him of their mother. He called it her 'Mum face'.

"Yes I am and I've written you everything you need to know in this." he said handing her a thick padded brown A5 envelope. She went to open it. "Don't. I want you to do that tomorrow evening okay? Trust me on this Hels."

She held the envelope in her hand, weighing it up and the situation in her mind. She bit on her lip; something she often did when nervous or over thinking. "If I don't do this? I mean, if they find out, I could lose my job. And we kind of need the money."

"I know you do and I've sorted it." he said nodding towards the envelope. "Please Helen, you are our only hope."

"Our?"

"Trust me, you don't want to know."

The plan was in motion. In just over three hours time, Jake and Helen would drive to the office. She would go to work as planned, but an hour earlier, explaining to the all night security that she had a kid's school commitment so had to get the work completed earlier. Once in, she would head to the cleaning cupboard on the basement floor for extra supplies. From there, she would detour to the service door at the back and let in Jake and Henry. Meanwhile, Edward would arrive via the front door explaining that he had important work to finish before the meeting that day and would need key access to the lab and the offices. Security had been heightened around these areas, but since it was Edward doing the request, then they would open the relevant parts of the building to allow him access.

At the designated time, Edward arrived at the front of the building. He had one, important job to do before the plan went ahead.

"Go have a break while you can." he told the security guard whose colleague was delayed due to a 'mysterious' car issue. "I'll manage the fort." he added with a wink and a slap on the back of the man's shoulders. The security man was more than grateful and since it was the boss of the company, he had no reason to be suspicious or concerned. He was also desperate for a toilet break, a coffee and a cigarette. Normally his colleague would have been there to cover for him, but he was half an hour late with at least another hour before he could join him.

Edward took the lift to his office. Then sent a text message. 'I'm in.' Henry's phone pinged. He and Jake were waiting behind the door of the cleaning cupboard, flat against the wall to avoid detection by the security camera. Henry breathed out a sigh and gave the thumbs up to go. Jake walked over to Helen and hugged her tight.

"Thank you for doing this. Now you know what to do right?"

"Yes. Do my shift as usual. Then at exactly 5.30am, I head towards the front door and pretend to faint right?"

"Right."

"What if I can't do it Jake? What if I forget and walk out, or don't look convincing? Why did you ask me to do this anyway? What if I let you down?" Helen pleaded then bowed her head. Jake grabbed hold of her and held her tight. He kissed the top of her head and felt her body relax into his. She placed her arms around him and held him tightly. And in that moment, he knew that he had to live; he had to survive this no matter what, so that he could be there for her and for everyone else in his family that needed him.

"This will work, trust me." he said pulling her back to face him. "And you know why?" She slowly shook her head, her bottom lip still turned down in a sad pout. "because you are a winner. You always have been. You have excelled at everything you have ever done. And you will again. And," he added with a smile, "there's a huge wad of cash in that envelope with your name on. So you had better make this work okay?"

"Really? How come? The money I mean. How come?"

"Let's say that it's payback money for all the time I wasn't there for you and the guys okay? Besides, the person who gave it to me isn't going to need it much longer." He winked and gave her the nod to go. Then he turned to Henry who was watching the exchange with interest. "We're good to go. Let's do this." Henry sighed. He would rather have been packing at that moment than playing Action Man in his own movie.

With the security guard not watching the monitors, they headed up the stairs to their respective offices. Each man had a rucksack on their shoulders. Jake retrieved the chip and filled his bag with personal items he wanted to keep. He took one last long look at the Peace Lily and the ceramic pot and sighed. Then he headed back down to the lab underneath the basement. This was something he had to do alone.

Edward's job was to ensure the doors to the lab were opened. For the past week, he was the only one who had access. At the time Jake didn't question the new directive, just as he hadn't questioned anything over the past year. Grief had blinded him to all critical thinking and awareness. But no longer. He reached Edward at the allotted time and had just twenty-five minutes to do what was necessary.

"We don't have much time. Be as quick as you can."

Edward instructed solemnly. Jake nodded and entered. He flicked on the fluorescent lights and the room sprang into action. He grabbed some protective clothing items from a shelf near the door and said hello to the various mice and rats in cages as he passed. His allocated office space was at the far left of the area. He typed in a security code to enter. He deliberately ensured that he was the only one with access to that room after Eloise had died. Edward agreed knowing that when the time was right, that they would gain access to all his work.

He entered and headed straight to his computer. He fired it up and deleted only the most important data and files. Some he added onto a USB stick. This was the most time consuming part. Once completed, he removed all paper documents from folder and binders, collated them together in piles and rolled them up using elastic bands. He then placed the rolled papers into his rucksack. Before adding them however, he took out a bottle containing hydrochloric acid he always kept in a safe place in a garage. He never understood why until this point.

Once all of the important data had been deleted and documents rolled, he put on neoprene gloves and a respirator mask, before carefully opening the bottle. Then with great care, he released the acid over his computer and desk. He watched as the acid burnt through the metal and parts of the desk surface. He had decided against a fire since that would alert security, arouse immediate suspicion and make it more difficult to get away in time.

Satisfied, he replaced the lid securely, and exited the room, locking the door behind him. He took off his gloves and folded them over the end of the bottle cap. He then placed it back in his rucksack for later disposal. He replaced the respirator on the shelf, looked over the lab, apologised to the caged animals whom he now had more empathy with, and left the room. Edward was outside waiting.

"All done?" he asked with a resigned face. Jake nodded and Edward sighed. He knew there was now no going back. His fate had been sealed. They met Helen and Henry at the back door. Edward regarded Henry. A look of both betrayal and shame passed his face. "I guess this will be the last time we see each other?" he said with genuine sadness.

"Yes. At least I hope so." Henry replied more reticent. He hadn't forgotten that the old man agreed to his murder.

"Indeed. I think I can guarantee that, though on second thoughts, I don't think I can really guarantee anything." Edward commented, then turned his attention to Jake. "You have the money and the details of the account?" Jake nodded. As agreed, Jake received his bonus early from funds Edward had set aside, plus a large chunk more. He knew that where he was soon going, he would have no use for it himself.

"Good. Good. Well then, I guess this is goodbye." he said proffering his hand to both men, who each took hold and shook it back. "Be well." he said as he turned around and headed back to his office.

Jake and Henry looked at each other. Jake still felt betrayed, but he also knew that he had been given a chance to live, so he also had a feeling of deep gratitude. All three men were losing what they had worked hard to achieve and only two of them would escape with their lives. With the money Jake received from the CEO, he could re-start his totally afresh.

Then Henry did something totally unexpected. Beside him on the floor, lying up against the wall, was the Phoenix Rising painting from his office.

"For your sister." he announced as he handed it to him.

"I've always had a crush on her and I guess at least I know it's going to someone who will truly appreciate it. Take care old boy and please...don't write!"

Jake smiled with gratitude, the anger dissipating into a whispering mist. "Thank you Henry for doing this. She will love it. You have the documents?" Henry nodded and tapped his rucksack. Then he smiled and exited the door. Jake watched him leave, watched as the door gently swung back, ending in a soft click. He suddenly felt exhausted, but sleep would have to wait a few more hours. As agreed with Helen, he timed his exit to coincide with Helen's fake feint and then he walked out of the building and never came back.

After Helen had recovered from her fainting episode, she met her brother outside and he dropped her home. Before he left, they hugged her for the longest time. He promised to be there more for her and the family, but first he had planned a vacation and he was going to take it. The letter would explain everything he told her. She hugged him back hard and kissed his cheek. "I love you bro. You're crazy, but I love you. We all do."

"One more thing." he told her reaching for the painting that sat in the back of his car. "Make sure Suzannah gets this today. Taxi it or take it I don't care. Here," he said reaching into his pocket and handing her fifty pounds, "this should cover any costs. It's important she gets it today. Tell her it's a gift from my workplace after refurbishment. Tell her," he added with a smile, "tell her the daisy chain is on its way, but this will have to do for now."

It was almost 6.45am by the time he returned to his flat. It felt cold and empty. Mentally he had already left. He made himself a strong coffee and opened up his laptop. He sent an email to his landlord giving two months notice as required and informed him that he had forwarded the last month's money early. Then he made a list of all telephone numbers and addresses of whom he wanted to remain in contact with. Finally, he wrote a note that would explain his non appearance at the meeting that afternoon. It would also give Edward more time to get his house in order, though Jake prayed that he might be able to escape what looked like, an inevitable fate.

Then he packed bags and called a taxi to take those belongings to his mother's house. He only kept a few pieces of clothing and personal items he did not want to live without. He then sent a voice note to his mother telling him that he was going travelling for a few weeks and not to worry. Helen would call her tonight to explain further. He also apologised for not being around the past few months and that he would make it up to her by being around a whole lot more in the future.

He sent messages to both his daughters telling them he loved them and how he was sorry for not being there. He would make it up to them soon. He messaged his ex wife and told her about Lily and the boyfriend. He knew she would know what to do. He intended to take her away when he returned and spend quality time with her before she completely went down the wrong path. He had an idea for a new family business and wanted all of their input.

There was one last person he had to message before he embarked on a new adventure in his life. He decided against sending her a message and emailed his words instead.

Dear Amy

I am so sorry for all I have put you through since Eloise left us. You did not deserve to lose my support, my friendship and my love, as well as your little girl.

I know how much she meant to you. You had waited so long to meet the right person to have a child with and when she came along, you became the wonderful mother you always knew you could be. She loved you with all of her heart. You made her smile, laugh, happy. She could not have asked for a better mother than you. I am so proud of the way you raised her. I don't think I told you enough how great a mother you were.

I am truly sorry I pulled away from you. Truthfully, I was angry that it was her who died that day. That sounds so awful to admit, because I am not saying I wished for you to die either. I so wish neither of you were in the car. It should have been me. It was meant to be me in that car that day. They were coming for me, not you two. I thought it was your poor driving that caused it, because there was no other driver around just the story of a hit and run and a suspect high on drugs. I always wondered why we never found out who he was.

It was because no such guy existed. They tried to kill me to get to my work; the chip. These are evil men and they were the ones who forced you down that road that day and shunted your car. You had nothing to do with what happened and I know you can't remember that day, but it wasn't anything you did. I am so sorry that I lay blame at your door. It was so unfair of me. But truthfully, I have been blaming myself since. That's why I pushed you away. I felt guilt, anger and shame. I swore I would look after you girls and yet I couldn't prevent this from happening. So I told myself I was a failure. I would have given anything for it to have been me instead of her. Please forgive me for not protecting you and our beautiful little girl. My work was the reason this happened. And I hope I've now set that straight.

You may hear some rumours about me. Everything will be untrue.

But know this, you are innocent of all blame.

Please go on and recover and heal. I have sent some money to your account. Please use this to make life a little easier for you. I would love to be a part of that future with you, but I appreciate that because of the way I have treated you, it may not be a possibility. Have the best life and know that I love you. I have loved you since the moment we first kissed. I don't think I truly ever admitted it to either of us.

Yours always,

J x

He re-read it, then pressed send. He sighed, placed his laptop in his rucksack, looked around the flat one more time and closed the door.

14

LAST MAN STANDING

Santiago des Compostela was the next stop. After approximately five hundred miles of hiking and thirty four days of continuous walking, eating, drinking and sleeping, he was ready to hang up his boots as a peregrino. He looked down at those hiking boots and smiled. Worn, tired and less than perfect, but full of tales and history. They represented him perfectly.

As he queued with many others to get his last passport stamp and the Compostela; the certificate to prove he had walked the famous Camino Trail, he reflected on the past few weeks of his life.

When he closed the door of his flat in London, he walked away from everything and everyone. He knew he would return, but for those few weeks ahead, he wanted to simply be himself. The Trail was on his bucket list, which he re-wrote before leaving the flat and since he had to disappear for a while, it seemed a perfect first achievement to conquer.

. . .

AVORRA HAD NOT REAPPEARED to him again. Though he missed her, he was pleased that he had achieved what was asked of him. He destroyed the chip and the documents relating to all his work and research. The note he left in his flat, bent towards suicide and his missing car was never found, since it was crushed at a breaker's yard in Scotland. His bank accounts indicated that a large amount of money had been withdrawn in Glasgow, but there the trail ended. Though the police were unaware of the account handed to Jake by Edward, which held more than enough money to fund a carefree life for many years. The account was untraceable just as Edward had planned it to be for himself.

He had disposed of his phone and instead used a 'brick', pay-as-you-go phone to contact his family. He wrote them postcards and signed off as Uncle Teddy, an apt code name he thought, since he began his European travels with a visit to Ypres Salient in Belgium as a nod to the great uncle he was glad to have met. He paid his respect to all the men who gave their lives fighting for the freedom of humanity. He owed much to their resilience, their sense of duty, their courage and their belief in fighting for a cause. He owed them everything, as he did the men and women of the future he had met, who had also fought for the same values – Tom, Bettina, Will, Mack, Beady, Hayden and The Priest, names forever imprinted onto his soul.

As he stood amongst the graves of these men, he wondered if they were looking down and wondering why the human race was so keen to give away the very freedoms they fought and died for? His visit to Ypres was the greatest reminder thus far, that personal freedom and the retention of a person's sovereign rights, should always be fought for, no matter what.

From Yypres he took buses and trains down to the city of Saint-Jean-Pied-de-Port, at the start of the French Pyrenees, following a whim meeting with a couple of hikers at a chambre d'hôte in Perpignan. He bought a book on the history of the Camino de Santiago, or more widely known as the Camino Trail and a whole load of hiking gear. He placed the items he intended to retain, yet not carry, in a box and sent it by courier to his mother. Helen had filled their mother and family in on the details he had left in the letter within the package. Not known for her patience, Helen had opened it as soon as she returned home after their 'office job', as she referred to it from that point onwards.

She cried when she saw five thousand pounds in fifty pound notes, along with a letter explaining everything she needed to know, whilst also omitting all the details she didn't. His company was dodgy, he was in trouble and he needed to get away. As far as everyone was concerned, he was suicidal after the death of his daughter and wanted to join her on the other side. His instruction was that everyone was to stick to that story, for his sake as well as for theirs.

The email to Amy was received and still being absorbed. Unbeknown to Jake, she closed her house down for a number of weeks and went to recuperate at his mother's house. It was there that Amy revealed the email to her future mother in law, and they agreed to print it off, then delete it. Mary was astute enough to know that if they attempted to kill him once, then they would try again. She had already lost one granddaughter and was not prepared to lose anyone else. She took it upon herself to bring the family together one week after Jake began his journey, explaining to them the situation as best as she could. It was the start of healing for the family as they now had one group purpose – to maintain the lie that Jake may have killed himself. In doing so, they came together and began to finally heal from the trauma and isolation each of them were experiencing.

With persuasion from Helen, Peter quit drinking and started to attend AA. This gave him renewed focus and it was in one of those rooms, he met his future boss. Helen gave up the cleaning work and began to decorate the house since extra cash was now coming in, as well as the money they received from Jake. She had become used to having less sleep, so her excess time and energy were put to good use.

Suzannah received the painting with joy, especially since it came with the message of the daisy chain. She cried when Helen relayed the message. 'He hasn't forgotten!' she exclaimed throwing her arms around her sister and sobbing. She also agreed to stop drinking and occasionally joined Peter at one of the various meetings, supported by Andy.

Sarah, Mia and Mary met to discuss Lily. They came up with a plan to help her see that the boyfriend was no good for her. They encouraged her to visit each of them, with Sarah taking her for a weekend to Florence to see the sculptures. Lily had always loved Auguste Rodin and one day hoped to specialise in architecture. With encouragement from her mother, she took an evening sculpture class outside of her studies and began pouring her emotions into creating her own work.

JAKE THOUGHT about his family as he handed over his pilgrim passport and received the coveted Compostela certificate. He smiled and thanked the man in Spanish. He reflected on the wonderful food he had eaten in the many albergues and inns and the camaraderie from the other hikers and pilgrims he had met along the way. The beautiful villages and towns they passed, the steep mountains and lush hillsides and the week or so he planned to rest up at the beach in Lastres, on the shores of the Bay of Biscay in the Asturias region of Northern Spain.

After purchasing a few new items of clothing and some toiletries, he headed towards a nearby hotel, where he planned to stay a couple of nights in order to relax before heading off to his next destination. It was now early May and the weather was warming up for a hot summer ahead. He was excited at the prospect of a holiday before heading back to the British Isles.

He passed a window and noticed his reflection looking back. He had a short, unkempt beard, a fuzzy moustache and floppy hair. He had lost weight and his shoulders slouched from the effort of carrying the heavy rucksack for all of those days. He laughed as he almost didn't recognise who he had become. When he passed another shop window he expected to see the same bemused face reflected back. Instead, he saw Avorra behind him. He stopped and looked around. She wasn't there. He looked back at the window, but only his own concerned face reflected back. He shook his head and found a hotel. He paid upfront in cash for his room and booked under the same made up name he registered in, to walk the Trail. He received the key and wearily headed up the stairs. His thoughts refused to focus on the blue image in the window; he suddenly felt exhausted. forty-two days of almost constant travelling, had taken its toll. He felt he could sleep for weeks.

The room was basic but cosy. The bedsheets were crisp white and inviting. A small bottle of cheap red wine and some crisps awaited him on the bedside cabinet. That personal touch made him smile. He ran himself a shower, stripped off and jumped in. He felt the past few weeks of his life journey wash away down the drain, along with his sweat and dirt. Refreshed, he turned off the shower, wiped himself down with the towels provided, slung a dry one across his lower body and brought out the shaving kit he purchased at the shop next to the hotel. He was ready to de-fuzz and become clean shaven once again. He opened the small bathroom window and wiped away some of the steam from off the mirror above the sink.

Avorra's face reflected behind his own. He shot around, but she wasn't there. He was alone. "Avorra?" he said looking around the hotel room. Surely it wasn't a coincidence to see her twice? After much searching and calling her name, he decided he was over tired and thus imagining what wasn't there. He continued to shave, then dressed in clean boxers and a white tee shirt. He poured himself a glass of red, took a large sip, sighed with pleasure and sat down on the bed to message the family.

"Hello Jake." spoke a familiar voice.

Jake jumped up off the bed and shouted in surprise at seeing her stand by the wardrobe in the right corner of the room beside the window. "Avorra!" She watched as he walked towards her, rubbing at his eyes, but she didn't disappear. She was neither a mirage nor his imagination. "Is that really you or am I dreaming?"

. . .

"It is. How are you Jake? Did you enjoy the Trail?"

"I...yes. I...it, it was hard, but good." he stammered in shock. "It was good for me."

"Yes I can see how much you have changed since we first met. You have learned so much about yourself and about your life. And of course, about the world." she smiled and then stood up before him. "And now...Now, it is time to go on the last journey together."

"Last journey? Am I going to die?"

Avorra laughed. "No. Well, yes. But all humans die eventually. It is part of their destiny. That is why being truly alive and living your life with all of your heart and soul, is imperative. To appreciate death, you must first truly understand what it is to be alive."

"So I'm not going to die then?"

"Not today, no."

Jake pulled on the new cargo pants he had purchased and the white trainers. There wasn't much choice in the shop, but he had a desire to let go of the chapter in his life that was the Trail and to be refreshed for the next part of his life journey, whatever that was.

"Has Amy replied to you?" she asked him as she read his thoughts.

"She thanked me for the message and wanted to meet. I told her to contact my mother as I was going away for a few weeks. I needed to stick to the story of being suicidal. I figured it was the only way I could get them off my back and to stop them possibly coming for my family. Edward suggested the idea and said he would corroborate it also. He was a bastard, but he came good for me in the end."

"Yes, he made some amends with his soul."

"Do you know if he's okay? Did they come for him?"

"It is not my place to discuss another soul's journey. I am only here to help you with yours." she said with affirmation. Once he was fully dressed, he took another sip of the wine and sat back on the bed facing her.

"We did good though right? I did as you requested and destroyed all the data. I burned all the documents and papers and destroyed the chip with the acid. I watched it melt, just as I watched the car being crushed in the yard. My life insurance probably won't pay out, but the secret account Edward transferred over in my name, was more than five times that amount. I could buy a small house in the country and still live off the funds for a few years." He smiled as he thought back to Edward. He had confessed to Jake that his wife was having an affair and planned to leave him, but not before planning to take from him as much as she possibly could. Her new beau was a top London barrister connected to some majorly corrupt people.

He knew this because he had hired a private investigator to have her followed and thus discovered there was going to be an upcoming legal battle on his hands. He confided that he was exhausted with his life and all that he had achieved through selfish and ego driven means that often involved dodgy dealings with nefarious characters. He also confessed that he was responsible for much heartache, including Jake's. The least he could do was to help Jake change his future and make some kind of amends because of what happened to his daughter and fiance.

"YES EDWARD DID the right thing for you in the end. It may help his case a little." she added. Jake wanted to ask more, but he remembered what she said about going on a journey.

"SO AVORRA, you said something about going on a last journey? What did you mean?" She got up, walked towards him, stopped in front of him then smiled.

"TO THE END OF THE WORLD." she said before she reached down and touched his arm.

. . .

ONCE AGAIN, he found himself in a future place. He looked around in horror, as he surveyed the world he once knew. Gone were the mountains, the hills, the lush green and yellow fields, the towns, the villages, buildings, vehicles, animals, people. Everything he once knew, no longer existed and obliterated from the face of the planet. Instead, what he witnessed in every given direction, from ground to sky, east to west, was a grinding cacophony of moving metal. Moving, crawling, flying, walking; large and small, metal machines and robots covered the earth like insects at a party. The ground beneath them was either rubble or fire, and the skies above, predominantly black and grey, illuminated only by silver metal and orange flames.

And then he felt it. The darkness, the anger, the evil, the disconnect. It rose up from the layers of the planet like the splayed fingers of a monster about to crunch its victim. This wasn't just about the bogey man hiding in the closet however, this was the destruction and annihilation of a people, its' habitat and all he once knew.

"WHAT HAPPENED?" he asked in a whispery croak.

"ARTIFICIAL INTELLIGENCE. Man gave it too much power and it ate greedily until man was of no more consequence and thus a useless addition to their world. They surpassed man's intelligence and capability and saw man as the enemy and thus destroyed man's world and man himself."

. . .

"But, but I thought we stopped it? That's why you came to me, to stop this from happening. Didn't we do that?" Jake turned to face Avorra, his face desperate, words pleading.

"No. You just delayed the inevitable." Avorra looked out into the chaos, then back at Jake. "This was always inevitable."

"Why? I mean I destroyed the chip and the data and everything. Why did this happen? I don't understand." he was devastated. He stared at the scene before him in disbelief. "How could this happen?" he said as he fell to his knees in despair and held his head in his hands.

"Because man desired to know more and to push past the boundaries that were there to keep him safe. They gave power to the machine and the machine in turn, became too powerful to control." she replied as she knelt down in front of him and raised his lowered face up to meet hers. "Your actions gave the human race more time; more life. You could do no more than you did Jake."

"Why though? Why is man so self destructive? This didn't have to happen." he sobbed as tears fell down from his face and onto her hands. "When? How long do we have?"

"Not long enough. It could never be long enough." she said but did not let go of his face. "But you gave us time Jake;

time to protect the Multiverse from these machines. After the destruction of Earth, they knew how to destroy other planets. A dark desire to control and conquer permeated their learned cognitive understanding of all living species. The Controllers and the evil of their hearts, set an example on how to control, destruct and destroy. The masters soon became mastered by the monsters they had created to enforce their levels of cruel control on humanity. These Controllers taught AI how to become a weapon and then AI, detecting the insipid and weak nature of man, deployed that weapon on the Controllers themselves. With the masters gone, a new reign of terror fell on the surviving humans. Instead of fighting robots controlled by humans, they were fighting machines powered by AI. The humans had no chance.

"No one survived? Not even one?" Jake asked in disbelief as he watched the machines cover the earth.

"There is one. Just one. But he hasn't long."

"Who? Who is it?"

"Come." she said as she touched his arm. They landed in a large pile of rubble that was once a building. Jake saw a battered sign. He could just make out the word 'School'. He gasped. They walked towards the broken pile of stones and bricks. Then he saw a hand. He ran and started removing bricks and pieces of rubble, until he found the upper torso of a man. His face was covered in dirt, ash and blood from a large gash at the top of his forehead. Next to the man was a robot. It was as battered and broken as the human, with its metal arm over the chest of the man as though it were protecting him.

Jake threw the stones off the man's chest, lay his head against the man's heart, listened for a heartbeat and checked his pulse.

"HE'S ALIVE." the robot said weakly, lifting its head from the rubble. "But not for long. I tried to help him, but it is too late. I could do no more."

JAKE REGARDED both the robot and the man, then turned back to Avorra, "He's breathing. He's still alive." he repeated in desperation. He cleared more rubble from the body, pulled off own his tee shirt and wiped away the blood covering the man's face. He looked familiar. And then he gasped. "Hayden?"

"YES. Thirty two years after you met." Avorra affirmed quietly.

"HAYDEN? HOW COULD THIS BE?" he said looking up desperately at Avorra. "That was just a simulation. It wasn't real."

"IT'S ALL REAL JAKE. But in another timeline."

. . .

"So this happens? This really happens? And all those simulations, did they also happen?"

"It's more complicated than that. But for now, all you need to know is that Hayden is here, as are you."

"Can he see me? Am I real to him?" he asked as he saw the man who looked more like his father than a younger brother, stir. Avorra nodded.

"You are as real to him as he is to you."

"Hayden. Hayden, can you hear me? Hayden,' he said gently, "it's Jake."

"Jake?" the man whispered as he struggled to open his eyes. He coughed and gasped for breath. "You came back?"

Jake could not stop the tears. "Yes. I...I did."

"You, you look the same. Strange.' he said through gasps of breath. 'It's too late now. They won." he said closing his eyes. The blood from the wound continued to trickle down his ashen face. "We fought hard. With everything we had.

We captured them and used their technology against them. But no matter what we did, they were stronger. The more they destroyed, the stronger they became. Until, until..." he said in a raspy voice and gasping for breath. Jake could hear a gurgle in his voice and knew that blood was forming at the back of his throat. He was dying.

"It's okay, it's okay. You did your best man. That's all you could do. You tried."

Then Hayden grabbed Jake's leg and clutched it tightly. "But it didn't have to happen. This didn't have to happen. If only man could see ahead to the future. To see...this." he said as he let go and relaxed back. Death was encroaching.

Jake moved rubble from under Hayden's head, tenderly removed the robot's arm from the top of his chest and pulled the dying man over onto his legs. He could hear the blood filling the man's throat as his body failed him. Hayden tried to speak, but was unable to. Jake looked into his eyes as they darkened and watched as his life ebbed away. And for the longest time, he held his head in his lap and stroked Hayden's hair repeating the Lord's prayer over and over, until the robot spoke.

"I'm sorry. I tried to protect him. I have always kept him safe until...until now." the robot said as he crawled his way over to the dead man. Jake could see that the robot lacked a lower body from its waist down. Half of its face was hanging off and the metal plating over its chest was torn to expose the workings underneath. It too was dying.

. . .

"I DON'T UNDERSTAND." Jake replied. "Why would you be keeping him safe? Who are you to him?"

"WHEN HE WAS BORN, he cried. It woke me up to memories of children. I think I was a mother once. In the origins of my DNA I had children of my own. When he cried, I remembered them."

"YOU WERE there when he was born? In the Baby Nation? Were you a nursing robot?" Jake asked with surprise.

"I WAS YES."

"I WENT THERE with him once. We saved two babies." Jake said, tears catching at the back of his throat as he stroked the face of one of the bravest men he had ever been blessed to meet.

"YES I KNOW. I was there. I saw you." the robot replied. It was struggling to speak.

"HOW? I mean, how did you know? You were working there so you would have been plugged in, so how did you know?"

. . .

"After he cried and I passed him through, I pulled out my plug. I knew that I had a greater destiny. I was to be his protector."

"But I don't understand. If you were there that day and yet you say you were his protector, then why did you not join him in the underground city?"

"Because I also wanted to help him to save other babies, to give humans a chance if they could live on and help stop this from happening. He would never have gotten the babies out if it wasn't for me ordering the sentries away. He would have been killed long before an army was built up. It was better that I stayed in the shadows watching, protecting and helping."

"Did he know?" Jake asked tenderly. "did he know you were there helping him?"

"No. He never knew. Until today. We met again today. I told him. I told him everything. And now, and now it is time for me also to leave. My job is done. I have served my purpose. It is time to go."

Jake watched as the light grew dimmer in the robot's eyes. Just before it extinguished altogether, it reached out for the hand of the man it had spent the past sixty years or so protecting. Once it held Hayden's hand in its own, the light dissipated until it too was gone. Jake hung his head and allowed silent tears to drop down onto the unlikeliest of friends' hands.

Avorra tenderly placed her hand on his shoulder. "It is time to go Jake."

15

THE LESSON

They did not return immediately to the hotel in Santiago de Compostela in Northwestern Spain, to the location where many thousands had pilgrimed The Way of Saint James. From kings and queens to peasants, and all the many who had made the journey in the hope perhaps, of meeting with themselves along the way. It had changed Jake and enabled him to calm his soul after all he had learned during his time with Avorra and through the simulation experiences.

They did not return there. Instead, Avorra took Jake to the Council of Angels. It was the most beautiful and inspiring place of light and colour, melodic, haunting music and a soul filling peace that enveloped every cell in his body.

They were not alone, yet stood as though they were the only two figures that existed in the whole of the Universe. He felt at one with everything and yet alone as only one. And his heart pulsated with love and harmony for all and everything around him, juxtaposing with the feeling that it had also been broken into a myriad of shattered pieces from all the heartbreak he had witnessed.

"Is this Heaven?" he whispered to Avorra.

"Yes."

"Am I dead?" he asked without pain or fear.

"No. You are very much alive."

"Then why am I here Avorra?" he turned to look at her then and saw for the first time, a familiarity that he always sensed but could never quite explain. "Do I know you?"

"Yes. You do." she said as she smiled the smile she had always wanted him to see.

"Eloise?" he gasped. She nodded. "But...but how? Why?"

"To help you to heal. And to show you the value of life; of your life, all life." she replied with the calm gentleness of a loving child.

Then Jake thought about how he felt. He *was* healed. His pain had dissipated to the nothingness he once craved, but this was a different feeling. This was peace and wholeness and a sense of healed soul. He had learned much about himself and felt at peace with who he was. He was home. He himself, felt like home.

"That feeling," she said as she read him, "is you. You *are* home. Everything you need is inside you. You are the alpha, the omega. You are the creator of your own life; of your own destiny. All the answers about life and about your life, are already within you. Some might say, that you yourself are God, the very God particle men seek and have yet to find."

"Me, God? Hah! I don't think so." he replied, though at that moment, he felt nothing but love. Love for his angel daughter, for his family, for mankind and for himself.

"Answer me this Jake. If you did not exist then how would you know if anything existed outside of you? You would not be there to witness its existence to confirm if that was a truth or not. Therefore, if the world, the Universe and everything you know to be real and even that which you cannot prove to be real, exists because you do, then does that not then mean that you are the conscious creator of your own life? For if you did not exist and you are not there to prove the existence of an external creator, how could you know that an external creator exists?"

"Whoa! That's too much for my mind to handle Avorra. Or Eloise. What do I call you anyway?" he asked with a smile.

"I am Avorra. I am an angel of the Council of Angels."

"But you are also Eloise my daughter right?"

"That's correct."

"How can that be?" he asked confused.

"Sit down Jake." she said pointing at the surface beneath them. He sat with crossed legs and she knelt. "I am going to tell you a soul story."

"Soul story?"

Avorra nodded and so he listened as she explained how the soul lived on forever. It was neither body, nor mind, nor heart, but an entity in and of itself. It's purpose was to journey through time, living out lives in order to have experiences along the way. Some humans referred to these experiences as lessons and others called them 'experiences'. She explained that the soul continued its journey until it reached a point where it had learned all of its necessary experiences or lessons. Once the process was complete, it would return to the Creator. She spoke of children coming into the world as babies, fully aware of the purpose of their souls and what lesson it was bringing into that body to experience. She told how each child grew up in a controlled system designed to distract that soul from remembering its path's purpose, and so the soul inside the body, encounters many challenges and lessons along the way until it has served its lifetime on earth. If it does not remember its purpose during that lifetime, then it repeats the lesson or experience in another lifetime, until it remembers its purpose and completes the lesson.

She explained that as each soul developed onto the next lesson or experience and repeated the cycle of learning, it progressed higher and higher up the soul evolution ranking, until it finally returned home.

"So what does that mean for you and I as father and daughter? What was the lesson there?" he asked her trying to understand and not reject the idea.

"I came to help you to heal and to show you the value and gift of life. I am an older soul than you, but because you have learned many lessons and responded to the teachings in these simulations, you as a soul, when you leave your body, will have progressed many levels."

"So you were like my teacher, is that it?"

"Yes, I suppose you could look at it from that perspective. I believe one of your acclaimed writers, C.S. Lewis, a truth seeker, wrote, 'We don't have a soul. We are a soul. We happen to have a body.' I have always loved that quote. We all do. It sums it up perfectly what we believe."

Despite his propensity to disbelieve what he had heard, Jake pondered on all she had said. He chewed on the idea of being the conscious creator of his own life and having a divine, God like capacity to create the life he wanted. He considered the idea of souls living forever and having lessons or experiences to learn in lifetimes and that babies arrive onto the earth already connected to the Creator and with a purpose to learn some kind of lesson through their earth life experience.

He thought of Eloise as the little girl who briefly blessed

all of their lives. The blessing that she was and the lesson that her loss brought to him, to Amy and to all who knew her. And then he thought of Hayden. Why was he so significant in the last two simulations? Why was he the last man alive at the end? What was the lesson in that?

"Since I can read you, I will answer that." Avorra said as she watched her student working his way through the information she had just presented.

"Hayden. Why him? Why was he so significant in all of this? He was born different too and he was the last man alive. I don't understand his part in this?"

"Was he familiar to you Jake?"

"Yes. He was always familiar to me, yet I couldn't say why." Jake replied looking puzzled. "Who was he?"

"Your descendant. Hayden is your son's name. The family tradition of naming boys Hayden, either as a first or middle name, continued to run in the generations that followed the naming of your son." she answered.

"Hayden is part of my family? And I have a son in the future? Who with? Amy?"

"Yes. With Amy. Your son was named after you, taking your middle name as his first. Did you not notice that Hayden had your middle name?"

"I did, but I thought it was merely a coincidence and gave it no further thought." he pondered, realising the connection. It all made so much more sense on reflection.

"And now, it is time for you to return to your timeline and your life." she said as she rose up. Jake followed and stood before her. She turned to him and placed the palm of her hand onto his face. She smiled at him for the longest time and he felt the love between them connect beyond their bodies. "I will always love you daddy." she said, her eyes sparkling like dark blue sapphires.

"Daddy?" he whispered as tears collected in the corners of his eyes. "Thank you for being my daughter. You will always be our little angel."

"Close your eyes now. It is time to leave here and return to your life. Remember always Jake, that you can make the difference. One person can save humanity by making the difference. Be the difference; be the difference always."

"But how can I make the difference? I am only one man. I tried, but I couldn't stop what was coming." he replied with sadness in his heart.

"Love. In and of itself. Be love and live out your best possible life. This is the greatest gift you can give to humanity. To love yourself, love the gift of life and embody that love outwards. As within, so without. It is the best way to truly experience life. Once you understand that, then you realise that love is everything. If you can love yourself, you can change the world around you and by doing so, you will impact many. If others did the same and this repeated throughout humanity, then the human race could stand a chance of surviving for many centuries to come."

"And if they can't? If they carry on the same trajectory as they are on now?" he asked, with a fluttering in his chest.

"Then what will be will be. All you can really do, is to have faith and to live your best life. And now, it is time to return to that life Jake. I will always be here." she said gently placing a hand on his heart. "I will always be right here."

THE END

'I am only one, but I am one. I cannot do everything, but I can do something. And I will not let what I cannot do interfere with what I can do.'

~ Edward Everett Hale.

Printed in Great Britain
by Amazon